SALUTE TO ADVENTURERS

John Buchan's stirring tale is set in the days when America was newly colonised, half by transported criminals and half by pioneers, men with the courage and vision to carve out their future from a hard land, where Indians were still active and hostile and the King's justice was a long sea voyage away.

Andrew Garvald is a young Scottish merchant, deadly with a pistol and tenacious as a bulldog, come to Virginia to establish his fortune. He is outlawed from Virginian society for opposing the London traders' monopoly, and finds his friends in strange places as a result. But with Red Ringan, the pirate and gentleman adventurer, finest blade in the Five Seas, and Shalah, the exiled Indian prince, his second shadow, Garvald finds himself fighting a deadly foe for higher stakes than trade – for the love of a dark-eyed lady and for the very existence of Virginia.

This is John Buchan at his thrilling best: he re-creates the spirit of those wild days of enterprise, when anything seemed possible to a man who would dare to fight for it, and tells a tale of hazard and adventure which will keep you spellbound.

BY THE SAME AUTHOR

The Thirty-Nine Steps
Greenmantle
Mr Standfast
The Courts of the Morning
The Path of the King
Huntingtower
The Gap in the Curtain
Midwinter
The Three Hostages
John MacNab
A Prince of the Captivity
The Dancing Floor
Witch Wood
The Runagates Club
Castle Gay
The Blanket of the Dark
The Free Fishers
The House of the Four Winds
The Island of Sheep
The Half-Hearted
The Moon Endureth
Prester John

JOHN BUCHAN

Salute to Adventurers

HUTCHINSON OF LONDON

Hutchinson & Co (Publishers) Ltd
3 Fitzroy Square, London W1

London Melbourne Sydney Auckland
Wellington Johannesburg and agencies
throughout the world

First published by Thomas Nelson & Sons Ltd 1915
This edition 1976

Printed in Great Britain by litho by
The Anchor Press Ltd and bound by
Wm Brendon & Son Ltd
both of Tiptree, Essex

ISBN 0 09 127750 7

TO MAJOR-GENERAL THE
HON. SIR REGINALD TALBOT, K.C.B.

I tell of old Virginian ways;
  And who more fit my tale to scan
Than you, who knew in far-off days
  The eager horse of Sheridan;
Who saw the sullen meads of fate,
  The tattered scrub, the blood-drenched sod,
When Lee, the greatest of the great,
  Bent to the storm of God?

I tell lost tales of savage wars;
  And you have known the desert sands,
The camp beneath the silver stars,
  The rush at dawn of Arab bands,
The fruitless toil, the hopeless dream,
  The fainting feet, the faltering breath,
While Gordon by the ancient stream
  Waited at ease on death.

And now, aloof from camp and field,
  You spend your sunny autumn hours
Where the green folds of Chiltern shield
  The nooks of Thames amid the flowers:
You who have borne that name of pride,
  In honour clean from fear or stain,
Which Talbot won by Henry's side
  In vanquished Aquitaine.

The reader is asked to believe that most of the characters in this tale and many of the incidents have good historical warrant. The figure of Muckle John Gib will be familiar to the readers of Patrick Walker.

CONTENTS

SALUTE TO ADVENTURERS

CHAPTER I

THE SWEET-SINGERS

WHEN I was a child in short-coats a spaewife came to the town-end, and for a silver groat paid by my mother she riddled my fate. It came to little, being no more than that I should miss love and fortune in the sunlight and find them in the rain. The woman was a haggard, black-faced gipsy, and when my mother asked for more she turned on her heel and spoke gibberish ; for which she was presently driven out of the place by Tam Roberton, the bailie, and the village dogs. But the thing stuck in my memory, and together with the fact that I was a Thursday's bairn, and so, according to the old rhyme, " had far to go," convinced me long ere I had come to man's estate that wanderings and surprises would be my portion.

It is in the rain that this tale begins. I was just turned of eighteen, and in the back-end of a dripping September set out from our moorland house of Auchencairn to complete my course at Edinburgh College. The year was 1685, an ill year for our countryside; for the folk were at odds with the King's Government about religion, and the land was full of covenants and repressions. Small wonder that I was backward with my colleging, and at an age when most lads are buckled to a calling was still attending the prelections of the Edinburgh masters. My father had blown hot and cold in politics, for he was fiery and unstable by nature, and swift to judge a cause by its latest professor. He had cast out with the Hamilton gentry, and, having broken the head of a dragoon in the change-house of Lesmahagow, had his little estate mulcted in fines. All of which, together with some natural curiosity and a family love of fighting, sent him to the ill-fated field of Bothwell Brig, from which he was lucky to escape with a bullet in the shoulder. Thereupon he had been put to the horn, and was now lying hid in a den in the mosses of Douglas Water. It was a sore business for my mother, who had the task of warding off prying eyes from our ragged household and keeping the fugitive in life. She was a Tweedside woman, as strong and staunch as an oak, and with a heart in her like Robert Bruce. And she was cheerful, too, in the worst days, and would go about the place with a bright eye and a song on her ·lips. But the thing was beyond a woman's bearing; so I had perforce to forsake my colleging and take a hand with our family vexations. The life made me hard and watchful, trusting no man, and brusque and stiff towards the world. And yet all the while youth was working in me like yeast, so that a spring day or a west wind would make me forget my troubles and thirst to be about a kindlier business than skulking in a moorland dwelling.

My mother besought me to leave her. "What," she would say, "has young blood to do with this bickering of kirks and old wives' lamentations? You have to learn and see and do, Andrew. And it's time you were beginning." But I would not listen to her, till by the mercy of God we got my father safely forth of Scotland, and heard that he was dwelling snugly at Leyden in as great patience as his nature allowed. Thereupon I bethought me of my neglected colleging, and, leaving my books and plenishing to come by the Lanark carrier, set out on foot for Edinburgh.

The distance is only a day's walk for an active man, but I started late, and purposed to sleep the night at a cousin's house by Kirknewton. Often in bright summer days I had travelled the road, when the moors lay yellow in the sun and larks made a cheerful chorus. In such weather it is a pleasant road, with long prospects to cheer the traveller, and kindly ale-houses to rest his legs in. But that day it rained as if the floodgates of heaven had opened. When I crossed Clyde by the bridge at Hyndford the water was swirling up to the keystone. The ways were a foot deep in mire, and about Carnwath the bog had overflowed and the whole neighbourhood swam in a loch. It was pitiful to see the hay afloat like water-weeds, and the green oats scarcely showing above the black floods. In two minutes after starting I was wet to the skin, and I thanked Providence I had left my little Dutch *Horace* behind me in the book-box. By three in the afternoon I was as unkempt as any tinkler, my hair plastered over my eyes, and every fold of my coat running like a gutter.

Presently the time came for me to leave the road and take the short-cut over the moors ; but in the deluge, where the eyes could see no more than a yard or two into a grey wall of rain, I began to misdoubt my knowledge of the way. On the left I saw a stone dovecot and a cluster of trees about a gateway ; so, knowing how few and remote were the dwellings on the moorland, I judged it wiser to seek guidance before I strayed too far.

The place was grown up with grass and sore neglected. Weeds made a carpet on the avenue, and the dykes were broke by cattle at a dozen places. Suddenly through the falling water there stood up the gaunt end of a house. It was no cot or farm, but a proud mansion, though badly needing repair. A low stone wall bordered a pleasance, but the garden had fallen out of order, and a dial-stone lay flat on the earth.

My first thought was that the place was tenant-less, till I caught sight of a thin spire of smoke struggling against the downpour. I hoped to come on some gardener or groom from whom I could seek direction, so I skirted the pleasance to find the kitchen door. A glow of fire in one of the rooms cried welcome to my shivering bones, and on the far side of the house I found signs of better care. The rank grasses had been mown to make a walk, and in a corner flourished a little group of pot-herbs. But there was no man to be seen, and I was about to retreat and try the farm-town, when out of the doorway stepped a girl.

She was maybe sixteen years old, tall and well-grown, but of her face I could see little, since she was all muffled in a great horseman's cloak. The hood of it covered her hair, and the wide flaps were folded over her bosom. She sniffed the chill wind, and held her head up to the rain, and all the while, in a clear childish voice, she was singing.

It was a song I had heard, one made by the great Montrose, who had suffered shameful death in Edinburgh thirty years before. It was a man's song, full of pride and daring, and not for the lips of a young maid. But that hooded girl in the wild weather sang it with a challenge and a fire that no cavalier could have bettered.

> " My dear and only love, I pray
>   That little world of thee
> Be governed by no other sway
>   Than purest monarchy.
> For if confusion have a part,
>   Which virtuous souls abhor,
> And hold a synod in thy heart,
>   I'll never love thee more."

So she sang, like youth daring fortune to give it aught but the best. The thing thrilled me, so that I stood gaping. Then she looked aside and saw me.

"Your business, man ? " she cried, with an imperious voice.

I took off my bonnet, and made an awkward bow.

"Madam, I am on my way to Edinburgh," I stammered, for I was mortally ill at ease with women. "I am uncertain of the road in this weather, and come to beg direction."

"You left the road three miles back," she said.

"But I am for crossing the moors," I said.

She pushed back her hood and looked at me with laughing eyes. I saw how dark those eyes were, and how raven black her wandering curls of hair.

"You have come to the right place," she cried. "I can direct you as well as any Jock or Sandy about the town. Where are you going to ? "

I said Kirknewton for my night's lodging.

"Then march to the right, up by yon planting, till you come to the Howe Burn. Follow it to the top, and cross the hill above its well-head. The wind is blowing from the east, so keep it on your right cheek. That will bring you to the springs of the Leith Water, and in an hour or two from there you will be back on the highroad."

She used a manner of speech foreign to our parts, but very soft and pleasant in the ear. I thanked her, clapped on my dripping bonnet, and made for the dykes beyond the garden. Once I looked back, but she had no further interest in

me. In the mist I could see her peering once more
skyward, and through the drone of the deluge
came an echo of her song.

> " I'll serve thee in such noble ways,
>   As never man before ;
> I'll deck and crown thy head with bays,
>   And love thee more and more."

The encounter cheered me greatly, and lifted
the depression which the eternal drizzle had settled
on my spirits. That bold girl singing a martial
ballad to the storm and taking pleasure in the
snellness of the air, was like a rousing summons
or a cup of heady wine. The picture ravished
my fancy. The proud dark eye, the little wanton
curls peeping from the hood, the whole figure alert
with youth and life—they cheered my recollection
as I trod that sour moorland. I tried to remember her song, and hummed it assiduously till
I got some kind of version, which I shouted in
my tuneless voice. For I was only a young lad,
and my life had been bleak and barren. Small
wonder that the call of youth set every fibre of me
a-quiver.

I had done better to think of the road. I found
the Howe Burn readily enough, and scrambled
up its mossy bottom. By this time the day was
wearing late, and the mist was deepening into the
darker shades of night. It is an eerie business to
be out on the hills at such a season, for they are
deathly quiet except for the lashing of the storm.
You will never hear a bird cry or a sheep bleat or

a weasel scream. The only sound is the drum of
the rain on the peat or its plash on a boulder, and
the low surge of the swelling streams. It is the
place and time for dark deeds, for the heart grows
savage ; and if two enemies met in the hollow of
the mist only one would go away.

I climbed the hill above the Howe burn-head,
keeping the wind on my right cheek as the girl
had ordered. That took me along a rough ridge
of mountain pitted with peat-bogs into which I
often stumbled. Every minute I expected to
descend and find the young Water of Leith, but
if I held to my directions I must still mount. I
see now that the wind must have veered to the
south-east, and that my plan was leading me into
the fastnesses of the hills ; but I would have
wandered for weeks sooner than disobey the word
of the girl who sang in the rain. Presently I was
on a steep hill-side, which I ascended only to drop
through a tangle of screes and juniper to the mires
of a great bog. When I had crossed this more
by luck than good guidance, I had another scramble
on the steeps where the long, tough heather clogged
my footsteps.

About eight o'clock I awoke to the conviction
that I was hopelessly lost, and must spend the
night in the wilderness. The rain still fell un-
ceasingly through the pit-mirk, and I was as sodden and bleached as the bent I trod on. A night
on the hills had no terrors for me ; but I was
mortally cold and furiously hungry, and my
temper grew bitter against the world. I had

(2,301)

forgotten the girl and her song, and desired above
all things on earth a dry bed and a chance of
supper.

I had been plunging and slipping in the dark
mosses for maybe two hours when, looking down
from a little rise, I caught a gleam of light.
Instantly my mood changed to content. It could
only be a herd's cottage, where I might hope for
a peat fire, a bicker of brose, and, at the worst,
a couch of dry bracken.

I began to run, to loosen my numbed limbs, and
presently fell headlong over a little scaur into a
moss-hole. When I crawled out, with peat plas-
tering my face and hair, I found I had lost my
notion of the light's whereabouts. I strove to
find another hillock, but I seemed now to be in
a flat space of bog. I could only grope blindly
forwards away from the moss-hole, hoping that
soon I might come to a lift of the hill.

Suddenly from the distance of about half a
mile there fell on my ears the most hideous wailing.
It was like the cats on a frosty night; it was like
the clanging of pots in a tinkler's cart; and it
would rise now and then to a shriek of rhapsody
such as I have heard at field-preachings. Clearly
the sound was human, though from what kind of
crazy human creature I could not guess. Had I
been less utterly forwandered and the night less
wild, I think I would have sped away from it as
fast as my legs had carried me. But I had little
choice. After all, I reflected, the worst bedlamite
must have food and shelter, and, unless the gleam

had been a will-o'-the-wisp, I foresaw a fire. So I hastened in the direction of the noise.

I came on it suddenly in a hollow of the moss. There stood a ruined sheepfold, and in the corner of two walls some plaids had been stretched to make a tent. Before this burned a big fire of heather roots and bogwood, which hissed and crackled in the rain. Round it squatted a score of women, with plaids drawn tight over their heads, who rocked and moaned like a flight of witches, and two-three men were on their knees at the edge of the ashes. But what caught my eye was the figure that stood before the tent. It was a long fellow, who held his arms to heaven, and sang in a great throaty voice the wild dirge I had been listening to. He held a book in one hand, from which he would pluck leaves and cast them on the fire, and at every burnt-offering a wail of ecstasy would go up from the hooded women and kneeling men. Then with a final howl he hurled what remained of his book into the flames, and with upraised hands began some sort of prayer.

I would have fled if I could ; but Providence willed it otherwise. The edge of the bank on which I stood had been rotted by the rain, and the whole thing gave under my feet. I slithered down into the sheepfold, and pitched head-foremost among the worshipping women. And at that, with a yell, the long man leaped over the fire, and had me by the throat.

My bones were too sore and weary to make resistance. He dragged me to the ground before

the tent, while the rest set up a skirling that
deafened my wits. There he plumped me down,
and stood glowering at me like a cat with a sparrow.

" Who are ye, and what do ye here, disturbing
the remnant of Israel ? " says he.

I had no breath in me to speak, so one of the
men answered.

" Some gangrel body, precious Mr. John," he
said.

" Nay," said another ; " it's a spy o' the Amalekites."

" It's a herd frae Linton way," spoke up a
woman. " He favours the look of one Zebedee
Linklater."

The long man silenced her. " The word of
the Lord came unto His prophet Gib, saying,
Smite and spare not, for the cup of the abominations of Babylon is now full. The hour cometh,
yea, it is at hand, when the elect of the earth,
meaning me and two-three others, will be enthroned above the Gentiles, and Dagon and Baal
will be cast down. Are ye still in the courts of
bondage, young man, or seek ye the true light
which the Holy One of Israel has vouchsafed to
me, John Gib, His unworthy prophet ? "

Now I knew into what rabble I had strayed.
It was the company who called themselves the
Sweet-Singers, led by one Muckle John Gib, once
a mariner of Borrowstoneness-on-Forth. He had
long been a thorn in the side of the preachers,
holding certain strange heresies that discomforted
even the wildest of the hill-folk. They had clapped

him into prison ; but the man, being three parts
mad, had been let go, and ever since had been
making strife in the westland parts of Clydesdale.
I had heard much of him, and never any good.
It was his way to draw after him a throng of
demented women, so that the poor, draggle-tailed
creatures forgot husband and bairns and followed
him among the mosses. There were deeds of
violence and blood to his name, and the look of
him was enough to spoil a man's sleep. He was
about six and a half feet high, with a long, lean
head and staring cheek bones. His brows grew
like bushes, and beneath glowed his evil and
sunken eyes. I remember that he had monstrous
long arms, which hung almost to his knees, and a
great hairy breast which showed through a rent
in his seaman's jerkin. In that strange place,
with the dripping spell of night about me, and the
fire casting weird lights and shadows, he seemed
like some devil of the hills awakened by magic
from his ancient grave.

But I saw it was time for me to be speaking up.

" I am neither gangrel, nor spy, nor Amalekite,
nor yet am I Zebedee Linklater. My name is
Andrew Garvald, and I have to-day left my home
to make my way to Edinburgh College. I tried
a short road in the mist, and here I am."

" Nay, but what seek ye ? " cried Muckle John.
" The Lord has led ye to our company by His
own good way. What seek ye ? I say again, and
yea, a third time."

" I go to finish my colleging," I said.

He laughed a harsh, croaking laugh. " Little ye ken, young man. We travel to watch the surprising judgment which is about to overtake the wicked city of Edinburgh. An angel hath revealed it to me in a dream. Fire and brimstone will descend upon it as on Sodom and Gomorrah, and it will be consumed and wither away, with its cruel Ahabs and its painted Jezebels, its subtle Doegs and its lying Balaams, its priests and its judges, and its proud men of blood, its Bible-idolaters and its false prophets, its purple and damask, its gold and its fine linen, and it shall be as Tyre and Sidon, so that none shall know the site thereof. But we who follow the Lord and have cleansed His word from human abominations, shall leap as he-goats upon the mountains, and enter upon the heritage of the righteous from Beth-peor even unto the crossings of Jordan."

In reply to this rigmarole I asked for food, since my head was beginning to swim from my long fast. This, to my terror, put him into a great rage.

" Ye are carnally minded, like the rest of them. Ye will get no fleshly provender here ; but if ye be not besotted in your sins ye shall drink of the Water of Life that floweth freely and eat of the honey and manna of forgiveness."

And then he appeared to forget my very exist-ence. He fell into a sort of trance, with his eyes fixed on vacancy. There was a dead hush in the place, nothing but the crackle of the fire and the steady drip of the rain. I endured it as well as

I might, for though my legs were sorely cramped, I did not dare to move an inch.

After nigh half an hour he seemed to awake. "Peace be with you," he said to his followers. "It is the hour for sleep and prayer. I, John Gib, will wrestle all night for your sake, as Jacob strove with the angel." With that he entered the tent.

No one spoke to me, but the ragged company sought each their sleeping-place. A woman with a friendly face jogged me on the elbow, and from the neuk of her plaid gave me a bit of oatcake and a piece of roasted moorfowl. This made my supper, with a long drink from a neighbouring burn. None hindered my movements, so, liking little the smell of wet, uncleanly garments which clung around the fire, I made my bed in a heather bush in the lee of a boulder, and from utter weariness fell presently asleep.

CHAPTER II

OF A HIGH-HANDED LADY

THE storm died away in the night, and I awoke to a clear, rain-washed world and the chill of an autumn morn. I was as stiff and sore as if I had been whipped, my clothes were sodden and heavy, and not till I had washed my face and hands in the burn and stretched my legs up the hill-side did I feel restored to something of my ordinary briskness.

The encampment looked weird indeed as seen in the cruel light of day. The women were cooking oatmeal on iron girdles, but the fire burned smokily, and the cake I got was no better than dough. They were a disjaskit lot, with tousled hair and pinched faces, in which shone hungry eyes. Most were barefoot, and all but two-three were ancient beldames who should have been at home in the chimney corner. I noticed one decent-looking young woman, who had the air of a farm servant ; and two were well-fed country wives who had probably left a brood of children to mourn them. The men were little better. One had the sallow look of a weaver, another was a hind with a big, foolish face, and there was a slip of a lad who might once have been a student of divinity. But each had a daftness in the eye and something weak and unwholesome in the visage, so that they were an offence to the fresh, gusty moorland.

All but Muckle John himself. He came out of his tent and prayed till the hill-sides echoed. It was a tangle of bedlamite ravings, with long screeds from the Scriptures intermixed like currants in a bag-pudding. But there was power in the creature, in the strange lift of his voice, in his grim jowl, and in the fire of his sombre eyes. The others I pitied, but him I hated and feared. On him and his kind were to be blamed all the madness of the land, which had sent my father overseas and desolated our dwelling. So long as crazy prophets preached brimstone and fire, so long would rough-shod soldiers and cunning lawyers profit by their folly ; and often I prayed in those days that the two evils might devour each other.

It was time that I was cutting loose from this ill-omened company and continuing my road Edinburgh-wards. We were lying in a wide trough of the Pentland Hills, which I well remembered. The folk of the place called it the Cauldstaneslap, and it made an easy path for sheep and cattle between the Lothians and Tweeddale. The camp had been snugly chosen, for, except by the gleam of a fire in the dark, it was

invisible from any distance. Muckle John was
so filled with his vapourings that I could readily
slip off down the burn and join the southern
highway at the village of Linton.

I was on the verge of going when I saw that
which pulled me up. A rider was coming over
the moor. The horse leaped the burn lightly, and
before I could gather my wits was in the midst
of the camp, where Muckle John was vociferating
to heaven.

My heart gave a great bound, for I saw it was
the girl who had sung to me in the rain. She
rode a fine sorrel, with the easy seat of a skilled
horsewoman. She was trimly clad in a green
riding-coat, and over the lace collar of it her hair
fell in dark, clustering curls. Her face was grave,
like a determined child's; but the winds of the
morning had whipped it to a rosy colour, so that
into that clan of tatterdemalions she rode like
Proserpine descending among the gloomy Shades.
In her hand she carried a light riding-whip.

A scream from the women brought Muckle John
out of his rhapsodies. He stared blankly at the
slim girl who confronted him with hand on hip.

"What seekest thou here, thou shameless
woman?" he roared.

"I am come," said she, "for my tirewoman,
Janet Somerville, who left me three days back
without a reason. Word was brought me that
she had joined a mad company called the Sweet-
Singers, that lay at the Cauldstaneslap. Janet's
a silly body, but she means no ill, and her mother

is demented at the loss of her. So I have come for Janet." *

Her cool eyes ran over the assembly till they lighted on the one I had already noted as more decent-like than the rest. At the sight of the girl the woman bobbed a curtsy.

"Come out of it, silly Janet," said she on the horse ; "you'll never make a Sweet-Singer, for there's not a notion of a tune in your head."

"It's not singing that I seek, my leddy," said the woman, blushing. "I follow the call o' the Lord by the mouth o' His servant, John Gib."

"You'll follow the call of your mother by the mouth of me, Elspeth Blair. Forget these havers, Janet, and come back like a good Christian soul. Mount and be quick. There's room behind me on Bess."

The words were spoken in a kindly, wheedling tone, and the girl's face broke into the prettiest of smiles. Perhaps Janet would have obeyed, but Muckle John, swift to prevent defection, took up the parable.

"Begone, ye daughter of Heth ! " he bellowed, "ye that are like the devils that pluck souls from the way of salvation. Begone, or it is strongly borne in upon me that ye will dree the fate of the women of Midian, of whom it is written that they were slaughtered and spared not."

The girl did not look his way. She had her coaxing eyes on her halting maid. "Come, Janet, woman," she said again. "It's no job for a decent lass to be wandering at the tail of a crazy warlock."

The word roused Muckle John to fury. He sprang forward, caught the sorrel's bridle, and swung it round. The girl did not move, but looked him square in the face, the young eyes fronting his demoniac glower. Then very swiftly her arm rose, and she laid the lash of her whip roundly over his shoulders.

The man snarled like a beast, leaped back and plucked from his seaman's belt a great horse-pistol. I heard the click of it cocking, and the next I knew it was levelled at the girl's breast. The sight of her and the music of her voice had so enthralled me that I had made no plan as to my own conduct. But this sudden peril put fire into my heels, and in a second I was at his side. I had brought from home a stout shepherd's staff, with which I struck the muzzle upwards. The pistol went off in a great stench of powder, but the bullet wandered to the clouds.

Muckle John let the thing fall into the moss, and plucked another weapon from his belt. This was an ugly knife, such as a cobbler uses for paring hides. I knew the seaman's trick of throwing, having seen their brawls at the pier of Leith, and I had no notion for the steel in my throat. The man was far beyond me in size and strength, so I dared not close with him. Instead, I gave him the point of my staff with all my power straight in the midriff. The knife slithered harmlessly over my shoulder, and he fell backwards into the heather.

There was no time to be lost, for the whole clan

came round me like a flock of daws. One of the men, the slim lad, had a pistol, but I saw by the way he handled it that it was unprimed. I was most afraid of the women, who with their long claws would have scratched my eyes out, and I knew they would not spare the girl. To her I turned anxiously, and, to my amazement, she was laughing. She recognized me, for she cried out, " Is this the way to Kirknewton, sir ? " And all the time she shook with merriment. In that hour I thought her as daft as the Sweet-Singers, whose nails were uncommonly near my cheek.

I got her bridle, tumbled over the countryman with a kick, and forced her to the edge of the sheepfold. But she wheeled round again, crying, " I must have Janet," and faced the crowd with her whip. That was well enough, but I saw Muckle John staggering to his feet, and I feared desperately for his next move. The girl was either mad or extraordinarily brave.

" Get back, you pitiful knaves," she cried. " Lay a hand on me, and I will cut you to ribbons. Make haste, Janet, and quit this folly."

It was gallant talk, but there was no sense in it. Muckle John was on his feet, half the clan had gone round to our rear, and in a second or two she would have been torn from the saddle. A headstrong girl was beyond my management, and my words of entreaty were lost in the babel of cries.

But just then there came another sound. From the four quarters of the moor there closed in upon us horsemen. They came silently and were about us before I had a hint of their presence. It was a troop of dragoons in the king's buff and scarlet, and they rode us down as if we had been hares in a field. The next I knew of it I was sprawling on the ground with a dizzy head, and horses trampling around me. I had a glimpse of Muckle John with a pistol at his nose, and the sorrel curveting and plunging in a panic. Then I bethought myself of saving my bones, and crawled out of the mellay behind the sheepfold.

Presently I realized that this was the salvation I had been seeking. Gib was being pinioned, and two of the riders were speaking with the girl. The women hung together like hens in a storm, while the dragoons laid about them with the flat of their swords. There was one poor creature came running my way, and after her followed on foot a long fellow, who made clutches at her hair. He caught her with ease, and proceeded to bind her hands with great brutality.

" Ye beldame," he said, with many oaths, " I'll pare your talons for ye."

Now I, who a minute before had been in danger from this very crew, was smitten with a sudden compunction. Except for Muckle John, they were so pitifully feeble, a pack of humble, elderly folk, worn out with fasting and marching and ill weather. I had been sickened by their crazy devotions, but I was more sickened by this man's barbarity. It was the woman, too, who had given me food the night before.

So I stepped out, and bade the man release her.

He was a huge, sunburned ruffian, and for answer aimed a clour at my head. " Take that, my mannie," he said. " I'll learn ye to follow the petticoats."

His scorn put me into a fury, in which anger at his brutishness and the presence of the girl on the sorrel moved my pride to a piece of naked folly. I flew at his throat, and since I had stood on a little eminence, the force of my assault toppled him over. My victory lasted scarcely a minute. He flung me from him like a feather, then picked me up and laid on to me with the flat of his sword.

" Ye thrawn jackanapes," he cried, as he beat me. " Ye'll pay dear for playing your pranks wi' John Donald."

I was a child in his mighty grasp, besides having no breath left in me to resist. He tied my hands and legs, haled me to his horse, and flung me sack-like over the crupper. There was no more shamefaced lad in the world than me at that moment, for coming out of the din I heard a girl's light laughter.

CHAPTER III

" NEVER daunton youth " was, I remember,
a saying of my grandmother's ; but it was
the most dauntoned youth in Scotland that now
jogged over the moor to the Edinburgh highroad.
I had a swimming head, and a hard crupper to
grate my ribs at every movement, and my captor
would shift me about with as little gentleness as if
I had been a bag of oats for his horse's feed. But
it was the ignominy of the business that kept me
on the brink of tears. First, I was believed to be
one of the maniac company of the Sweet-Singers,
whom my soul abhorred ; *item*, I had been worsted
by a trooper with shameful ease, so that my manhood cried out against me. Lastly, I had cut the
sorriest figure in the eyes of that proud girl. For
a moment I had been bold, and fancied myself her
saviour, but all I had got by it was her mocking
laughter.

They took us down from the hill to the highroad
a little north of Linton village, where I was dumped
on the ground, my legs untied, and my hands

strapped to a stirrup leather. The women were given a country cart to ride in, but the men, including Muckle John, had to run each by a trooper's leg. The girl on the sorrel had gone, and so had the maid Janet, for I could not see her among the dishevelled wretches in the cart. The thought of that girl filled me with bitter animosity. She must have known that I was none of Gib's company, for had I not risked my life at the muzzle of his pistol ? I had taken her part as bravely as I knew how, and she had left me to be dragged to Edinburgh without a word. Women had never come much my way, but I had a boy's distrust of the sex ; and as I plodded along the highroad, with every now and then a cuff from a trooper's fist to cheer me, I had hard thoughts of their heartlessness.

We were a pitiful company as, in the bright autumn sun, we came in by the village of Liberton, to where the reek of Edinburgh rose straight into the windless weather. The women in the cart kept up a continual lamenting, and Muckle John, who walked between two dragoons with his hands tied to the saddle of each, so that he looked like a crucified malefactor, polluted the air with hideous profanities. He cursed everything in nature an ! beyond it, and no amount of clouts on the head would stem the torrent. Sometimes he would fall to howling like a wolf, and folk ran to their cottage doors to see the portent. Groups of children followed us from every wayside clachan, so that we gave great entertainment to the dwellers

in Lothian that day. The thing infuriated the
dragoons, for it made them a laughing-stock, and
the sins of Gib were visited upon the more silent
prisoners. We were hurried along at a cruel
pace, so that I had often to run to avoid the dragging at my wrists, and behind us bumped the
cart full of wailful women. I was sick from fatigue
and lack of food, and the South Port of Edinburgh
was a welcome sight to me. Welcome, and yet
shameful, for I feared at any moment to see the
face of a companion in the jeering crowd that
lined the causeway. I thought miserably of my
pleasant lodgings in the Bow, where my landlady,
Mistress Macvittie, would be looking at the boxes
the Lanark carrier had brought, and wondering
what had become of their master. I saw no light
for myself in the business. My father's ill-repute
with the Government would tell heavily in my
disfavour, and it was beyond doubt that I had
assaulted a dragoon. There was nothing before
me but the plantations or a long spell in some
noisome prison.

The women were sent to the House of Correc-
tion to be whipped and dismissed, for there was
little against them but foolishness ; all except
one, a virago called Isobel Bone, who was herded
with the men. The Canongate Tolbooth was our
portion, the darkest and foulest of the city prisons ;
and presently I found myself forced through a
gateway and up a narrow staircase, into a little
chamber in which a score of beings were already
penned. A small unglazed window with iron

bars high up on one wall gave us such light and air as was going, but the place reeked with human breathing, and smelled as rank as a kennel. I have a delicate nose, and I believed on my entrance that an hour of such a hole would be the death of me. Soon the darkness came, and we were given a tallow dip in a horn lantern hung on a nail to light us to food. Such food I had never dreamed of. There was a big iron basin of some kind of broth, made, as I judged, from offal, from which we drank in pannikins; and with it were hunks of mildewed rye-bread. One mouthful sickened me, and I preferred to fast. The behaviour of the other prisoners was most seemly, but not so that of my company. They scrambled for the stuff like pigs round a trough, and the woman Isobel threatened with her nails any one who would prevent her. I was black ashamed to enter prison with such a crew, and withdrew myself as far distant as the chamber allowed me.

I had no better task than to look round me at those who had tenanted the place before our coming. There were three women, decent-looking bodies, who talked low in whispers and knitted. The men were mostly country-folk, culled, as I could tell by their speech, from the west country, whose only fault, no doubt, was that they had attended some field-preaching. One old man, a minister by his dress, sat apart on a stone bench, and with closed eyes communed with himself. I ventured to address him, for in that horrid place he had a welcome air of sobriety and sense.

He asked me for my story, and when he heard
it looked curiously at Muckle John, who was now
reciting gibberish in a corner.

" So that is the man Gib," he said musingly.
" I have heard tell of him, for he was a thorn in
the flesh of blessed Mr. Cargill. Often have I
heard him repeat how he went to Gib in the moors
to reason with him in the Lord's name, and got
nothing but a mouthful of devilish blasphemies.
He is without doubt a child of Belial, as much
as any proud persecutor. Woe is the Kirk, when
her foes shall be of her own household, for it is
with the words of the Gospel that he seeks to over-
throw the Gospel work. And how is it with you,
my son ? Do you seek to add your testimony to
the sweet savour which now ascends from moors,
mosses, peat-bogs, closes, kennels, prisons, dun-
geons, ay, and scaffolds in this distressed land of
Scotland ? You have not told me your name."

When he heard it he asked for my father, whom
he had known in old days at Edinburgh College.
Then he inquired into my religious condition with
so much fatherly consideration that I could take
no offence, but told him honestly that I was little
of a partisan, finding it hard enough to keep my
own feet from temptation without judging others.
" I am weary," I said, " of all covenants and
resolutions and excommunications and the con-
straining of men's conscience either by Government or sectaries. Some day, and I pray that
it may be soon, both sides will be dead of their
wounds, and there will arise in Scotland men

who will preach peace and tolerance, and heal the grievously irritated sores of this land."

He sighed as he heard me. "I fear you are still far from grace, lad," he said. "You are shaping for a Laodicean, of whom there are many in these latter times. I do not know. It may be that God wills that the Laodiceans have their day, for the fires of our noble Covenant have flamed too smokily. Yet those fires die not, and sometime they will kindle up, purified and strengthened, and will burn the trash and stubble and warm God's feckless people."

He was so old and gentle that I had no heart for disputation, and could only beseech his blessing. This he gave me and turned once more to his devotions. I was very weary, my head was splitting with the foul air of the place, and I would fain have got me to sleep. Some dirty straw had been laid round the walls of the room for the prisoners to lie on, and I found a neuk close by the minister's side.

But sleep was impossible, for Muckle John got another fit of cursing. He stood up by the door with his eyes blazing like a wild-cat's, and delivered what he called his "testimony." His voice had been used to shout orders on shipboard, and not one of us could stop his ears against it. Never have I heard such a medley of profane nonsense. He cursed the man Charles Stuart, and every councillor by name; he cursed the Persecutors, from His Highness of York down to one Welch of Borrowstoneness, who had been the means of his first imprisonment; he cursed the indulged and tolerated ministers; and he cursed every man of the hill-folk whose name he could remember. He testified against all dues and cesses, against all customs and excises, taxes and burdens; against beer and ale and wines and tobacco; against mumming and peep-shows and dancing, and every sort of play; against Christmas and Easter and Pentecost and Hogmanay. Then most nobly did he embark on theology. He made short work of hell and shorter work of heaven. He raved against idolaters of the Kirk and of the Bible, and against all preachers who, by his way of it, had perverted the Word. As he went on, I began to fancy that Muckle John's true place was with the Mussulmans, for he left not a stick of Christianity behind him.

Such blasphemy on the open hill-side had been shocking enough, but in that narrow room it was too horrid to be borne. The minister stuck his fingers in his ears, and, advancing to the maniac, bade him be silent before God should blast him. But what could his thin old voice do against Gib's bellowing? The mariner went on undisturbed, and gave the old man a blow with his foot which sent him staggering to the floor.

The thing had become too much for my temper. I cried on the other men to help me, but none stirred, for Gib seemed to cast an unholy spell on ordinary folk. But my anger and discomfort banished all fear, and I rushed at the prophet in a whirlwind. He had no eyes for my coming till my head took him fairly in the middle, and drove the breath out of his chest. That quieted his noise, and he turned on me with something like wholesome human wrath in his face.

Now, I was no match for this great being with my ungrown strength, but the lesson of my encounter with the dragoon was burned on my mind, and I was determined to keep out of grips with him. I was light on my feet, and in our country bouts had often worsted a heavier antagonist by my quickness in movement. So when Muckle John leaped to grab me, I darted under his arm, and he staggered half-way across the room. The women scuttled into a corner, all but the besom Isobel, who made clutches at my coat.

Crying " The sword of the Lord and of Gideon," Gib made a great lunge at me with his fist. But the sword of Gideon missed its aim, and skinned its knuckles on the stone wall. I saw now to my great comfort that the man was beside himself with fury, and was swinging his arms wildly like a flail. Three or four times I avoided his rushes, noting with satisfaction that one of the countrymen had got hold of the shrieking Isobel. Then my chance came, for as he lunged I struck from the side with all my force on his jaw. I am left-handed, and the blow was unlooked for. He staggered back a step, and I deftly tripped him up, so that he fell with a crash on the hard floor.

In a second I was on the top of him, shouting to the others to lend me a hand. This they did at last, and so amazed was he with the fall, being a mighty heavy man, that he scarcely resisted. "If you want a quiet night," I cried, "we must silence this mountebank." With three leathern belts, one my own and two borrowed, we made fast his feet and arms. I stuffed a kerchief into his mouth, and bound his jaws with another, but not so tight as to hinder his breathing. Then we rolled him into a corner, where he lay peacefully making the sound of a milch cow chewing her cud. I returned to my quarters by the minister's side, and presently from utter weariness fell into an uneasy sleep.

I woke in the morning greatly refreshed for all the closeness of the air, and, the memory of the night's events returning, was much concerned as to the future. I could not be fighting with Muckle John all the time, and I made no doubt that once his limbs were freed he would try to kill me. The others were still asleep while I tip-toed over to his corner. At first sight I got a fearsome shock, for I thought he was dead of suf-focation. He had worked the gag out of his mouth, and lay as still as a corpse. But soon I saw that he was sleeping quietly, and in his slumbers the madness had died out of his face. He looked like any other sailorman, a trifle ill-favoured of counte-nance, and dirty beyond the ordinary of sea-folk.

When the gaoler came with food, we all wakened up, and Gib asked very peaceably to be released. The gaoler laughed at his predicament, and in-quired the tale of it; and when he heard the truth, called for a vote as to what he should do. I was satisfied, from the look of Muckle John, that his dangerous fit was over, so I gave my voice for release. Gib shook himself like a great dog, and fell to his breakfast without a word. I found the thin brose provided more palatable than the soup of the evening before, and managed to consume a pannikin of it. As I finished, I perceived that Gib had squatted by my side. There was clearly some change in the man, for he gave the woman Isobel some very ill words when she started ranting.

Up in the little square of window one could see a patch of clear sky, with white clouds crossing it, and a gust of the clean air of morning was blown into our cell. Gib sat looking at it with his eyes abstracted, so that I feared a renewal of his daftness.

" Can ye whistle ' Jenny Nettles,' sir ? " he asked me civilly.

It was surely a queer request in that place and from such a fellow. But I complied, and to the best of my skill rendered the air.

He listened greedily. " Ay, you've got it," he said, humming it after me, " I aye love the way of it. Yon's the tune I used to whistle mysel' on shipboard when the weather was clear."

He had the seaman's trick of thinking of the weather first thing in the morning, and this little thing wrought a change in my view of him. His madness was seemingly like that of an epileptic, and when it passed he was a simple creature with a longing for familiar things.

"The wind's to the east," he said. "I could
wish I were beating down the Forth in the *Loupin'
Jean*. She was a trim bit boat for him that could
handle her."

"Man," I said, "what made you leave a clean
job for the ravings of yesterday ? "

"I'm in the Lord's hands," he said humbly.
"I'm but a penny whistle for His breath to blow
on." This he said with such solemnity that the
meaning of a fanatic was suddenly revealed to me.
One or two distorted notions, a wild imagination,
and fierce passions, and there you have the ingre-
dients ready. But moments of sense must come,
when the better nature of the man revives. I had
a thought that the clout he got on the stone floor
had done much to clear his wits.

"What will they do wi' me, think ye ? " he
asked. "This is the second time I've fallen
into the hands o' the Amalekites, and it's no likely
they'll let me off sae lightly."

"What will they do with us all ? " said I. "The
Plantations maybe, or the Bass ! It's a bonny
creel you've landed me in, for I'm as innocent as
a new-born babe."

The notion of the Plantations seemed to comfort him. "I've been there afore, once in the
brig *John Rolfe* o' Greenock, and once in the *Luck-
penny* o' Leith. It's a het land but a bonny, and
full o' all manner o' fruits. You can see tobacco
growin' like aits, and mair big trees in one plantin'
than in all the shire o' Lothian. Besides——"

But I got no more of Muckle John's travels,

for the door opened on that instant, and the gaoler appeared. He looked at our heads, then singled me out, and cried on me to follow. " Come on, you," he said. " Ye're wantit in the captain's room."

I followed in bewilderment ; for I knew something of the law's delays, and I could not believe that my hour of trial had come already. The man took me down the turret stairs and through a long passage to a door where stood two halberdiers. Through this he thrust me, and I found myself in a handsome panelled apartment with the city arms carved above the chimney. A window stood open, and I breathed the sweet, fresh air with delight. But I caught a reflection of myself in the polished steel of the fireplace, and my spirits fell, for a more woebegone ruffian my eyes had never seen. I was as dirty as a collier, my coat was half off my back from my handling on the moor, and there were long rents at the knees of my breeches.

Another door opened, and two persons entered. One was a dapper little man with a great wig, very handsomely dressed in a plum-coloured silken coat, with a snowy cravat at his neck. At the sight of the other my face crimsoned, for it was the girl who had sung Montrose's song in the rain.

The little gentleman looked at me severely, and then turned to his companion. " Is this the fellow, Elspeth ? " he inquired. " He looks a sorry rascal."

The minx pretended to examine me carefully. Her colour was high with the fresh morning, and she kept tapping her boot with her whip handle.

"Why, yes, Uncle Gregory," she said. "It is the very man, though none the better for your night's attentions."

"And you say he had no part in Gib's company, but interfered on your behalf when the madman threatened you?"

"Such was his impertinence," she said, "as if I were not a match for a dozen crazy hill-folk. But doubtless the lad meant well."

"It is also recorded against him that he assaulted one of His Majesty's servants, to wit, the trooper John Donald, and offered to hinder him in the prosecution of his duty."

"La, uncle!" cried the girl, "who is to distinguish friend from foe in a mellay? Have you never seen a dog in a fight bite the hand of one who would succour him?"

"Maybe, maybe," said the gentleman. "Your illustrations, Elspeth, would do credit to His Majesty's Advocate. Your plea is that this young man, whose name I do not know and do not seek to hear, should be freed or justice will miscarry? God knows the law has enough to do without clogging its wheels with innocence."

The girl nodded. Her wicked, laughing eyes roamed about the apartment with little regard for my flushed face.

"Then the Crown assoilzies the panel and deserts the diet," said the little gentleman.

"Speak, sir, and thank His Majesty for his clemency and this lady for her intercession."

I had no words, for if I had been sore at my imprisonment, I was black angry at this manner of release. I did not reflect that Miss Elspeth Blair must have risen early and ridden far to be in the Canongate at this hour. 'Twas justice only that moved her, I thought, and no gratitude or kindness. To her I was something so lowly that she need not take the pains to be civil, but must speak of me in my presence as if it were a question of a stray hound. My first impulse was to refuse to stir, but happily my good sense returned in time and preserved me from playing the fool.

"I thank you, sir," I said gruffly—"and the lady. Do I understand that I am free to go?"

"Through the door, down the left stairway, and you will be in the street," said the gentleman.

I made some sort of bow and moved to the door. "Farewell, Mr. Whiggamore," the girl cried. "Keep a cheerful countenance, or they'll think you a Sweet-Singer. Your breeches will mend, man."

And with her laughter most unpleasantly in my ears I made my way into the Canongate, and so to my lodgings at Mrs. Macvittie's.

Three weeks later I heard that Muckle John was destined for the Plantations in a ship of Mr. Barclay of Urie's, which traded to New Jersey.

I had a fancy to see him before he went, and after much trouble I was suffered to visit him. His gaoler told me he had been mighty wild during his examination before the Council, and had had frequent bouts of madness since, but for the moment he was peaceable. I found him in a little cell by himself, outside the common room of the gaol. He was sitting in an attitude of great dejection, and when I entered could scarcely recall me to his memory. I remember thinking that, what with his high cheek-bones, and lank black hair, and brooding eyes, and great muscular frame, Scotland could scarcely have furnished a wilder figure for the admiration of the Carolinas, or wherever he went to. I did not envy his future master.

But with me he was very friendly and quiet. His ailment was home-sickness ; for though he had been a great voyager, it seemed he was loath to quit our bleak countryside for ever. " I used aye to think o' the first sight o' Inchkeith and the Lomond hills, and the smell o' herrings at the pier o' Leith. What says the Word ? ' *Weep not for the dead, neither bemoan him ; but weep sore for him that goeth away, for he shall return no more, nor see his native country.*' "

I asked him if I could do him any service.

"There's a woman at Cramond," he began timidly. " She might like to ken what had become o' me. Would ye carry a message ? "

I did better, for at Gib's dictation I composed for her a letter, since he could not write. I wrote

it on some blank pages from my pocket which
I used for College notes.   It was surely the queerest
love-letter ever indited, for the most part of it
was theology, and the rest was instructions for
the disposing of his scanty plenishing. I have
forgotten now what I wrote, but I remember that
the woman's name was Alison Steel.

CHAPTER IV

OF A STAIRHEAD AND A SEA-CAPTAIN

WITH the escapade that landed me in the Tolbooth there came an end to the nightmare years of my first youth. A week later I got word that my father was dead of an ague in the Low Countries, and I had to be off post-haste to Auchencairn to see to the ordering of our little estate. We were destined to be bitter poor, what with dues and regalities incident on the passing of the ownership, and I thought it best to leave my mother to farm it, with the help of Robin Gilfillan the grieve, and seek employment which would bring me an honest penny. Her one brother, Andrew Sempill, from whom I was named, was a merchant in Glasgow, the owner of three ships that traded to the Western Seas, and by repute a man of a shrewd and venturesome temper. He was single, too, and I might reasonably look to be his heir ; so when a letter came from him offering me a hand in his business, my mother was instant for my going. I was little loath myself, for I saw nothing now to draw me to the profes-

sion of the law, which had been my first notion.
" Hame's hame," runs the proverb, " as the devil
said when he found himself in the Court of Session,"
and I had lost any desire for that sinister company. Besides, I liked the notion of having to
do with ships and far lands ; for I was at the
age when youth burns fiercely in a lad, and his
fancy is as riotous as a poet's.

Yet the events I have just related had worked
a change in my life. They had driven the un-
thinking child out of me and forced me to reflect
on my future. Two things rankled in my soul
—a wench's mocking laughter and the treatment
I had got from the dragoon. It was not that I
was in love with the black-haired girl ; indeed,
I think I hated her ; but I could not get her face
out of my head or her voice out of my ears. She
had mocked me, treated me as if I was no more
than a foolish servant, and my vanity was raw.
I longed to beat down her pride, to make her
creep humbly to me, Andrew Garvald, as her
only deliverer ; and how that should be com-
passed was the subject of many hot fantasies in
my brain. The dragoon, too, had tossed me about
like a silly sheep, and my manhood cried out at
the recollection. What sort of man was I if any
lubberly soldier could venture on such liberties ?

I went into the business with the monstrous
solemnity of youth, and took stock of my equip-
ment as if I were casting up an account. Many
a time in those days I studied my appearance
in the glass like a foolish maid. I was not well

featured, having a freckled, square face, a biggish head, a blunt nose, grey, colourless eyes, and a sandy thatch of hair. I had great square shoulders, but my arms were too short for my stature, and —from an accident in my nursing days—of indifferent strength. All this stood on the debit side of my account. On the credit side I set down that I had unshaken good health and an uncommon power of endurance, especially in the legs. There was no runner in the Upper Ward of Lanark who was my match, and I had travelled the hills so constantly in all weathers that I had acquired a gipsy lore in the matter of beasts and birds and wild things. I had long, clear, unerring eyesight, which had often stood me in good stead in the time of my father's troubles. Of moral qualities, Heaven forgive me, I fear I thought less ; but I believed, though I had been little proved, that I was as courageous as the common run of men.

All this looks babyish in the writing, but there was a method in this self-examination. I believed that I was fated to engage in strange ventures, and I wanted to equip myself for the future. The pressing business was that of self-defence, and I turned first to a gentleman's proper weapon, the sword. Here, alas ! I was doomed to a bitter disappointment. My father had given me a lesson now and then, but never enough to test me, and when I came into the hands of a Glasgow master my unfitness was soon manifest. Neither with broadsword nor small sword could I acquire any skill. My short arm lacked reach and vigour, and there seemed to be some stiffness in wrist and elbow and shoulder which compelled me to yield to smaller men. Here was a pretty business, for though gentleman born I was as loutish with a gentleman's weapon as any country hind.

This discovery gave me some melancholy weeks, but I plucked up heart and set to reasoning. If my hand were to guard my head it must find some other way of it. My thoughts turned to powder and shot, to the musket and the pistol. Here was a weapon which needed only a stout nerve, a good eye, and a steady hand; one of these I possessed to the full, and the others were not beyond my attainment. There lived an armourer in the Gallowgate, one Weir, with whom I began to spend my leisure. There was an alley by the Molendinar Burn, close to the archery butts, where he would let me practise at a mark with guns from his store. Soon, to my delight, I found that here was a weapon with which I need fear few rivals. I had a natural genius for the thing, as some men have for sword-play, and Weir was a zealous teacher, for he loved his flintlocks.

" See, Andrew," he would cry, " this is the true leveller of mankind. It will make the man his master's equal, for though your gentleman may cock on a horse and wave his Andrew Ferrara, this will bring him off it. Brains, my lad, will tell in coming days, for it takes a head to shoot well, though any flesher may swing a sword."

The better marksman I grew the less I liked

the common make of guns, and I cast about to
work an improvement. I was especially fond of
the short gun or pistol, not the bell-mouthed thing
which shot a handful of slugs, and was as little
precise in its aim as a hailstorm, but the light
foreign pistol which shot as true as a musket.
Weir had learned his trade in Italy, and was a neat
craftsman, so I employed him to make me a pistol
after my own pattern. The butt was of light,
tough wood, and brass-bound, for I did not care
to waste money on ornament. The barrel was
shorter than the usual, and of the best Spanish
metal, and the pan and the lock were set after my
own device. Nor was that all, for I became an
epicure in the matter of bullets, and made my own
with the care of a goldsmith. I would weigh out
the powder charges as nicely as an apothecary
weighs his drugs, for I had discovered that with
the pistol the weight of bullet and charge meant
much for good marksmanship. From Weir I got
the notion of putting up ball and powder in cartouches, and I devised a method of priming much
quicker and surer than the ordinary. In one way
and another I believe I acquired more skill in the
business than anybody then living in Scotland.
I cherished my toy like a lover ; I christened it
" Elspeth " ; it lay by my bed at night, and lived
by day in a box of sweet-scented foreign wood
given me by one of my uncle's skippers. I doubt
I thought more of it than of my duty to my
Maker.

All the time I was very busy at Uncle Andrew's

counting-house in the Candleriggs, and down by
the river-side among the sailors. It was the day
when Glasgow was rising from a cluster of streets
round the High Kirk and College to be the chief
merchants' resort in Scotland. Standing near the
Western Seas, she turned her eyes naturally to
the Americas, and a great trade was beginning
in tobacco and raw silk from Virginia, rich woods
and dye-stuffs from the Main, and rice and fruits
from the Summer Islands. The river was too
shallow for ships of heavy burthen, so it was the
custom to unload in the neighbourhood of Greenock
and bring the goods upstream in barges to the
quay at the Broomielaw. There my uncle, in
company with other merchants, had his warehouse,
but his counting-house was up in the town, near
by the College, and I spent my time equally between the two places. I became furiously interested in the work, for it has ever been my happy
fortune to be intent on whatever I might be doing
at the moment. I think I served my uncle well,
for I had much of the merchant's aptitude, and the
eye to discern far-away profits. He liked my bold-
ness, for I was impatient of the rule-of-thumb
ways of some of our fellow-traders. " We are
dealing with new lands," I would say, " and there
is need of new plans. It pays to think in trading
as much as in statecraft." There were plenty
that looked askance at us, and cursed us as troublers
of the peace, and there were some who prophesied
speedy ruin. But we discomforted our neighbours
by prospering mightily, so that there was talk of

Uncle Andrew for the Provost's chair at the next
vacancy.

They were happy years, the four I spent in
Glasgow, for I was young and ardent, and had
not yet suffered the grave miscarriage of hope
which is our human lot. My uncle was a busy
merchant, but he was also something of a scholar,
and was never happier than when disputing some
learned point with a college professor over a bowl
of punch. He was a great fisherman, too, and
many a salmon I have seen him kill between the
town and Rutherglen in the autumn afternoons.
He treated me like a son, and by his aid I completed my education by much reading of books
and a frequent attendance at college lectures.
Such leisure as I had I spent by the river-side
talking with the ship captains and getting news
of far lands. In this way I learned something
of the handling of a ship, and especially how to
sail a sloop alone in rough weather. I have ventured, myself the only crew, far down the river
to the beginning of the sea-lochs, and more than
once escaped drowning by a miracle. Of a Satur-
day I would sometimes ride out to Auchencairn
to see my mother and assist with my advice the
work of Robin Gilfillan. Once, I remember, I
rode to Carnwath, and looked again on the bleak
house where the girl Elspeth had sung to me in
the rain. I found it locked and deserted, and
heard from a countrywoman that the folk had
gone. " And a guid riddance," said the woman.
" The Blairs was aye a cauld and oppressive race,

and black Prelatists forbye. But I whiles miss yon hellicat lassie. She had a cheery word for a'body, and she keepit the place frae languor."

But I cannot linger over the tale of those peaceful years when I have so much that is strange and stirring to set down. Presently came the Revolution, when King James fled overseas, and the Dutch King William reigned in his stead. The event was a godsend to our trade, for with Scotland in a bicker with covenants and dragoonings, and new taxes threatened with each new Parliament, a merchant's credit was apt to be a brittle thing. The change brought a measure of security, and as we prospered I soon began to see that something must be done in our Virginian trade. Years before, my uncle had sent out a man, Lambie by name, who watched his interests in that country. But we had to face such fierce rivalry from the Bristol merchants that I had small confidence in Mr. Lambie, who from his letters was a sleepy soul. I broached the matter to my uncle, and offered to go myself and put things in order. At first he was unwilling to listen. I think he was sorry to part with me, for we had become close friends, and there was also the difficulty of my mother, to whom I was the natural protector. But his opposition died down when I won my mother to my side, and when I promised that I would duly return. I pointed out that Glasgow and Virginia were not so far apart. Planters from the colony would dwell with us for a season, and their sons often came to Glasgow for their school-

ing. You could see the proud fellows walking the
streets in brave clothes, and marching into the
kirk on Sabbath with a couple of servants carrying cushions and Bibles. In the better class of
tavern one could always meet with a Virginian or
two compounding their curious drinks, and swear-
ing their outlandish oaths. Most of them had
gone afield from Scotland, and it was a fine incen-
tive to us young men to see how mightily they
had prospered.

My uncle yielded, and it was arranged that I
should sail with the first convoy of the New Year.
From the moment of the decision I walked the
earth in a delirium of expectation. That February, I remember, was blue and mild, with soft
airs blowing up the river. Down by the Broomielaw I found a new rapture in the smell of tar and
cordage, and the queer foreign scents in my uncle's
warehouse. Every skipper and greasy sailor became for me a figure of romance. I scanned every
outland face, wondering if I should meet it again
in the New World. A negro in cotton drawers,
shivering in our northern clime, had more attrac-
tion for me than the fairest maid, and I was eager
to speak with all and every one who had crossed
the ocean. One bronzed mariner with silver ear-
rings I entertained to three stoups of usquebaugh,
hoping for strange tales, but the little I had from
him before he grew drunk was that he had once
voyaged to the Canaries. You may imagine that
I kept my fancies to myself, and was outwardly
only the sober merchant with a mind set on freights

and hogsheads. But whoever remembers his youth will know that such terms to me were not the common parlance of trade. The very names of the tobaccos—Negro's Head, Sweet-scented, Oronoke, Carolina Red, Gloucester Glory, Golden Rod —sang in my head like a tune, that told of green forests and magic islands.

But an incident befell ere I left which was to have unforeseen effects on my future. One afternoon I was in the shooting alley I have spoken of, making trial of a new size of bullet I had moulded. The place was just behind Parlane's tavern, and some gentlemen, who had been drinking there, came out to cool their heads and see the sport. Most of them were cock-lairds from the Lennox, and after the Highland fashion, had in their belts heavy pistols of the old kind which folk called "dags." They were cumbrous, illmade things, gaudily ornamented with silver and Damascus work, fit ornaments for a savage Highland chief, but little good for serious business, unless a man were only a pace or two from his opponent. One of them, who had drunk less than the others, came up to me and very civilly proposed a match. I was nothing loath, so a course was fixed, and a mutchkin of French *eau de vie* named as the prize. I borrowed an old hat from the landlord which had stuck in its side a small red cockade. The thing was hung as a target in a leafless cherry tree at twenty paces, and the cockade was to be the centre mark. Each man was to fire three shots apiece.

Barshalloch—for so his companions called my opponent after his lairdship—made a great to-do about the loading, and would not be content till he had drawn the charge two-three times. The spin of a coin gave him first shot, and he missed the mark and cut the bole of the tree.

" See," I said, " I will put my ball within a finger's-breadth of his." Sure enough, when they looked, the two bullets were all but in the same hole.

His second shot took the hat low down on its right side, and clipped away a bit of the brim. I saw by this time that the man could shoot, though he had a poor weapon and understood little about it. So I told the company that I would trim the hat by slicing a bit from the other side. This I achieved, though by little, for my shot removed only half as much cloth as its predecessor. But the performance amazed the onlookers. " Ye've found a fair provost at the job, Barshalloch," one of them hiccupped. " Better quit and pay for the mutchkin."

My antagonist took every care with his last shot, and, just missing the cockade, hit the hat about the middle, cut the branch on which it rested, and brought it fluttering to the ground a pace or two farther on. It lay there, dimly seen through a low branch of the cherry tree, with the cockade on the side nearest me. It was a difficult mark, but the light was good and my hand steady. I walked forward and brought back the hat with a hole drilled clean through the cockade.

At that there was a great laughter, and much jocosity from the cock-lairds at their friend's expense. Barshalloch very handsomely complimented me, and sent for the mutchkin. His words made me warm towards him, and I told him that half the business was not my skill of shooting but the weapon I carried.

He begged for a look at it, and examined it long and carefully.

"Will ye sell, friend ? " he asked. "I'll give ye ten golden guineas and the best filly that ever came out o' Strathendrick for that pistol." But I told him that the offer of Strathendrick itself would not buy it.

"No ? " said he. "Well, I won't say ye're wrong. A man should cherish his weapon like his wife, for it carries his honour."

Presently, having drunk the wager, they went indoors again, all but a tall fellow who had been a looker-on, but had not been of the Lennox company. I had remarked him during the contest, a long, lean man with a bright, humorous blue eye and a fiery red head. He was maybe ten years older than me, and though he was finely dressed in town clothes, there was about his whole appearance a smack of the sea. He came forward, and, in a very Highland voice, asked my name.

"Why should I tell you ? " I said, a little nettled.

"Just that I might carry it in my head. I have seen some pretty shooting in my day, but

none like yours, young one. What's your trade
that ye've learned the pistol game so cleverly ? "

Now I was flushed with pride, and in no
mood for a stranger's patronage. So I told him
roundly that it was none of his business, and
pushed by him to Parlane's back-door. But
my brusqueness gave no offence to this odd being.
He only laughed and cried after me that, if my
manners were the equal of my marksmanship, I
would be the best lad he had seen since his home-
coming.

I had dinner with my uncle in the Candleriggs,
and sat with him late afterwards casting up accounts, so it was not till nine o'clock that I set
out on my way to my lodgings. These were in
the Saltmarket, close on the river front, and to
reach them I went by the short road through the
Friar's Vennel. It was an ill-reputed quarter of
the town, and not long before had been noted as
a haunt of coiners ; but I had gone through it
often, and met with no hindrance.

In the vennel stood a tall dark bit of masonry
called Gilmour's Lordship, which was pierced
by long closes from which twisting stairways
led to the upper landings. I was noting its
gloomy aspect under the dim February moon,
when a man came towards me and turned
into one of the closes. He swung along with
a free, careless gait that marked him as no
townsman, and ere he plunged into the darkness I had a glimpse of fiery hair. It was the
stranger who had accosted me in Parlane's alley,

and he was either drunk or in wild spirits, for he
was singing :—

> " We're a' dry wi' the drinkin' o't,
> We're a' dry wi' the drinkin' o't.
> The minister kissed the fiddler's wife,
> And he couldna preach for thinkin' o't."

The ribald chorus echoed from the close mouth.

Then I saw that he was followed by three others,
bent, slinking fellows, who slipped across the
patches of moonlight, and eagerly scanned the
empty vennel. They could not see me, for I was
in shadow, and presently they too entered the
close.

The thing looked ugly, and, while I had no love
for the red-haired man, I did not wish to see
murder or robbery committed and stand idly by.
The match of the afternoon had given me a fine
notion of my prowess, though, had I reflected, my
pistol was in its case at home, and I had no weapon
but a hazel staff. Happily in youth the blood is
quicker than the brain, and without a thought I
ran into the close and up the long stairway.

The chorus was still being sung ahead of me,
and then it suddenly ceased. In dead silence and
in pitchy darkness I struggled up the stone steps,
wondering what I should find at the next turning.
The place was black as night, the steps were un-
even, and the stairs corkscrewed most wonderfully.
I wished with all my heart that I had not come,
as I groped upwards hugging the wall.

Then a cry came and a noise of hard breathing.

At the same moment a door opened somewhere above my head, and a faint glow came down the stairs. Presently with a great rumble a heavy man came rolling past me, butting with his head at the stair-side. He came to anchor on a landing below me, and, finding his feet, plunged downwards as if the devil were at his heels. He left behind him a short Highland knife, which I picked up and put in my pocket.

On his heels came another with his hand clapped to his side, and he moaned as he slithered past me. Something dripped from him on the stone steps.

The light grew stronger, and as I rounded the last turning a third came bounding down, stumbling from wall to wall like a drunk man. I saw his face clearly, and if ever mortal eyes held baffled murder it was that fellow's. There was a dark mark on his shoulder.

Above me as I blinked stood my red-haired friend on the top landing. He had his sword drawn, and was whistling softly through his teeth, while on the right hand was an open door and an old man holding a lamp.

" Ho ! " he cried. " Here comes a fourth. God's help, it's my friend the marksman ! "

I did not like that naked bit of steel, but there was nothing for it but to see the thing through. When he saw that I was unarmed he returned his weapon to its sheath, and smiled broadly down on me.

" What brings my proud gentleman up these long stairs ? " he asked.

" I saw you enter the close and three men following you. It looked bad, so I came up to see
fair play."

" Did ye so ? And a very pretty intention, Mr.
What's-your-name. But ye needna have fashed
yourself. Did ye see any of our friends on the
stairs ? "

" I met a big man rolling down like a football,"
I said.

" Ay, that would be Angus. He's a clumsy stot,
and never had much sense."

" And I met another with his hand on his side,"
I said.

" That would be little James. He's a fine lad
with a skean-dhu on a dark night, but there was
maybe too much light here for his trade."

" And I met a third who reeled like a drunk
man," I said.

" Ay," said he meditatively, " that was Long
Colin. He's the flower o' the flock, and I had to
pink him. At another time and in a better place
I would have liked a bout with him, for he has
some notion of sword-play."

" Who were the men ? " I asked, in much confusion, for this laughing warrior perplexed me.

" Who but just my cousins from Glengyle.
There has long been a sort of bicker between us,
and they thought they had got a fine chance of
ending it."

" And who, in Heaven's name, are you," I said,
" that treats murder so lightly ? "

" Me ? " he repeated. " Well, I might give ye

the answer you gave me this very day when I speired the same question. But I am frank by nature, and I see you wish me well. Come in bye, and we'll discuss the matter."

He led me into a room where a cheerful fire crackled, and got out from a press a bottle and glasses. He produced tobacco from a brass box and filled a long pipe.

" Now," said he, " we'll understand each other better. Ye see before you a poor gentleman of fortune, whom poverty and a roving spirit have driven to outland bits o' the earth to ply his lawful trade of sea-captain. They call me by different names. I have passed for a Dutch skipper, and a Maryland planter, and a French trader, and, in spite of my colour, I have been a Spanish don in the Main. At Tortuga you will hear one name, and another at Port o' Spain, and a third at Cartagena. But, seeing we are in the city o' Glasgow in the kindly kingdom o' Scotland, I'll be honest with you. My father called me Ninian Campbell, and there's no better blood in Breadalbane."

What could I do after that but make him a present of the trivial facts about myself and my doings ? There was a look of friendly humour about this dare-devil which captured my fancy. I saw in him the stuff of which adventurers are made, and, though I was a sober merchant, I was also young. For days I had been dreaming of foreign parts and an Odyssey of strange fortunes, and here on a Glasgow stairhead I had found Ulysses himself.

" Is it not the pity," he cried, " that such talents as yours should rust in a dark room in the Candleriggs ? Believe me, Mr. Garvald, I have seen some pretty shots, but I have never seen your better."

Then I told him that I was sailing within a month for Virginia, and he suddenly grew solemn.

" It looks like Providence," he said, " that we two should come together. I, too, will soon be back in the Western Seas, and belike we'll meet. I'm something of a rover, and I never bide long in the same place, but I whiles pay a visit to James Town, and they ken me well on the Eastern Shore and the Accomac beaches."

He fell to giving me such advice as a traveller gives to a novice. It was strange hearing for an honest merchant, for much of it was concerned with divers ways of outwitting the law. By and by he was determined to convoy me to my lodgings, for he pointed out that I was unarmed ; and I think, too, he had still hopes of another meeting with Long Colin, his cousin.

" I leave Glasgow the morrow's morn," he said, " and it's no likely we'll meet again in Scotland. Out in Virginia, no doubt, you'll soon be a great man, and sit in Council, and hob-nob with the Governor. But a midge can help an elephant, and I would gladly help you, for you had the goodwill to help me. If ye need aid you will go to Mercer's Tavern at James Town down on the water front, and you will ask news of Ninian Campbell. The man will say that he never heard tell of the name, and then you will speak these words to him. You will say, ' The lymphads are on the loch, and the horn of Diarmaid has sounded.' Keep them well in mind, for some way or other they will bring you and me together."

Without another word he was off, and as I committed the gibberish to memory I could hear his song going up the Saltmarket :—

> " The minister kissed the fiddler's wife,
>   And he couldna preach for thinkin' o't."

CHAPTER V

THERE are few moments in life to compare
with a traveller's first sight of a new land
which is destined to be for short or long his home.
When, after a fair and speedy voyage, we passed
Point Comfort, and had rid ourselves of the revenue
men, and the tides bore us up the estuary of a
noble river, I stood on deck and drank in the
heady foreign scents with a boyish ecstasy. Presently we had opened the capital city, which
seemed to me no more than a village set amid
gardens, and Mr. Lambie had come aboard and
greeted me. He conveyed me to the best ordinary
in the town, which stood over against the Court-
house. Late in the afternoon, just before the dark
fell, I walked out to drink my fill of the place.

You are to remember that I was a country lad
who had never set foot forth of Scotland. I was
very young, and hot on the quest of new sights
and doings. As I walked down the unpaven street
and through the narrow tobacco-grown lanes, the
strange smell of it all intoxicated me like wine.

There was a great red sunset burning over the blue river and kindling the far forests till they glowed like jewels. The frogs were croaking among the reeds, and the wild duck squattered in the dusk. I passed an Indian, the first I had seen, with cock's feathers on his head, and a curiously tattooed chest, moving as light as a sleep-walker. One or two townsfolk took the air, smoking their long pipes, and down by the water a negro girl was singing a wild melody. The whole place was like a mad, sweet-scented dream to one just come from the unfeatured ocean, and with a memory only of grim Scots cities and dour Scots hills. I felt as if I had come into a large and generous land, and I thanked God that I was but twenty-three.

But as I was mooning along there came a sudden interruption on my dreams. I was beyond the houses, in a path which ran among tobacco-sheds and little gardens, with the river lapping a stone's-throw off. Down a side alley I caught a glimpse of a figure that seemed familiar.

'Twas that of a tall, hulking man, moving quickly among the tobacco plants, with something stealthy in his air. The broad, bowed shoulders and the lean head brought back to me the rainy moorlands about the Cauldstaneslap and the mad fellow whose prison I had shared. Muckle John had gone to the Plantations, and 'twas Muckle John or the devil that was moving there in the half light.

I cried on him, and ran down the side alley.

But it seemed that he did not want company, for he broke into a run.

Now in those days I rejoiced in the strength of my legs, and I was determined not to be thus balked. So I doubled after him into a maze of tobacco and melon beds.

But it seemed he knew how to run. I caught a glimpse of his hairy legs round the corner of a shed, and then lost him in a patch of cane. Then I came out on a sort of causeway floored with boards which covered a marshy sluice, and there I made great strides on him. He was clear against the sky now, and I could see that he was clad only in shirt and cotton breeches, while at his waist flapped an ugly sheath-knife.

Rounding the hut corner I ran full into a man.

" Hold you," cried the stranger, and laid hands on my arm ; but I shook him off violently, and continued the race. The collision had cracked my temper, and I had a mind to give Muckle John a lesson in civility. For Muckle John it was beyond doubt ; not two men in the broad earth had that ungainly bend of neck.

The next I knew we were out on the river bank on a shore of hard clay which the tides had created. Here I saw him more clearly, and I began to doubt. I might be chasing some river-side ruffian, who would give me a knife in my belly for my pains.

The doubt slackened my pace, and he gained on me. Then I saw his intention. There was a flat-bottomed wherry tied up by the bank, and for this he made. He flung off the rope, seized a long pole, and began to push away.

The last rays of the westering sun fell on his face, and my hesitation vanished. For those pent-house brows and deep-set, wild-cat eyes were fixed for ever in my memory.

I cried to him as I ran, but he never looked my road. Somehow it was borne in on me that at all costs I must have speech with him. The wherry was a yard or two from the shore when I jumped for its stern.

I lighted firm on the wood, and for a moment looked Muckle John in the face. I saw a coun-tenance lean like a starved wolf, with great weals as of old wounds on cheek and brow. But only for a second, for as I balanced myself to step for-ward he rammed the butt of the pole in my chest, so that I staggered and fell plump in the river.

The water was only up to my middle, but before I could clamber back he had shipped his oars, and was well into the centre of the stream.

I stood staring like a zany, while black anger filled my heart. I plucked my pistol forth, and for a second was on the verge of murder, for I could have shot him like a rabbit. But God mercifully restrained my foolish passion, and pres-ently the boat and the rower vanished in the evening haze.

" This is a bonny beginning ! " thought I, as I waded through the mud to the shore. I was wearing my best clothes in honour of my arrival, and they were all fouled and plashing.

Then on the bank above me I saw the fellow who had run into me and hindered my catching Muckle John on dry land. He was shaking with laughter.

I was silly and hot-headed in those days, and my wetting had not disposed me to be laughed at. In this fellow I saw a confederate of Gib's, and if I had lost one I had the other. So I marched up to him and very roundly damned his insolence.

He was a stern, lantern-jawed man of forty or so, dressed very roughly in leather breeches and a frieze coat. Long grey woollen stockings were rolled above his knees, and slung on his back was an ancient musket.

"Easy, my lad," he said. "It's a free country, and there's no statute against mirth."

"I'll have you before the sheriff," I cried. "You tripped me up when I was on the track of the biggest rogue in America."

"So!" said he, mocking me. "You'll be a good judge of rogues. Was it a runaway redemptioner, maybe? You'd be looking for the twenty hogsheads reward."

This was more than I could stand. I was carrying a pistol in my hand, and I stuck it to his ear. "March, my friend," I said. "You'll walk before me to a Justice of the Peace, and explain your doings this night."

I had never threatened a man with a deadly weapon before, and I was to learn a most unforgettable lesson. A hand shot out, caught my wrist, and forced it upwards in a grip of steel.

And when I would have used my right fist in his face another hand seized that, and my arms were padlocked.

Cool, ironical eyes looked into mine.

"You're very free with your little gun, my lad. Let me give you a word in season. Never hold a pistol to a man unless you mean to shoot. If your eyes waver you had better had a porridge stick."

He pressed my wrist back till my fingers relaxed, and he caught my pistol in his teeth. With a quick movement of the head he dropped it inside his shirt.

"There's some would have killed you for that trick, young sir," he said. "It's trying to the temper to have gunpowder so near a man's brain. But you're young, and, by your speech, a newcomer. So instead I'll offer you a drink."

He dropped my wrists, and motioned me to follow him. Very crestfallen and ashamed, I walked in his wake to a little shanty almost on the water-edge. The place was some kind of inn, for a negro brought us two tankards of apple-jack, and tobacco pipes, and lit a foul-smelling lantern, which he set between us.

"First," says the man, "let me tell you that I never before clapped eyes on the long piece of rascality you were seeking. He looked like one that had cheated the gallows."

"He was a man I knew in Scotland," I said grumpily.

"Likely enough. There's a heap of Scots re-

demptioners hereaways. I'm out of Scotland myself, or my forbears were, but my father was
settled in the Antrim Glens. There's wild devils
among them, and your friend looked as if he had
given the slip to the hounds in the marshes.
There was little left of his breeches. . . . Drink,
man, or you'll get fever from your wet duds."

I drank, and the strong stuff mounted to my
unaccustomed brain ; my tongue was loosened,
my ill-temper mellowed, and I found myself telling
this grim fellow much that was in my heart.

"So you're a merchant," he said. "It's not
for me to call down an honest trade, but we could
be doing with fewer merchants in these parts.
They're so many leeches that suck our blood.
Are you here to make siller ? "

I said I was, and he laughed. "I never heard
of your uncle's business, Mr. Garvald, but you'll
find it a stiff task to compete with the lads from
Bristol and London. They've got the whole
dominion by the scruff of the neck."

I replied that I was not in awe of them, and
that I could hold my own with anybody in a fair
trade.

"Fair trade ! " he cried scornfully. "That's
just what you won't get. That's a thing un-
kenned in Virginia. Look you here, my lad. The
Parliament in London treats us Virginians like so
many puling bairns. We cannot sell our tobacco
except to English merchants, and we cannot buy
a horn spoon except it comes in an English ship.
What's the result of that ? You, as a merchant,

can tell me fine. The English fix what price they like for our goods, and it's the lowest conceivable, and they make their own price for what they sell us, and that's as high as a Jew's. There's a fine profit there for the gentlemen-venturers of Bristol, but it's starvation and damnation for us poor Virginians."

" What's the result ? " he cried again. " Why, that there's nothing to be had in the land except what the merchants bring. There's scarcely a smith or a wright or a cobbler between the James and the Potomac. If I want a bed to lie in, I have to wait till the coming of the tobacco convoy, and go down to the wharves and pay a hundred pounds of sweet-scented for a thing you would buy in the Candleriggs for twenty shillings. How, in God's name, is a farmer to live if he has to pay usury for every plough and spade and yard of dimity ! "

" Remember you're speaking to a merchant," I said. " You've told me the very thing to encourage me. If prices are high, it's all the better for me."

" It would be," he said grimly, " if your name werena what it is, and you came from elsewhere than the Clyde. D'you think the proud English corporations are going to let you inside ? Not them. The most you'll get will be the scraps that fall from their table, my poor Lazarus, and for these you'll have to go hat in hand to Dives."

His face grew suddenly earnest, and he leaned on the table and looked me straight in the eyes.

" You're a young lad and a new-comer, and the accursed scales of Virginia are not yet on your eyes. Forbye, I think you've spirit, though it's maybe mixed with a deal of folly. You've your choice before you, Mr. Garvald. You can become a lickspittle like the rest of them, and no doubt you'll gather a wheen bawbees, but it will be a poor shivering soul will meet its Maker in the hinder end. Or you can play the man and be a good Virginian. I'll not say it's an easy part. You'll find plenty to cry you down, and there will be hard knocks going ; but by your face I judge you're not afraid of that. Let me tell you this land is on the edge of hell, and there's sore need for stout men. They'll declare in this town that there's no Indians on this side the mountains that would dare to lift a tomahawk. Little they ken ! "

In his eagerness he had gripped my arm, and his dark, lean face was thrust close to mine.

" I was with Bacon in '76, in the fray with the Susquehannocks. I speak the Indian tongues, and there's few alive that ken the tribes like me. The folk here live snug in the Tidewater, which is maybe a hundred miles wide from the sea, but of the West they ken nothing. There might be an army thousands strong concealed a day's journey from the manors, and never a word would be heard of it."

" But they tell me the Indians are changed nowadays," I put in. " They say they've settled down to peaceful ways like any Christian."

" Put your head into a catamount's mouth, if

you please," he said grimly, " but never trust an
Indian. The only good kind is the dead kind. I
tell you we're living on the edge of hell. It may
come this year or next year or five years hence,
but come it will. I hear we are fighting the
French, and that means that the tribes of the
Canadas will be on the move. Little you know
the speed of a war-party. They would cut my
throat one morning, and be hammering at the
doors of James Town before sundown. There
should be a line of forts in the West from the
Roanoke to the Potomac, and every man within
fifty miles should keep a gun loaded and a horse
saddled. But think you the Council will move ?
It costs money, say the wiseacres, as if money
were not cheaper than a slit wizzand ! "

I was deeply solemnized, though I scarce understood the full drift of his words, and the queer
thing was that I was not ill-pleased. I had come
out to seek for trade, and it looked as if I were to
find war. And all this when I was not four hours
landed.

" What think you of that ? " he asked, as I
kept silent. " I've been warned. A man I know
on the Rappahannock passed the word that the
Long House was stirring. Tell that to the gentry
in James Town. What side are you going for,
young sir ? "

" I'll take my time," I said, " and see for myself. Ask me again this day six months."

He laughed loud. " A very proper answer for
a Scot," he cried. " See for yourself, travel the

country, and use the wits God gave you to form your judgment."

He paid the lawing, and said he would put me on the road back. "These alleys are not very healthy at this hour for a young gentleman in braw clothes."

Once outside the tavern he led me by many curious by-paths till I found myself on the riverside just below the Court-house. It struck me that my new friend was not a popular personage in the town, for he would stop and reconnoitre at every turning, and he chose the darkest side of the road.

"Good-night to you," he said at length. "And when you have finished your travels come west to the South Fork River and ask for Simon Frew, and I'll complete your education."

I went to bed in a glow of excitement. On the morrow I should begin a new life in a world of wonders, and I rejoiced to think that there was more than merchandise in the prospect.

CHAPTER VI

TELLS OF MY EDUCATION

I HAD not been a week in the place before I saw one thing very clear—that I should never get on with Mr. Lambie. His notion of business was to walk down the street in a fine coat, and to sleep with a kerchief over his face in some shady veranda. There was no vice in the creature, but there was mighty little sense. He lived in awe of the great and rich, and a nod from a big planter would make him happy for a week. He used to deafen me with tales of Colonel Randolph, and worshipful Mr. Carew, and Colonel Byrd's new house at Westover, and the rare fashion in cravats that young Mr. Mason showed at the last Surrey horse-racing. Now when a Scot chooses to be a lickspittle, he is more whole-hearted in the job than any one else on the globe, and I grew very weary of Mr. Lambie. He was no better than an old wife, and as timid as a hare forbye. When I spoke of fighting the English merchants, he held up his hands as if I had uttered blasphemy. So, being determined to find out for myself the truth about this wonderful new land, I left him the business in the town, bought two good horses, hired a servant, by name John Faulkner, who had worked out his time as a redemptioner, and set out on my travels.

This is a history of doings, not of thoughts, or I would have much to tell of what I saw during those months, when, lean as a bone, and brown as a hazel-nut, I tracked the course of the great rivers. The roads were rough, where roads there were, but the land smiled under the sun, and the Virginians, high and low, kept open house for the chance traveller. One night I would eat pork and hominy with a rough fellow who was carving a farm out of the forest; and the next I would sit in a fine panelled hall and listen to gentlefolks' speech, and dine off damask and silver. I could not tire of the green forests, or the marshes alive with wild fowl, or the noble orchards and gardens, or even the salty dunes of the Chesapeake shore. My one complaint was that the land was desperate flat to a hill-bred soul like mine. But one evening, away north in Stafford county, I cast my eyes to the west and saw, blue and sharp against the sunset, a great line of mountains. It was all I sought. Somewhere in the west Virginia had her high lands, and one day, I promised myself, I would ride the road of the sun and find their secret.

In these months my thoughts were chiefly of trade, and I saw enough to prove the truth of what the man Frew had told me. This richest

land on earth was held prisoner in the bonds of
a foolish tyranny. The rich were less rich than
their estates warranted, and the poor were ground
down by bitter poverty. There was little coin
in the land, tobacco being the sole means of payment, and this meant no trade in the common
meaning of the word. The place was slowly
bleeding to death, and I had a mind to try and
stanch its wounds. The firm of Andrew Sempill
was looked on jealously, in spite of all the bowings
and protestations of Mr. Lambie. If we were to
increase our trade, it must be at the Englishmen's
expense, and that could only be done by offering
the people a better way of business.

When the harvest came and the tobacco fleet
arrived, I could see how the thing worked out.
Our two ships, the *Blackcock* of Ayr and the *Dun-
can Davidson* of Glasgow, had some trouble getting their cargoes. We could only deal with the
smaller planters, who were not thirled to the big
merchants, and it took us three weary weeks up
and down the river-side wharves to get our holds
filled. There was a madness in the place for
things from England, and unless a man could
label his wares "London-made," he could not
hope to catch a buyer's fancy. Why, I have
seen a fellow at a fair at Henricus selling common
Virginian mocking-birds as the "best English
mocking-birds"! My uncle had sent out a quantity of Ayrshire cheeses, mutton hams, pickled
salmon, Dunfermline linens, Paisley dimity, Alloa
worsted, sweet ale from Tranent, Kilmarnock

cowls, and a lot of fine feather-beds from the
Clydeside. There was nothing common or trashy
in the whole consignment; but the planters preferred some gewgaws from Cheapside or some
worthless London furs which they could have
bettered any day by taking a gun and hunting their
own woods. When my own business was over, I
would look on at some of the other ladings. There
on the wharf would be the planter with his wife
and family, and every servant about the place.
And there was the merchant skipper, showing off
his goods, and quoting for each a weight of tobacco.
The planter wanted to get rid of his crop, and knew
that this was his only chance, while the merchant
could very well sell his leavings elsewhere. So the
dice were cogged from the start, and I have seen
a plain kitchen chair sold for fifty pounds of sweet-
scented, or something like the price at which a
joiner in Glasgow would make a score and leave
himself a handsome profit.

The upshot was that I paid a visit to the Governor, Mr. Francis Nicholson, whom my lord Howard
had left as his deputy. Governor Nicholson had
come from New York not many months before
with a great repute for ill-temper and harsh dealing; but I liked the look of his hard-set face and
soldierly bearing, and I never mind choler in a
man if he have also honesty and good sense. So
I waited upon him at his house close by Middle
Plantation, on the road between James Town
and York River.

I had a very dusty reception. His Excellency sat in his long parlour among a mass of books and papers and saddle-bags, and glared at me from beneath lowering brows. The man was sore harassed by the King's Government on one side and the Virginian Council on the other, and he treated every stranger as a foe.

"What do you seek from me?" he shouted. "If it is some merchants' squabble, you can save your breath, for I am sick of the Shylocks."

I said, very politely, that I was a stranger not half a year arrived in the country, but that I had been using my eyes, and wished to submit my views to his consideration.

"Go to the Council," he rasped; "go to that silken fool, His Majesty's Attorney. My politics are not those of the leather-jaws that prate in this land."

"That is why I came to you," I said.

Then without more ado I gave him my notions on the defence of the colony, for from what I had learned I judged that would interest him most. He heard me with unexpected patience.

"Well, now, supposing you are right? I don't deny it. Virginia is a treasure-house with two of the sides open to wind and weather. I told the Council that, and they would not believe me. Here are we at war with France, and Frontenac is hammering at the gates of New York. If that falls, it will soon be the turn of Maryland and next of Virginia. England's possessions in the West are indivisible, and what threatens one endangers all. But think you our Virginians can see it ? When I presented my scheme for setting forts along the northern line, I could not screw a guinea out of the miscreants. The colony was poor, they cried, and could not afford it, and then the worshipful councillors rode home to swill Madeira and loll on their London beds. God's truth! were I not a patriot, I would welcome M. Frontenac to teach them decency."

Now I did not think much of the French danger, being far more concerned with the peril in the West; but I held my peace on that subject. It was not my cue to cross his Excellency in his present humour.

"What makes the colony poor ? " I asked. "The planters are rich enough, but the richest man will grow tired of bearing the whole burden of the government. I submit that His Majesty and the English laws are chiefly to blame. When the Hollanders were suffered to trade here, they paid five shillings on every anker of brandy they brought hither, and ten shillings on every hogshead of tobacco they carried hence. Now every penny that is raised must come out of the Virginians, and the Englishmen who bleed the land go scot-free."

"That's true," said he, "and it's a damned disgrace. But how am I to better it ? "

"Clap a tax on every ship that passes Point Comfort outward bound," I said. "The merchants can well afford to pay it."

"Listen to him ! " he laughed. "And what

kind of answer would I get from my lord Howard
and His Majesty ? Every greasy member would
be on his feet in Parliament in defence of what
he called English rights. Then there would come
a dispatch from the Government consigning the
poor Deputy-Governor of Virginia to the devil ! "

He looked at me curiously, screwing up his
eyes.

" By the way, Mr. Garvald, what is your trade ? "

" I am a merchant like the others," I said ;
" only my ships run from Glasgow instead of
Bristol."

" A very pretty merchant," he said quizzically.
" I have heard that hawks should not pick out
hawks' eyes. What do you propose to gain, Mr.
Garvald ? "

" Better business," I said. " To be honest
with you, sir, I am suffering from the close monopoly of the Englishmen, and I think the country
is suffering worse. I have a notion that things
can be remedied. If you cannot put on a levy,
good and well ; that is your business. But I
mean to make an effort on my own account."

Then I told him something of my scheme, and
he heard me out with a puzzled face.

" Of all the brazen Scots——" he cried.

" Scot yourself," I laughed, for his face and
speech betrayed him.

" I'll not deny that there's glimmerings of
sense in you, Mr. Garvald. But how do you,
a lad with no backing, propose to beat a strong
monopoly buttressed by the whole stupidity and

idleness of Virginia ?   You'll be stripped of your
last farthing, and you'll be lucky if it ends there.
Don't think I'm against you. I'm with you in
your principles, but the job is too big for you."

"We will see," said I. "But I can take it
that, provided I keep within the law, His Majesty's
Governor will not stand in my way ? "

"I can promise you that. I'll do more, for
I'll drink success to your enterprise." He filled
me a great silver tankard of spiced sack, and I
emptied it to the toast of " Honest Men."

All the time at the back of my head were other
thoughts than merchandise. The picture which
Frew had drawn of Virginia as a smiling garden
on the edge of a burning pit was stamped on my
memory. I had seen on my travels the Indians
that dwelled in the Tidewater, remnants of the
old great clans of Doeg and Powhatan and
Pamunkey. They were civil enough fellows, following their own ways, and not molesting their
scanty white neighbours, for the country was
wide enough for all. But so far as I could learn,
these clanlets of the Algonquin house were no more
comparable to the fighting tribes of the West than
a Highland caddie in an Edinburgh close is to a
hill Macdonald with a claymore. But the common Virginian would admit no peril, though now
and then some rough landward fellow would lay
down his spade, spit moodily, and tell me a grim
tale. I had ever the notion to visit Frew and
finish my education.

It was not till the tobacco ships had gone and the autumn had grown late that I got the chance. The trees were flaming scarlet and saffron as I rode west through the forests to his house on the South Fork River. There, by a wood fire in the October dusk, he fed me on wild turkey and barley bread, and listened silently to my tale.

He said nothing when I spoke of my schemes for getting the better of the Englishmen and winning Virginia to my side. Profits interested him little, for he grew his patch of corn and pumpkins, and hunted the deer for his own slender needs. Once he broke in on my rigmarole with a piece of news that fluttered me.

" You mind the big man you were chasing that night you and me first forgathered ? Well, I've seen him."

" Where ? " I cried, all else forgotten.

" Here, in this very place, six weeks syne. He stalked in about ten o' the night, and lifted half my plenishing. When I got up in my bed to face him he felled me. See, there's the mark of it," and he showed a long scar on his forehead. " He went off with my best axe, a gill of brandy and a good coat. He was looking for my gun, too, but that was in a hidy-hole. I got up next morning with a dizzy head, and followed him nigh ten miles. I had a shot at him, but I missed, and his legs were too long for me. Yon's the dangerous lad."

" Where did he go, think you ? " I asked.

" To the hills. To the refuge of every ne'erdo-weel. Belike the Indians have got his scalp, and I'm not regretting it."

I spent three days with Frew, and each day I had the notion that he was putting me to the test. The first day he took me over the river into a great tangle of meadow and woodland beyond which rose the hazy shapes of the western mountains. The man was twenty years my elder, but my youth was of no avail against his iron strength. Though I was hard and spare from my travels in the summer heat, 'twas all I could do to keep up with him, and only my pride kept me from crying halt. Often when he stopped I could have wept with fatigue, and had no breath for a word, but his taciturnity saved me from shame.

In a hollow among the woods we came to a place which sent him on his knees, peering and sniffing like a wild-cat.

" What make you of that ? " he asked.

I saw nothing but a bare patch in the grass, some broken twigs, and a few ashes.

" It's an old camp," I said.

" Ay," said he. " Nothing more ? Use your wits, man."

I used them, but they gave me no help.

" This is the way I read it, then," he said. " Three men camped here before midday. They were Cherokees, of the Matabaw tribe, and one was a maker of arrows. They were not hunting, and they were in a mighty hurry. Just now they're maybe ten miles off, or maybe they're watching us This is no healthy country for you and me."

He took me homeward at a speed which well-nigh foundered me, and, when I questioned him, he told me where he got his knowledge.

They were three men, for there were three different footmarks in the ashes' edge, and they were Cherokees because they made their fire in the Cherokee way, so that the smoke ran in a tunnel into the scrub. They were Matabaws from the pattern of their moccasins. They were in a hurry, for they did not wait to scatter the ashes and clear up the place; and they were not hunting, for they cooked no flesh. One was an arrow-maker, for he had been hardening arrow-points in the fire, and left behind him the arrow-maker's thong.

" But how could you know how long back this happened ? " I asked.

" The sap was still wet in the twigs, so it could not have been much above an hour since they left. Besides, the smoke had blown south, for the grass smelt of it that side. Now the wind was more to the east when we left, and, if you remember, it changed to the north about midday."

I said it was a marvel, and he grunted. " The marvel is what they've been doing in the Tide-water, for from the Tidewater I'll swear they came."

Next day he led me eastward, away back in the direction of the manors. This was an easier day, for he went slow, as if seeking for something. He picked up some kind of a trail, which we followed through the long afternoon. Then he found

something, which he pocketed with a cry of satisfaction. We were then on the edge of a ridge,
whence we looked south to the orchards of Henricus.

" That is my arrow-maker," he cried, showing
me a round stone whorl. " He's a careless lad,
and he'll lose half his belongings ere he wins to
the hills."

I was prepared for the wild Cherokees on our
journey of yesterday, but it amazed me that the
savages should come scouting into the Tidewater
itself. He smiled grimly when I said this, and
took from his pocket a crumpled feather.

" That's a Cherokee badge," he said. " I found
that a fortnight back on the river-side an hour's
ride out of James Town. And it wasna there
when I had passed the same place the day before.
The Tidewater thinks it has put the fear of God
on the hill tribes, and here's a red Cherokee
snowking about its back doors."

The last day he took me north up a stream
called the North Fork, which joined with his own
river. I had left my musket behind, for this heavy
travel made me crave to go light, and I had no
use for it. But that day it seemed we were to go
hunting.

He carried an old gun, and slew with it a deer
in a marshy hollow—a pretty shot, for the animal
was ill-placed. We broiled a steak for our midday
meal, and presently clambered up a high woody
ridge which looked down on a stream and a piece
of green meadow.

Suddenly he stopped. "A buck," he whispered. "See what you can do, you that were so ready with your pistol." And he thrust his gun into my hand.

The beast was some thirty paces off in the dusk of the thicket. It nettled me to have to shoot with a strange weapon, and I thought too lightly of the mark. I fired, and the bullet whistled over its back. He laughed scornfully.

I handed it back to him. "It throws high, and you did not warn me. Load quick, and I'll try again."

I heard the deer crashing through the hillside thicket, and guessed that presently it would come out in the meadow. I was right, and before the gun was in my hands again the beast was over the stream.

It was a long range and a difficult mark, but I had to take the risk, for I was on my trial. I allowed for the throw of the musket and the steepness of the hill, and pulled the trigger. The shot might have been better, for I had aimed for the shoulder, and hit the neck. The buck leaped into the air, ran three yards, and toppled over. By the grace of God, I had found the single chance in a hundred.

Frew looked at me with sincere respect. "That's braw shooting," he said. "I can't say I ever saw its equal."

That night in the smoky cabin he talked freely for once. "I never had a wife or bairn, and I lean on no man. I can fend for myself, and cook my dinner, and mend my coat when it's wanting it. When Bacon died I saw what was coming to this land, and I came here to await it. I've had some sudden calls from the red gentry, but they havena got me yet, and they'll no get me before my time. I'm in the Lord's hands, and He has a job for Simon Frew. Go back to your money-bags, Mr. Garvald. Beat the English merchants, my lad, and take my blessing with you. But keep that gun of yours by your bedside, for the time is coming when a man's hands will have to keep his head."

CHAPTER VII

I BECOME AN UNPOPULAR CHARACTER

I DID not waste time in getting to work. I had already written to my uncle, telling him my plans, and presently I received his consent. I arranged that cargoes of such goods as I thought most suitable for Virginian sales should arrive at regular seasons independent of the tobacco harvest. Then I set about equipping a store. On the high land north of James Town, by the road to Middle Plantation, I bought some acres of cleared soil, and had built for me a modest dwelling. Beside it stood a large brick building, one half fitted as a tobacco shed, where the leaf could lie for months, if need be, without taking harm, and the other arranged as a merchant's store with roomy cellars and wide garrets. I relinquished the warehouse by the James Town quay, and to my joy I was able to relinquish Mr. Lambie. That timid soul had been on thorns ever since I mooted my new projects. He implored me to put them from me ; he drew such pictures of the power of the English traders, you would have thought them the prince merchants of Venice ; he saw all his hard-won gentility gone at a blow, and himself an outcast precluded for ever from great men's recognition. He could not bear it, and though he was loyal to my uncle's firm in his own way, he sought a change. One day he announced that he had been offered a post as steward to a big planter at Henricus, and when I warmly bade him accept it, he smiled wanly, and said he had done so a week agone. We parted very civilly, and I chose as manager my servant, John Faulkner.

This is not a history of my trading ventures, or I would tell at length the steps I took to found a new way of business. I went among the planters, offering to buy tobacco from the coming harvest, and to pay for it forthwith in bonds which could be exchanged for goods at my store. I also offered to provide shipment in the autumn for tobacco and other wares, and I fixed the charge for freight—a very moderate one—in advance. My plan was to clear out my store before the return of the ships, and to have thereby a large quantity of tobacco mortgaged to me. I hoped that thus I would win the friendship and custom of the planters, since I offered them a more convenient way of sale and higher profits. I hoped by breaking down the English monopoly to induce a continual and wholesome commerce in the land. For this purpose it was necessary to get coin into the people's hands, so, using my uncle's credit, I had a parcel of English money from the New York goldsmiths.

In a week I found myself the most-talked-of man

in the dominion, and soon I saw the troubles that credit brings. I had picked up a very correct notion of the fortunes of most of the planters, and the men who were most eager to sell to me were just those I could least trust. Some fellow who was near bankrupt from dice and cock-fighting would offer me five hundred hogsheads, when I knew that his ill-guided estate could scarce produce half. I was not a merchant out of charity, and I had to decline many offers, and so made many foes. Still, one way and another, I was not long in clearing out my store, and I found myself with some three times the amount of tobacco in prospect that I had sent home at the last harvest.

That was very well, but there was the devil to pay besides. Every wastrel I sent off empty-handed was my enemy; the agents of the Englishmen looked sourly at me; and many a man who was swindled grossly by the Bristol buyers saw me as a marauder instead of a benefactor. For this I was prepared; but what staggered me was the way that some of the better sort of the gentry came to regard me. It was not that they did not give me their custom; that I did not expect, for gunpowder alone would change the habits of a Virginian Tory. But my new business seemed to them such a downcome that they passed me by with a cock of the chin. Before they had treated me hospitably, and made me welcome at their houses. I had hunted the fox with them—very little to my credit; and shot wild-fowl in their company with better success. I had dined with them, and danced in their halls at Christmas. Then I had been a gentleman ; now I was a shopkeeper, a creature about the level of a redemptioner. The thing was so childish that it made me angry. It was right for one of them to sell his tobacco on his own wharf to a tarry skipper who cheated him grossly, but wrong for me to sell kebbucks and linsey-woolsey at an even bargain. I gave up the puzzle. Some folks' notions of gentility are beyond my wits.

I had taken to going to the church in James Town, first at Mr. Lambie's desire, and then because I liked the sermons. There on a Sunday you would see the fashion of the neighbourhood, for the planters' ladies rode in on pillions, and the planters themselves, in gold-embroidered waistcoats and plush breeches and new-powdered wigs, leaned on the tombstones, and exchanged snuff-mulls and gossip. In the old ramshackle graveyard you would see such a parade of satin bodices and tabby petticoats and lace headgear as made it blossom like the rose. I went to church one Sunday in my second summer, and, being late, went up the aisle looking for a place. The men at the seat-ends would not stir to accommodate me, and I had to find rest in the cock-loft. I thought nothing of it, but the close of the service was to enlighten me. As I went down the churchyard not a man or woman gave me greeting, and when I spoke to any I was not answered. These were men with whom I had been on the friendliest terms ; women, too, who only a week before had

chaffered with me at the store. It was clear that
the little society had marooned me to an isle by
myself. I was a leper, unfit for gentlefolks' company, because, forsooth, I had sold goods, which
every one of them did also, and had tried to sell
them fair.

The thing made me very bitter. I sat in my
house during the hot noons when no one stirred,
and black anger filled my heart. I grew as peevish as a slighted girl, and would no doubt have
fretted myself into some signal folly, had not an
event occurred which braced my soul again. This
was the arrival of the English convoy.

When I heard that the ships were sighted, I
made certain of trouble. I had meantime added
to my staff two other young men, who, like Faulkner, lived with me at the store. Also I had got
four stalwart negro slaves who slept in a hut in
my garden. 'Twas a strong enough force to repel
a drunken posse from the plantations, and I had
a fancy that it would be needed in the coming
weeks.

Two days later, going down the street of James
Town, I met one of the English skippers, a red-
faced, bottle-nosed old ruffian called Bulteel. He
was full of apple-jack, and strutted across the way
to accost me.

"What's this I hear, Sawney?" he cried.
"You're setting up as a pedlar, and trying to
cut in on our trade. Od twist me, but we'll put
an end to that, my bully-boy. D'you think the
King, God bless him, made the laws for a red-

haired, flea-bitten Sawney to diddle true-born Englishmen ? What'll the King's Bench say to that,
think ye ? "

He was very abusive, but very uncertain on his
legs. I said good-humouredly that I welcomed
process of law, and would defend my action. He
shook his head, and said something about law not
being everything, and England being a long road
off. He had clearly some great threat to be delivered of, but just then he sat down so heavily
that he had no breath for anything but curses.

But the drunkard had given me a notion. I
hurried home and gave instructions to my men to
keep a special guard on the store. Then I set off
in a pinnace to find my three ships, which were
now lading up and down among the creeks.

That was the beginning of a fortnight's struggle,
when every man's hand was against me, and I
enjoyed myself surprisingly. I was never at rest
by land or water. The ships were the least of the
business, for the dour Scots seamen were a match
for all comers. I made them anchor at twilight
in mid-stream for safety's sake, for in that drouthy
clime a firebrand might play havoc with them.
The worst that happened was that one moonless
night a band of rascals, rigged out as Indian
braves, came yelling down to the quay where
some tobacco was waiting to be shipped, and
before my men were warned had tipped a couple
of hogsheads into the water. They got no further,
for we fell upon them with marlingspikes and
hatchets, stripped them of their feathers, and sent

them to cool their heads in the muddy river. The
ringleader I haled to James Town, and had the
pleasure of seeing him grinning through a collar in
the common stocks.

Then I hied me back to my store, which was
my worst anxiety. I was followed by ill names
as I went down the street, and one day in a tavern
a young fool drew his shabble on me. But I would
quarrel with no man, for that was a luxury beyond
a trader. There had been an attack on my tobacco shed by some of the English seamen, and
in the mellay one of my blacks got an ugly wound
from a cutlass. It was only a foretaste, and I set
my house in order.

One afternoon John Faulkner brought me word
that mischief would be afoot at the darkening. I
put each man to his station, and I had the sense
to picket them a little distance from the house.
The Englishmen were clumsy conspirators. We
watched them arrive, let them pass, and followed
silently on their heels. Their business was wreck-
age, and they fixed a charge of powder by the
tobacco shed, laid and lit a fuse, and retired dis-
creetly into the bushes to watch their handiwork.
Then we fell upon them, and the hindquarters of
all bore witness to our greeting.

I caught the fellow who had laid the charge,
tied the whole thing round his neck, clapped a
pistol to his ear, and marched him before me into
the town. "If you are minded to bolt," I said,
"remember you have a charge of gunpowder lob-
bing below your chin. I have but to flash my

pistol into it, and they will be picking the bits of you off the high trees."

I took the rascal, his knees knocking under him, straight to the ordinary where the English merchants chiefly forgathered. A dozen of them sat over a bowl of punch, when the door was opened and I kicked my Guy Fawkes inside. I may have misjudged them, but I thought every eye looked furtive as they saw my prisoner. " Gentlemen," said I, " I restore you your property. This is a penitent thief who desires to make a confession."

My pistol was at his temple, the powder was round his neck, and he must have seen a certain resolution in my face. Anyhow, sweating and quaking, he blurted out his story, and when he offered to halt I made rings with the barrel on the flesh of his neck.

" It is a damned lie," cried one of them, a handsome, over-dressed fellow who had been conspicuous for his public insolence towards me.

" Nay," said I, " our penitent's tale has the note of truth. One word to you, gentlemen. I am hospitably inclined, and if any one of you will so far honour me as to come himself instead of dispatching his servant, his welcome will be the warmer. I bid you good-night and leave you this fellow in proof of my goodwill. Keep him away from the candle, I pray you, or you will all go to hell before your time."

That was the end of my worst troubles, and presently my lading was finished and my store replenished. Then came the time for the return sailing, and the last enterprise of my friends was to go off without my three vessels. But I got an order from the Governor, delivered readily but with much profanity, to the commander of the frigates to delay till the convoy was complete. I breathed more freely as I saw the last hulls grow small in the estuary. For now, as I reasoned it out, the planters must begin to compare my prices with the Englishmen's, and must come to see where their advantage lay.

But I had counted my chickens too soon, and was to be woefully disappointed. At that time all the coast of America from New England to the Main was infested by pirate vessels. Some sailed under English letters of marque, and preyed only on the shipping of France, with whom we were at war. Some who had formed themselves into a company called the Brethren of the Coast robbed the Spanish treasure-ships and merchant-men in the south waters, and rarely came north to our parts save to careen or provision. They were mostly English and Welsh, with a few French-men, and though I have little to say for their doings, they left British ships in the main un-molested, and were welcomed as a godsend by our coast dwellers, since they smuggled goods to them which would have been twice the cost if bought at the convoy markets. Lastly, there were one or two horrid desperadoes who ravaged the seas like tigers. Such an one was the man Cosh, and that Teach, surnamed Blackbeard, of whom we hear too much to-day. But, on the whole, we of Virginia suffered not at all from these gentlemen of fortune, and piracy, though the common peril of the seas, entered but little into the estimation of the merchants.

Judge, then, of my disgust when I got news a week later that one of my ships, the Ayr brig, had straggled from the convoy, and been seized, rifled, and burned to the water by pirates almost in sight of Cape Charles. The loss was grievous, but what angered me was the mystery of such a happening. I knew the brig was a slow sailer, but how in the name of honesty could she be suffered in broad daylight to fall into such a fate ? I remembered the hostility of the Englishmen, and feared she had had foul play. Just after Christmas-tide I expected two ships to replenish the stock in my store. They arrived safe, but only by the skin of their teeth, for both had been chased from their first entrance into American waters, and only their big topsails and a favouring wind brought them off. I examined the captains closely on the matter, and they were positive that their assailant was not Cosh or any one of his kidney, but a ship of the Brethren, who ordinarily were on the best of terms with our merchantmen.

My suspicions now grew into a fever. I had long believed that there was some connivance between the pirates of the coast and the English traders, and small blame to them for it. 'Twas a sensible way to avoid trouble, and I for one would rather pay a modest blackmail every month or two than run the risk of losing a good ship and a twelvemonth's cargo. But when it came to using this connivance for private spite, the thing was not to be endured

In March my doubts became certainties. I had a parcel of gold coin coming to me from New York in one of the coasting vessels—no great sum, but more than I cared to lose. Presently I had news that the ship was aground on a sandspit on Accomac, and had been plundered by a pirate brigantine. I got a sloop and went down the river, and, sure enough, I found the vessel newly refloated, and the captain, an old New Hampshire fellow, in a great taking. Piracy there had been, but of a queer kind, for not a farthing's worth had been touched except my packet of gold. The skipper was honesty itself, and it was plain that the pirate who had chased the ship aground and then come aboard to plunder, had done it to do me hurt, and me alone.

All this made me feel pretty solemn. My uncle was a rich man, but no firm could afford these repeated losses. I was the most unpopular figure in Virginia, hated by many, despised by the genteel, whose only friends were my own servants and a few poverty-stricken landward folk. I had found out a good way of trade, but I had set a hornet's nest buzzing about my ears, and was on the fair way to be extinguished. This alliance between my rivals and the Free Companions was the last straw to my burden. If the sea was to be shut to him, then a merchant might as well put up his shutters.

It made me solemn, but also most mightily angry. If the stars in their courses were going to fight against Andrew Garvald, they should find

him ready. I went to the Governor, but he gave
me no comfort. Indeed, he laughed at me, and
bade me try the same weapon as my adversaries.
I left him, very wrathful, and after a night's sleep
I began to see reason in his words. Clearly the
law of Virginia or of England would give me no
redress. I was an alien from the genteel world ;
why should I not get the benefit of my ungentility ?
If my rivals went for their weapons into dark
places, I could surely do likewise. A line of Virgil
came into my head, which seemed to me to con-
tain very good counsel : " *Flectere si nequeo superos,
Acheronta movebo*," which means that if you cannot get Heaven on your side, you had better try
for the devil.

But how was I to get into touch with the devil ?
And then I remembered in a flash my meeting
with the sea-captain on the Glasgow stairhead
and his promise to help me. I had no notion
who he was or how he could aid, but I had a vague
memory of his power and briskness. He had
looked like the kind of lad who might conduct
me into the wild world of the Free Companions.

I sought Mercer's tavern by the water-side,
a melancholy place grown up with weeds, with a
yard of dark trees at the back of it. Old Mercer
was an elder in the little wooden Presbyterian kirk,
which I had taken to attending since my quarrels
with the gentry. He knew me and greeted me with
his doleful smile, shaking his foolish old beard.

" What's your errand this e'en, Mr. Garvald ? "
he said in broad Scots. " Will you drink a rummer

o' toddy, or try some fine auld usquebaugh I hae got frae my cousin in Buchan ? "

I sat down on the settle outside the tavern door. " This is my errand. I want you to bring me to a man or bring that man to me. His name is Ninian Campbell."

Mercer looked at me dully.

" There was a lad o' that name was hanged at Peebles i' '68 for stealin' twae hens and a wether."

" The man I mean is long and lean, and his head is as red as fire. He gave me your name, so you must know him."

His eyes showed no recognition. He repeated the name to himself, mumbling it toothlessly. " It sticks i' my memory," he said, " but when and where I canna tell. Certes, there's no man o' the name in Virginia."

I was beginning to think that my memory had played me false, when suddenly the whole scene in the Saltmarket leaped vividly to my brain. Then I remembered the something else I had been enjoined to say.

" Ninian Campbell," I went on, " bade me ask for him here, and I was to tell you that the lymphads are on the loch and the horn of Diarmaid has sounded."

In a twinkling his face changed from vacancy to shrewdness and from senility to purpose. He glanced uneasily round.

" For God's sake, speak soft," he whispered. " Come inside, man. We'll steek the door, and then I'll hear your business."

CHAPTER VIII

RED RINGAN

ONCE at Edinburgh College I had read the Latin tale of Apuleius, and the beginning stuck in my memory : "*Thraciam ex negotio petebam*"—"I was starting off for Thrace on business." That was my case now. I was about to plunge into a wild world for no more startling causes than that I was a trader who wanted to save his pocket. It is to those who seek only peace and a quiet life that adventures fall; the homely merchant, jogging with his pack train, finds the enchanted forest and the sleeping princess ; and Saul, busily searching for his father's asses, stumbles upon a kingdom.

"What seek ye with Ringan ?" Mercer asked, when we had sat down inside with locked doors.

"The man's name is Ninian Campbell," I said, somewhat puzzled.

"Well, it's the same thing. What did they teach you at Lesmahagow if ye don't know that Ringan is the Scots for Ninian ? Lord bless me, laddie, don't tell me ye've never heard of Red Ringan ?"

To be sure I had; I had heard of little else
for a twelvemonth. In every tavern in Virginia,
when men talked of the Free Companions, it was
the name of Red Ringan that came first to their
tongues. I had been too occupied by my own
affairs to listen just then to fireside tales, but I
could not help hearing of this man's exploits.
He was a kind of leader of the buccaneers, and by
all accounts no miscreant like Cosh, but a mirth-
ful fellow, striking hard when need be, but at
other times merciful and jovial. Now I set little
store by your pirate heroes. They are for lads
and silly girls and sots in an ale-house, and a merchant can have no kindness for those who are the
foes of his trade. So when I heard that the man
I sought was this notorious buccaneer I showed my
alarm by dropping my jaw.

Mercer laughed. "I'll not conceal from ye
that ye take a certain risk in going to Ringan.
Ye need not tell me your business, but it should
be a grave one to take ye down to the Carolina
keys. There's time to draw back, if ye want;
but ye've brought me the master word, and I'm
bound to set ye on the road. Just one word to
ye, Mr. Garvald. Keep a stout face whatever
ye see, for Ringan has a weakness for a bold man.
Be here the morn at sunrise, and if ye're wise bring
no weapon. I'll see to the boat and the pro-
visioning."

I was at the water-side next day at cock-crow,
while the mist was still low on the river. Mercer
was busy putting food and a keg of water into a

light sloop, and a tall Indian was aboard redding out the sails. My travels had given me some knowledge of the red tribes, and I spoke a little of their language, but this man was of a type not often seen in the Virginian lowlands. He was very tall, with a skin clear and polished like bronze, and, unlike the ordinary savage, his breast was unmarked, and his hair unadorned. He was naked to the waist, and below wore long leather breeches, dyed red, and fringed with squirrels' tails. In his wampum belt were stuck a brace of knives and a tomahawk. It seemed he knew me, for as I approached he stood up to his full height and put his hands on his forehead. "Brother," he said, and his grave eyes looked steadily into mine.

Then I remembered. Some months before I had been riding back the road from Green Springs, and in a dark, woody place had come across an Indian sore beset by three of the white scum which infested the river-side. What the quarrel was I know not, but I liked little the villainous look of the three, and I liked much the clean, lithe figure of their opponent. So I rode my horse among them, and laid on to them with the butt of my whip. They had their knives out, but I managed to disarm the one who attacked me, and my horse upset a second, while the Indian, who had no weapon but a stave, cracked the head of the last. I got nothing worse than a black eye, but the man I had rescued bled from some ugly cuts which I had much ado stanching. He shook hands with me gravely when I had done, and vanished into the thicket. He was a Seneca Indian, and I wondered what one of that house was doing in the Tidewater.

Mercer told me his name. " Shalah will take ye to the man ye ken. Do whatever he tells ye, Mr. Garvald, for this is a job in which ye're nothing but a bairn." We pushed off, the Indian taking the oars, and in five minutes James Town was lost in the haze.

On the Surrey shore we picked up a breeze, and with the ebbing tide made good speed down the estuary. Shalah the Indian had the tiller, and I sat luxuriously in the bows, smoking my cob pipe, and wondering what the next week held in store for me. The night before I had had qualms about the whole business, but the air of morning has a trick of firing my blood, and I believe I had forgotten the errand which was taking me to the Carolina shores. It was enough that I was going into a new land and new company. Last night I had thought with disfavour of Red Ringan the buccaneer ; that morning I thought only of Ninian Campbell, with whom I had forgathered on a Glasgow landing.

My own thoughts kept me silent, and the Indian never opened his mouth. Like a statue he crouched by the tiller, with his sombre eyes looking to the sea. That night, when we had rounded Cape Henry in fine weather, we ran the sloop into a little bay below a headland, and made camp for the night beside a stream of cold water. Next morning it blew hard from the north, and in a driving rain we crept down the Carolina coast. One incident of the day I remember. I took in a reef or two, and adjusted the sheets, for this was a game I knew and loved. The Indian watched me closely, and made a sign to me to take the helm. He had guessed that I knew more than himself about the handling of a boat in wind, and since we were in an open sea where his guidance was not needed, he preferred to trust the thing to me. I liked the trait in him, for I take it to be a mark of a wise man that he knows what he can do, and is not ashamed to admit what he cannot.

That evening we had a cold bed ; but the storm blew out in the night, and the next day the sun was as hot as summer, and the wind a point to the east. Shalah once again was steersman, for we were inside some very ugly reefs, which I took to be the beginning of the Carolina keys. On shore forests straggled down to the sea, so that sometimes they almost had their feet in the surf ; but now and then would come an open, grassy space running far inland. These were the great savannahs where herds of wild cattle and deer roamed, and where the Free Companions came to fill their larders. It was a wilder land than the Tidewater, for only once did we see a human dwelling. Far remote on the savannahs I could pick out twirls of smoke rising into the blue weather, the signs of Indian hunting fires. Shalah began now to look for landmarks, and to take bearings of a sort. Among the maze of creeks and shallow

bays which opened on the land side it needed an
Indian to pick out a track.

The sun had all but set when, with a grunt
of satisfaction, he swung round the tiller and
headed shorewards. Before me in the twilight I
saw only a wooded bluff which, as we approached,
divided itself into two. Presently a channel
appeared, a narrow thing about as broad as a
cable's length, into which the wind carried us.
Here it was very dark, the high sides with their
gloomy trees showing at the top a thin line of
reddening sky. Shalah hugged the starboard
shore, and as the screen of the forest caught the
wind it weakened and weakened till it died away,
and we moved only with the ingoing tide. I had
never been in so eerie a place. It was full of the
sharp smell of pine trees, and as I sniffed the air
I caught the savour of wood smoke. Men were
somewhere ahead of us in the gloom.

Shalah ran the sloop into a little creek so overgrown with vines that we had to lie flat on the
thwarts to enter. Then, putting his mouth to
my ear, he spoke for the first time since we had
left James Town. "It is hard to approach the
Master, and my brother must follow me close as
the panther follows the deer. Where Shalah puts
his foot let my brother put his also. Come."

He stepped from the boat to the hill-side, and
with incredible speed and stillness began to ascend.
His long, soft strides were made without noise or
effort, whether the ground were moss, or a tangle
of vines, or loose stones. or the trunks of fallen

trees. I had prided myself on my hill-craft, but
beside the Indian I was a blundering child. I
might have made shift to travel as fast, but it was
the silence of his progress that staggered me. I
plunged, and slipped, and sprawled, and my
heart was bursting before the ascent ceased and
we stole to the left along the hill shoulder.

Presently came a gap in the trees, and I looked
down in the last greyness of dusk on a strange
and beautiful sight. The channel led to a land-
locked pool, maybe a mile around, and this was
as full of shipping as a town's harbour. The
water was but a pit of darkness, but I could make
out the masts rising into the half light, and I
counted more than twenty vessels in that port.
No light was shown, and the whole place was
quiet as a grave.

We entered a wood of small hemlocks, and I
felt rather than saw the ground slope in front of
us. About two hundred feet above the water
the glen of a little stream shaped itself into a flat
cup, which was invisible from below, and girdled
on three sides by dark forest. Here we walked
more freely, till we came to the lip of the cup, and
there, not twenty paces below me, I saw a wonderful thing. The hollow was lit with the glow of
a dozen fires, round which men clustered. Some
were busy boucanning meat for ship's food, some
were cooking supper, some sprawled in idleness,
and smoked or diced. The night had now grown
very black around us, and we were well protected,
for the men in the glow had their eyes dazed, and

could not spy into the darkness. We came very close above them, so that I could hear their talk. The smell of roasting meat pricked my hunger, and I realized that the salt air had given me a noble thirst. They were common seamen from the pirate vessels, and, as far as I could judge, they had no officer among them. I remarked their fierce, dark faces, and the long knives with which they slashed and trimmed the flesh for their boucanning.

Shalah touched my hand, and I followed him into the wood. We climbed again, and from the tinkle of the stream on my left I judged that we were ascending to a higher shelf in the glen. The Indian moved very carefully, as noiseless as the flight of an owl, and I marvelled at the gift. In after days I was to become something of a woodsman, and track as swiftly and silently as any man of my upbringing. But I never mastered the Indian art by which the foot descending in the darkness on something that will crackle checks before the noise is made. I could do it by day, when I could see what was on the ground, but in the dark the thing was beyond me. It is an instinct like a wild thing's, and possible only to those who have gone all their days light-shod in the forests.

Suddenly the slope and the trees ceased, and a new glare burst on our eyes. This second shelf was smaller than the first, and as I blinked at the light I saw that it held about a score of men. Torches made of pine boughs dipped in tar blazed at the four corners of the assembly, and in the middle, on a boulder, a man was sitting. He was speaking, and with passion, but I could not make him out. Once more Shalah put his mouth to my ear, with a swift motion like a snake, and whispered, " The Master."

We crawled flat on our bellies round the edge of the cup. The trees had gone, and the only cover was the long grass and the low sumach bushes. We moved a foot at a time, and once the Indian turned in his tracks and crawled to the left almost into the open. My sense of smell, as sharp almost as a dog's, told me that horses were picketed in the grass in front of us. Our road took us within hearing of the speaker, and though I dared not raise my head, I could hear the soft Highland voice of my friend. He seemed now to be speaking humorously, for a laugh came from the hearers.

Once at the crossing of a little brook, I pulled a stone into the water, and we instantly lay as still as death. But men preoccupied with their own concerns do not keep anxious watch, and our precautions were needless. Presently we had come to the far side of the shelf abreast of the boulder on which he sat who seemed to be the chief figure. Now I could raise my head, and what I saw made my eyes dazzle.

Red Ringan sat on a stone with a naked cutlass across his knees. In front stood a man, the most evil-looking figure that I had ever beheld. He was short but very sturdily built, and wore a

fine laced coat not made for him, which hung to
his knees, and was stretched tight at the armpits.
He had a heavy pale face, without hair on it.
His teeth had gone, all but two buck-teeth which
stuck out at each corner of his mouth, giving him
the look of a tusker. I could see his lips moving
uneasily in the glare of the pine boughs, and his
eyes darted about the company as if seeking
countenance.

Ringan was speaking very gravely, with his
eyes shining like sword points. The others were
every make and manner of fellow, from well-
shaped and well-clad gentlemen to loutish seamen in leather jerkins. Some of the faces were
stained dark with passion and crime, some had
the air of wild boys, and some the hard sobriety
of traders. But one and all were held by the
dancing eyes of the man that spoke.

" What is the judgment," he was saying, " of
the Free Companions ? By the old custom of the
Western Seas I call upon you, gentlemen all, for
your decision."

Then I gathered that the evil-faced fellow had
offended against some one of their lawless laws,
and was on his trial.

No one spoke for a moment, and then one
grizzled seaman raised his hand. " The dice must
judge," he said. " He must throw for his life
against the six."

Another exclaimed against this. " Old wives'
folly," he cried, with an oath. " Let Cosh go his
ways, and swear to amend them. The Brethren

of the Coast cannot be too nice in these little
matters. We are not pursy justices or mooning
girls."

But he had no support. The verdict was for
the dice, and a seaman brought Ringan a little
ivory box, which he held out to the prisoner.
The latter took it with shaking hand, as if he did
not know how to use it.

"You will cast thrice," said Ringan. "Two
even throws, and you are free."

The man fumbled a little and then cast. It
fell a four.

A second time he threw, and the dice lay five.

In that wild place, in the black heart of night,
the terror of the thing fell on my soul. The savage
faces, the deadly purpose in Ringan's eyes, the
fumbling miscreant before him, were all heavy
with horror. I had no doubt that Cosh was
worthy of death, but this cold and merciless treatment froze my reason. I watched with starting
eyes the last throw, and I could not hear Ringan
declare it. But I saw by the look on Cosh's face
what it had been.

"It is your privilege to choose your manner
of death and to name your successor," I heard
Ringan say.

But Cosh did not need the invitation. Now
that his case was desperate, the courage in him
revived. He was fully armed, and in a second
he had drawn a knife and leaped for Ringan's
throat.

Perhaps he expected it, perhaps he had learned

the art of the wild beast so that his body was answerable to his swiftest wish. I do not know, but I saw Cosh's knife crash on the stone and splinter, while Ringan stood by his side.

" You have answered my question," he said quietly. " Draw your cutlass, man. You have maybe one chance in ten thousand for your life."

I shut my eyes as I heard the steel clash. Then very soon came silence. I looked again, and saw Ringan wiping his blade on a bunch of grass, and a body lying before him.

He was speaking—speaking, I suppose, about the successor to the dead man, whom two negroes had promptly removed. Suddenly at my shoulder Shalah gave the hoot of an owl, followed at a second's interval by a second and a third. I suppose it was some signal agreed with Ringan, but at the time I thought the man had gone mad.

I was not very sane myself. What I had seen had sent a cold grue through me, for I had never before seen a man die violently, and the circumstances of the place and hour made the thing a thousandfold more awful. I had a black fright on me at that whole company of merciless men, and especially at Ringan, whose word was law to them. Now the worst effect of fear is that it obscures good judgment, and makes a man in desperation do deeds of a foolhardiness from which at other times he would shrink. All I remembered in that moment was that I had to reach Ringan, and that Mercer had told me that the safest plan was to show a bold front. I never remembered that I had also been bidden to follow Shalah, nor did I reflect that a secret conclave of pirates was no occasion to choose for my meeting. With a sudden impulse I forced myself to my feet, and stalked, or rather shambled, into the light.

"Ninian," I cried, "Ninian Campbell! I'm here to claim your promise."

The whole company turned on me, and I was gripped by a dozen hands and flung on the ground. Ringan came forward to look, but there was no recognition in his eyes. Some one cried out, "A spy!" and there was a fierce murmur of voices, which were meaningless to me, for fear had got me again, and I had neither ears nor voice. Dimly it seemed that he gave some order, and I was trussed up with ropes. Then I was conscious of being carried out of the glare of torches into the cool darkness. Presently I was laid in some kind of log-house, carpeted with fir boughs, for the needles tickled my face. Bit by bit my senses came back to me, and I caught hold of my vagrant courage.

A big negro in seaman's clothes, with a scarlet sash round his middle, was squatted on the floor watching me by the light of a ship's lantern. He had a friendly, foolish face, and I remember yet how he rolled his eyeballs.

"I won't run away," I said, "so you might slacken these ropes and let me breathe easy."

Apparently he was an accommodating gaoler, for he did as I wished.

" And give me a drink," I said, " for my tongue's like a stick."

He mixed me a pannikin of rum and water. Perhaps he hocussed it, or maybe 'twas only the effect of spirits on a weary body ; but three minutes after I had drunk I was in a heavy sleep.

CHAPTER IX

VARIOUS DOINGS IN THE SAVANNAH

I AWOKE in broad daylight, and when my wits came back to me, I saw I was in a tent of skins, with my limbs unbound, and a pitcher of water beside me placed by some provident hand. Through the tent door I looked over a wide space of green savannah. How I had got there I knew not; but, as my memory repeated the events of the night, I knew I had travelled far, for the sea showed miles away at a great distance beneath me. On the water I saw a ship in full sail, diminished to a toy size, careering northward with the wind.

Outside a man was seated whistling a cheerful tune. I got to my feet and staggered out to clear my head in the air, and found the smiling face of Ringan.

" Good morning, Andrew," he cried, as I sat down beside him. " Have you slept well ? "

I rubbed my eyes and took long draughts of the morning breeze.

" Are you a warlock, Mr. Campbell, that you

can spirit folk about the country at your pleasure ?
I have slept sound, but my dreams have been bad."

"Yes," he said ; " what sort of dreams, maybe ? "

"I dreamed I was in a wild place among wild
men, and that I saw murder done. The look of
the man who did it was not unlike your own."

"You have dreamed true," he said gravely ;
"but you have the wrong word for it. Others
would call it justice."

"What sort of justice ? " said I, "when you
had no court or law but just what you made
yourself."

"Is it not a stiff Whiggamore ? " he said, looking skywards. "Why, man, all justice is what
men make themselves. What hinders the Free
Companions from making as honest laws as any
cackling Council in the towns ? Did you see the
man Cosh ? Have you heard anything of his
doings, and will you deny that the world was well
quit of him ? There's a decency in all trades,
and Cosh fair stank to heaven. But I'm glad
the thing ended as it did. I never get to like a
cold execution. 'Twas better for everybody that
he should fly at my face and get six inches of
kindly steel in his throat. He had a gentleman's
death, which was more than his crimes warranted."

I was only half convinced. Here was I, a law-
abiding merchant, pitchforked suddenly into a
world of lawlessness. I could not be expected
to adjust my views in the short space of a night.

"You gave me a rough handling," I said.
"Where was the need of it ? "

" And you showed very little sense in bursting in on us the way you did ! Could you not have bided quietly till Shalah gave the word ? I had to be harsh with you, or they would have suspected something and cut your throat. Yon gentry are not to take liberties with. What made you do it, Andrew ? "

" Just that I was black afraid. That made me more feared of being a coward, so I forced myself to yon folly."

" A very honourable reason," he said.

" Are you the leader of those men ? " I asked. " They looked a scurvy lot. Do you call that a proper occupation for the best blood in Breadalbane ? "

It was a silly speech, and I could have bitten my tongue out when I had uttered it. But I was in a vile temper, for the dregs of the negro's rum still hummed in my blood. His face grew dark, till he looked like the man I had seen the night before.

" I allow no man to slight my race," he said in a harsh voice.

" It's the truth whether you like it or not. And you that claimed to be a gentleman ! What is it they say about the Highlands ? " And I quoted a ribald Glasgow proverb.

What moved me to this insolence I cannot say. I was in the wrong, and I knew it, but I was too much of a child to let go my silly pride.

Ringan got up very quickly and walked three steps. The blackness had gone from his face, and it was puzzled and melancholy.

"There's a precious lot of the bairn in you, Mr. Garvald," he said, "and an ugly spice of the Whiggamore. I would have killed another man for half your words, and I've got to make you pay for them somehow." And he knit his brow and pondered.

"I'm ready," said I, with the best bravado I could muster, though the truth is I was sick at heart. I had forced a quarrel like an ill-mannered boy on the very man whose help I had come to seek. And I saw, too, that I had gone just that bit too far for which no recantation would win pardon.

"What sort of way are you ready?" he asked politely. "You would fight me with your pistols, but you haven't got them, and this is no a matter that will wait. I could spit you in a jiffy with my sword, but it wouldna be fair. It strikes me that you and me are ill matched. We're like a shark and a wolf that cannot meet to fight in the same element."

Then he ran his finger down the buttons of his coat, and his eyes were smiling. "We'll try the old way that laddies use on the village green. Man, Andrew, I'm going to skelp you, as your mother skelped you when you were a breechless bairn." And he tossed his coat on the grass.

I could only follow suit, though I was black ashamed at the whole business. I felt the disgrace of my conduct, and most bitterly the disgrace of the penalty.

My arm was too short to make a fighter of me,

and I could only strive to close, that I might get the use of my weight and my great strength of neck and shoulder. Ringan danced round me, tapping me lightly on nose and cheek, but hard enough to make the blood flow. I defended myself as best I could, while my temper rose rapidly and made me forget my penitence. Time and again I looked for a chance to slip in, but he was as wary as a fox, and was a yard off before I could get my arm round him.

At last, in extreme vexation, I lowered my head and rushed blindly for his chest. Something like the sails of a windmill smote me on the jaw, and I felt myself falling into a pit of great darkness where little lights twinkled.

The next I knew I was sitting propped against the tent-pole with a cold bandage round my forehead, and Ringan with a napkin bathing my face.

"Cheer up, man," he cried; "you've got off light, for there's no a scratch on your lily-white cheek, and the blood-letting from the nose will clear out the dregs of Moro's hocus."

I blinked a little, and tried to recall what had happened. All my ill-humour had gone, and I was now in a hurry to set myself right with my conscience. He heard my apology with an embarrassed face.

"Say no more, Andrew. I was as muckle to blame as you, and I've been giving myself some ill names for that last trick. It was ower hard, but, man, the temptation was sore."

He elbowed me to the open air.

" Now for the questions you've a right to ask. We of the Brethren have not precisely a chief, as you call it, but there are not many of them would gainsay my word. Why ? you ask. Well, it's not for a modest man to be sounding his own trumpet. Maybe it's because I'm a gentleman, and there's that in good blood which awes the commonalty. Maybe it's because I've no fish of my own to fry. I do not rob for greed, like Calvert and Williams, or kill for lust, like the departed Cosh. To me it's a game, which I play by honest rules. I never laid finger on a bodle's worth of English stuff, and if now and then I ease the Dons of a pickle silver or send a Frenchman or two to purgatory, what worse am I doing than His Majesty's troops in Flanders, or your black frigates that lie off Port Royal ? If I've a clear conscience I can more easily take order with those that are less single-minded. But maybe the chief reason is that I've some little skill of arms, so that the lad that questions me is apt to fare like Cosh."

There was a kind of boastful sincerity about the man which convinced me. But his words put me in mind of my own business.

" I came seeking you to ask help. Your friends have been making too free with my belongings. I would never complain if it were the common risk of my trade, but I have a notion that there's some sort of design behind it." Then I told him of my strife with the English merchants.

" What are your losses ? " he asked.

" The Ayr brig was taken off Cape Charles, and

burned to the water. God help the poor souls in her, for I fear they perished."

He nodded. " I know. That was one of Cosh's exploits. He has paid by now for that and other things."

" Two of my ships were chased through the Capes and far up the Tidewater of the James not two months back," I went on.

He laughed. " I did that myself," he said.

Astonishment and wrath filled me, but I finished my tale.

" A week ago there was a ship ashore on Accomac. Pirates boarded her, but they took nothing away save a sum of gold that was mine. Was that your doing also, Mr. Campbell ? "

" Yes," he said ; " but the money's safe. I'll give you a line to Mercer, and he'll pay it you."

" I'm much obliged to you, Mr. Campbell," I said, choking with anger. " But who, in Heaven's name, asked you to manage my business ? I thought you were my friend, and I came to you as such, and here I find you the chief among my enemies."

" Patience, Andrew," he said, " and I'll explain everything, for I grant you it needs some explaining. First, you are right about the English merchants. They and the Free Companions have long had an understanding, and word was sent by them to play tricks on your ships. I was absent at the time, and though the thing was dirty work, as any one could see, some of the fools thought it a fair plòy, and Cosh was suffered to do his will. When

I got back I heard the story, and was black angry, so I took the matter into my own keeping. I have ways and means of getting the news of Virginia, and I know pretty well what you have been doing, young one. There's spirit in you and some wise notions, but you want help in the game. Besides, there's a bigger thing before you. So I took steps to bring you here."

"You took a roundabout road," said I, by no means appeased.

"It had to be. D'you think I could come marching into James Town and collogue with you in your counting-house? Now that you're here, you have my sworn word that the Free Companions will never lay hand again on your ventures. Will that content you?"

"It will," I said; "but you spoke of a bigger thing before me."

"Yes, and that's the price you are going to pay me for my goodwill. It's what the lawyers call *consideratio* for our bargain, and it's the reason I brought you here. Tell me, Andrew, d'you ken a man Frew who lives on the South Fork River?"

"A North Ireland fellow, with a hatchet face and a big scar? I saw him a year ago."

"It stuck in my mind that you had. And d'you mind the advice he gave you?"

I remembered it very well, for it was Frew who had clinched my views on the defencelessness of our West. "He spoke God's truth," I said, "but I cannot get a Virginian to believe it."

"They'll believe in time," he said, "though

maybe too late to save some of their scalps. Come
to this hillock, and I will show you something."

From the low swell of ground we looked west to
some little hills, and in the hollow of them a spire
of smoke rose into the blue.

" I'm going to take you there, that you may
hear and see something to your profit. Quick,
Moro," he cried to a servant. " Bring food, and
have the horses saddled."

We breakfasted on some very good beefsteaks,
and started at a canter for the hills. My head-
ache had gone, and I was now in a contented
frame of mind ; for I saw the purpose of my
errand accomplished, and I had a young man's
eagerness to know what lay before me. As we
rode Ringan talked.

" You'll have heard tell of Bacon's rising in '76 ?
Governor Berkeley had ridden the dominion with
too harsh a hand, and in the matter of its defence
against the Indians he was slack where he should
have been tight. The upshot was that Nathaniel
Bacon took up the job himself, and after giving
the Indians their lesson, turned his mind to the
government of Virginia. He drove Berkeley into
Accomac, and would have turned the whole place
tapsalteery if he had not suddenly died of a bowel
complaint. After that Berkeley and his tame
planters got the upper hand, and there were some
pretty hornings and hangings. There were two
men that were lieutenants to Bacon, and maybe
put the notion into his head. One was James
Drummond, a cousin of my own mother's, and he

got the gallows for his trouble. The other was a man Richard Lawrence, a fine scholar, and a grand hand at planning, though a little slow in a fight. He kept the ordinary at James Town, and was the one that collected the powder and kindled the fuse. Governor Berkeley had a long score to settle with him, but he never got him, for when the thing was past hope Mr. Richard rode west one snowy night to the hills, and Virginia saw him no more. They think he starved in the wilderness, or got into the hands of the wild Indians, and is long ago dead."

I knew all about Dick Lawrence, for I had heard the tale twenty times. " But surely they're right," I said. " It's fifteen years since any man had word of him."

" Well, you'll see him within an hour," said Ringan. " It's a queer story, but it seems he fell in with a Monacan war party, and since he and Bacon had been fighting their deadly foes, the Susquehannocks, they treated him well, and brought him south into Carolina. You must know, Andrew, that all this land hereaways, except for the little Algonquin villages on the shore, is Sioux country, with as many tribes as there are houses in Clan Campbell. But cheek by jowl is a long strip held by the Tuscaroras, a murdering lot of devils, of whom you and I'll get news sooner than we want. The Tuscaroras are bad enough in themselves, but the worst part is that all the back country in the hills belongs to their cousins the Cherokees, and God knows how far north their sway holds. The Long House of

the Iroquois controls everything west of the coast
land from Carolina away up through Virginia to
New York and the Canadas. That means that
Virginia has on two sides the most powerful tribes
of savages in the world, and if ever the Iroquois
found a general and made a common attack things
would go ill with the Tidewater. I tell you that
so that you can understand Lawrence's doings.
He hates the Iroquois like hell, and so he likes
their enemies. He has lived for fifteen years
among the Sioux, whiles with the Catawbas, whiles
with the Manahoacs, but mostly with the Monacans. We of the Free Companions see him pretty
often, and bring him the news and little comforts,
like good tobacco and *eau de vie*, that he cannot
get among savages. And we carry messages between him and the Tidewater, for he has many
friends still alive there. There's no man ever had
his knowledge of Indians, and I'm taking you to
him, for he has something to tell you."

By this time we had come to a place where a
fair-sized burn issued from a shallow glen in the
savannah. There was a peeled wand stuck in a
burnt tree above the water, and this Ringan took
and broke very carefully into two equal pieces,
and put them back in the hole. From this point
onwards I had the feeling that the long grass and
the clumps of bushes held watchers. They made
no noise, but I could have sworn to the truth of
my notion. Ringan, whose senses were keener
than mine, would stop every now and again and
raise his hand as if in signal. At one place we

halted dead for five minutes, and at another he dismounted and cut a tuft of sumach, which he laid over his saddle. Then at the edge of a thicket he stopped again, and held up both hands above his head. Instantly a tall Indian stepped from the cover, saluted, and walked by our side. In five minutes more we rounded a creek of the burn and were at the encampment.

'Twas the first time I had ever seen an Indian village. The tents, or teepees, were of skins stretched over poles, and not of bark, like those of the woodland tribes. At a great fire in the centre women were grilling deer's flesh, while little brown children strove and quarrelled for scraps. I saw few men, for the braves were out hunting or keeping watch at the approaches. One young lad took the horses, and led us to a teepee bigger than the others, outside of which stood a finely-made savage, with heron's feathers in his hair, and a necklace of polished shells. On his iron face there was no flicker of welcome or re-cognition, but he shook hands silently with the two of us, and struck a blow on a dry gourd. Instantly three warriors appeared, and took their place by his side. Then all of us sat down and a pipe was lit and handed by the chief to Ringan. He took a puff and gave it to one of the other Indians, who handed it to me. With that cere-mony over, the tongue of the chief seemed to be unloosed. " The Sachem comes," he said, and an old man sat himself down beside us.

He was a strange figure to meet in an Indian

camp. A long white beard hung down to his middle, and his unshorn hair draped his shoulders like a fleece. His clothing was of tanned skin, save that he had a belt of Spanish leather, and on his feet he wore country shoes and not the Indian moccasins. The eyes in his head were keen and youthful, and though he could not have been less than sixty he carried himself with the vigour of a man in his prime. Below his shaggy locks was a high, broad forehead, such as some college professor might have borne who had given all his days to the philosophies. He seemed to have been disturbed in reading, for he carried in his hand a little book with a finger marking his place. I caught a glimpse of the title, and saw that it was Mr. Locke's new *Essay on the Human Understanding.*

Ringan spoke to the chief in his own tongue, but the Sioux language was beyond me. Mr. Lawrence joined in, and I saw the Indian's eyes kindle. He shook his head, and seemed to deny something. Then he poured forth a flood of talk, and when he had finished Ringan spoke to me.

" He says that the Tuscaroras are stirring. Word has come down from the hills to be ready for a great ride between the Moon of Stags and the Corn-gathering."

Lawrence nodded. " That's an old Tuscarora habit ; but somehow these ridings never happen." He said something in Sioux to one of the warriors, and got an emphatic answer, which he translated to me. " He thinks that the Cherokees have had word from farther north. It looks like a general stirring of the Long House."

" Is it the fighting in Canada ? " I asked.

" God knows," he said, " but I don't think so If that were the cause we should have the Iroquois pushed down on the top of the Cherokees. But my information is that the Cherokees are to move north themselves, and then down to the Tidewater. It is not likely that the Five Nations have any plan of conquering the lowlands. They're a hill people, and they know the white man's mettle too well. My notion is that some devilry is going on in the West, and I might guess that there's a white man in it." He spoke to the chief, who spoke again to his companion, and Lawrence listened with contracting brows, while Ringan whistled between his teeth.

" They've got a queer story," said Lawrence at last. " They say that when last they hunted on the Roanoke their young men brought a tale that a tribe of Cherokees, who lived six days' journey into the hills, had found a great Sachem who had the white man's magic, and that God was moving him to drive out the palefaces and hold his hunting lodge in their dwellings. That is not like an ordinary Indian lie. What do you make of it, Mr. Campbell ? "

Ringan looked grave. " It's possible enough. There's a heap of renegades among the tribes, men that have made the Tidewater and even the Free Companies too warm for them. There's no knowing the mischief a strong-minded rascal might

work. I mind a man at Norfolk, a Scots redemptioner, who had the tongue of a devil and the
strength of a wolf. He broke out one night and
got clear into the wilderness."

Lawrence turned to me briskly. " You see the
case, sir. There's trouble brewing in the hills,
black trouble for Virginia, but we've some months'
breathing space. For Nat Bacon's sake, I'm loath
to see the war paint at James Town. The question is, are you willing to do your share ? "

" I'm willing enough," I said, " but what can I
do ? I'm not exactly a popular character in the
Tidewater. If you want me to hammer sense into
the planters, you could not get a worse man for
the job. I have told Governor Nicholson my fears,
and he is of my opinion, but his hands are tied by
a penurious Council. If he cannot screw money
for troops out of the Virginians, it's not likely that
I could do much."

Lawrence nodded his wise head. " All you say
is true, but I want a different kind of service from
you. You may have noticed in your travels, Mr.
Garvald—for they tell me you are not often out of
the saddle—that up and down the land there's a
good few folk that are not very easy in their minds.
Many of these are former troopers of Bacon, some
are new men who have eyes in their heads, some
are old settlers who have been soured by the folly
of the Government. With such poor means as I
possess I keep in touch with these gentlemen, and
in them we have the rudiments of a frontier army.
I don't say they are many ; but five hundred

resolute fellows, well horsed and well armed, and led by some man who knows the Indian ways, might be a stumbling-block in the way of an Iroquois raid. But to perfect this force needs time, and, above all, it needs a man on the spot; for Virginia is not a healthy place for me, and these savannahs are a trifle distant. I want a man in James Town who will receive word when I send it, and pass it on to those who should hear it. I want a discreet man, whose trade takes him about the country. Mr. Campbell tells me you are such an one. Will you accept the charge?"

I was greatly flattered, but a little perplexed. "I'm a law-abiding citizen," I said, "and I can have no hand in rebellions. I've no ambition to play Bacon's part."

Lawrence smiled. "A proof of your discretion, sir. But believe me, there is no thought of rebellion. We have no quarrel with the Council and less with His Majesty's Governor. We but seek to set the house in order against perils which we alone know fully. I approve of your scruples, and I give you my word they shall not be violated."

"So be it," I said. "I will do what I can."

"God be praised," said Mr. Lawrence. "I have here certain secret papers which will give you the names of the men we can trust. Messages will come to you, which I trust you to find the means of sending on. Mercer has our confidence, and will arrange with you certain matters of arms. He will also supply you with what money is needed. There are many in the Tidewater who would look

askance at this business, so it must be done in
desperate secrecy ; but if there should be trouble
I counsel you to play a bold hand with the Governor. They tell me that you and he are friendly,
and, unless I mistake the man, he can see reason
if he is wisely handled. If the worst comes to the
worst, you can take Nicholson into your confidence."

" How long have we to prepare ? " I asked.

" The summer months, according to my forecast. It may be shorter or longer, but I will know
better when I get nearer the hills."

" And what about the Carolina tribes ? " I
asked. " If we are to hold the western marches
of Virginia, we cannot risk being caught on the
flank."

" That can be arranged," he said.   " Our friends
the Sioux are not over-fond of the Long House.
If the Tuscaroras ride, I do not think they will
ever reach the James."

The afternoon was now ending, and we were
given a meal of corn-cakes and roast deer's flesh.
Then we took our leave, and Mr. Lawrence's last
word to me was to send him any English books of
a serious cast which came under my eye. This
request he made with so much hesitation, but with
so hungry a desire in his face, that I was moved
to pity this ill-fated scholar, wandering in Indian
lodges, and famished for lack of the society of his
kind.

Ringan took me by a new way which bore north
of that we had ridden, and though the dusk began

soon to fall, he never faltered in his guiding. Presently we left the savannah for the woods of the coast, and, dropping down hill by a very meagre path, we came in three hours to a creek of the sea. There by a little fire we found Shalah, and the sloop riding at anchor below a thick covert of trees.

" Good-bye to you, Andrew," cried Ringan. " You'll be getting news of me soon, and maybe see me in the flesh on the Tidewater. Remember the word I told you in the Saltmarket, for I never mention names when I take the road."

CHAPTER X

I HEAR AN OLD SONG

WHEN we sailed at daybreak next morning I had the glow of satisfaction with my own doings which is a safe precursor of misfortunes. I had settled my business with the Free Companions, and need look for no more trouble on that score. But what tickled my vanity was my talk with Ringan and Lawrence at the Monacan lodge and the momentous trust they had laid on me. With a young man's vanity, I saw myself the saviour of Virginia, and hailed as such by the proud folk who now scorned me. My only merits, as I was to learn in time, are a certain grasp of simple truths that elude cleverer men, and a desperate obstinacy which is reluctant to admit defeat. But it is the fashion of youth to glory in what it lacks, and I flattered myself that I had a natural gift for finesse and subtlety, and was a born deviser of wars. Again and again I told myself how I and Lawrence's Virginians—grown under my hand to a potent army—should roll back the invaders to the hills and beyond,

while the Sioux of the Carolinas guarded one flank
and the streams of the Potomac the other. In
those days the star of the great Marlborough had
not risen ; but John Churchill, the victor of Blen-
heim, did not esteem himself a wiser strategist
than the raw lad Andrew Garvald, now sailing
north in the long wash of the Atlantic seas.

The weather grew spiteful, and we were much
buffeted about by the contrary spring winds, so
that it was late in the afternoon of the third day
that we turned Cape Henry and came into the
Bay of Chesapeake. Here a perfect hurricane fell
upon us, and we sought refuge in a creek on the
shore of Norfolk county. The place was marshy,
and it was hard to find dry land for our night's
lodging. Our provisions had run low, and there
seemed little enough for two hungry men who had
all day been striving with salt winds. So, knowing that this was a neighbourhood studded with
great manors, and remembering the hospitality I
had so often found, I left Shalah by the fire with
such food as remained, and set out with our
lantern through the woods to look for a human
habitation.

I found one quicker than I had hoped. Almost
at once I came on a track which led me into a
carriage-road and out of the thickets to a big
clearing. The daylight had not yet wholly gone,
and it guided me to two gateposts, from which
an avenue of chestnut trees led up to a great
house. There were lights glimmering in the win-
dows, and when I reached the yard and saw the

size of the barns and outbuildings, I wished I had
happened on a place of less pretensions. But
hunger made me bold, and I tramped over the
mown grass of the yard, which in the dusk I could
see to be set with flower-beds, till I stood before
the door of as fine a mansion as I had found in the
dominion. From within came a sound of speech
and laughter, and I was in half a mind to turn
back to my cold quarters by the shore. I had no
sooner struck the knocker than I wanted to run
away.

The door was opened instantly by a tall negro
in a scarlet livery. He asked no questions, but
motioned me to enter as if I had been an invited
guest. I followed him, wondering dolefully what
sort of figure I must cut in my plain clothes soaked
and stained by travel; for it was clear that I had
lighted on the mansion of some rich planter, who
was even now entertaining his friends. The servant led me through an outer hall into a great room
full of people. A few candles in tall candlesticks
burned down the length of a table, round which
sat a score of gentlemen. The scarlet negro went
to the table-head, and said something to the
master, who rose and came to meet me.

" I am storm-stayed," I said humbly, " and I
left my boat on the shore and came inland to look
for a supper."

" You shall get it," he said heartily. " Sit down,
and my servants will bring you what you need."

" But I am not fit to intrude, sir. A weary
traveller is no guest for such a table."

"Tush, man," he cried, "when did a Virginian think the worse of a man for his clothes? Sit down and say no more. You are heartily welcome."

He pushed me into a vacant chair at the bottom of the table, and gave some orders to the negro. Now I knew where I was, for I had seen before the noble figure of my host. This was Colonel Beverley, who in his youth had ridden with Prince Rupert, and had come to Virginia long ago in the Commonwealth time. He sat on the Council, and was the most respected of all the magnates of the dominion, for he had restrained the folly of successive Governors, and had ever been ready to stand forth alike on behalf of the liberties of the settlers and their duties to the Crown. His name was highly esteemed at Whitehall, and more than once he had occupied the Governor's place when His Majesty was slow in filling it. His riches were large, but he was above all things a great gentleman, who had grafted on an old proud stock the tolerance and vigour of a new land.

The company had finished dining, for the table was covered with fruits and comfits, and wine in silver goblets. There was sack and madeira, and French claret, and white Rhenish, and ale and cider for those with homelier palates. I saw dimly around me the faces of the guests, for the few candles scarcely illumined the dusk of the great panelled hall hung with dark portraits. One man gave me good-evening, but as I sat at the extreme end of the table I was out of the circle of the com-

pany. They talked and laughed, and it seemed
to me that I could hear women's voices at the
other end. Meantime I was busy with my viands,
and no man ever punished a venison pie more
heartily. As I ate and drank, I smiled at the
strangeness of my fortunes—to come thus straight
from the wild seas and the company of outlaws
into a place of silver and damask and satin coats
and lace cravats and orderly wigs. The soft hum
of gentlefolks' speech was all around me, those
smooth Virginian voices compared with which my
Scots tongue was as strident as a raven's. But as
I listened, I remembered Ringan and Lawrence,
and, " Ah, my silken friends," thought I, " little
you know the judgment that is preparing. Some
day soon, unless God is kind, there will be blood
on the lace and the war-whoop in these pleasant
chambers."

Then a voice said louder than the rest, " Dulcinea will sing to us. She promised me this morning in the garden."

At this there was a ripple of " Bravas," and
presently I heard the tuning of a lute. The low
twanging went on for a little, and suddenly I was
seized with a presentiment. I set down my tankard, and waited with my heart in my mouth.

Very clear and pure the voice rose, as fresh as
the morning song of birds. There was youth in
it, and joy and pride—joy of the fairness of the
earth, pride of beauty and race and strength.
" *My dear and only love* " it sang, as it had sung
before ; but then it had been a girl's hope, and

now it was a woman's certainty. At the first note, the past came back to me like yesterday. I saw the moorland gables in the rain, I heard the swirl of the tempest, I saw the elfin face in the hood which had cheered the traveller on his way. In that dim light I could not see the singer, but I needed no vision. The strangeness of the thing clutched at my heart, for here was the voice which had never been out of my ears singing again in a land far from the wet heather and the driving mists of home.

As I sat dazed and dreaming, I knew that a great thing had befallen me. For me, Andrew Garvald, the prosaic trader, coming out of the darkness into this strange company, the foundations of the world had been upset. All my cares and hopes, my gains and losses, seemed in that moment no better than dust. Love had come to me like a hurricane. From now I had but the one ambition, to hear that voice say to me and to mean it truly, " My dear and only love." I knew it was folly and a madman's dream, for I felt most deeply my common clay. What had I to offer for the heart of that proud lady ? A dingy and battered merchant might as well enter a court of steel-clad heroes and contend for the love of a queen. But I was not downcast. I do not think I even wanted to hope. It was enough to know that so bright a thing was in the world, for at one stroke my drab horizon seemed to have broadened into the infinite heavens.

The song ended in another chorus of " Bravas."

" Bring twenty candles, Pompey," my host called
out, " and the great punch-bowl. We will pledge
my lady in the old Beverley brew."

Servants set on the table a massive silver dish,
into which sundry bottles of wine and spirits
were poured. A mass of cut fruit and sugar was
added, and the whole was set alight, and leaped
almost to the ceiling in a blue flame. Colonel
Beverley, with a long ladle, filled the array of
glasses on a salver, which the servants carried
round to the guests. Large branching candelabra
had meantime been placed on the table, and in
a glow of light we stood to our feet and honoured
the toast.

As I stood up and looked to the table's end,
I saw the dark, restless eyes and the heavy blue
jowl of Governor Nicholson. He saw me, for I
was alone at the bottom end, and when we were
seated, he cried out to me,—

" What news of trade, Mr. Garvald ? You're
an active packman, for they tell me you're never
off the road."

At the mention of my name every eye turned
towards me, and I felt, rather than saw, the disfavour of the looks. No doubt they resented a
storekeeper's intrusion into well-bred company,
and some were there who had publicly cursed me
for a meddlesome upstart. But I was not looking
their way, but at the girl who sat on my host's
right hand, and in whose dark eyes I thought I
saw a spark of recognition.

She was clad in white satin, and in her hair

and bosom spring flowers had been set. Her little hand played with the slim glass, and her eyes had all the happy freedom of childhood. But now she was a grown woman, with a woman's pride and knowledge of power. Her exquisite slimness and grace, amid the glow of silks and silver, gave her the air of a fairy-tale princess. There was a grave man in black seated next her, to whom she bent to speak. Then she looked towards me again, and smiled with that witching mockery which had pricked my temper in the Canongate Tolbooth.

The Governor's voice recalled me from my dream.

"How goes the Indian menace, Mr. Garvald?" he cried. "You must know," and he turned to the company, "that our friend combines commerce with high policy, and shares my apprehensions as to the safety of the dominion."

I could not tell whether he was mocking at me or not. I think he was, for Francis Nicholson's moods were as mutable as the tides. In every word of his there lurked some crabbed irony.

The company took the speech for satire, and many laughed. One young gentleman, who wore a purple coat and a splendid brocaded vest, laughed very loud.

"A merchant's nerves are delicate things," he said, as he fingered his cravat. "I would have said 'like a woman's,' had I not seen this very day Miss Elspeth's horsemanship." And he bowed to her very neatly.

Now I was never fond of being quizzed, and in that company I could not endure it.

" We have a saying, sir," I said, " that the farmyard fowl does not fear the eagle. The men who look grave just now are not those who live snugly in coast manors, but the outland folk who have to keep their doors with their own hands."

It was a rude speech, and my hard voice and common clothes made it ruder. The gentleman fired in a second, and with blazing eyes asked me if I intended an insult. I was about to say that he could take what meaning he pleased, when an older man broke in with, " Tush, Charles, let the fellow alone. You cannot quarrel with a shopman."

" I thank you, George, for a timely reminder," said my gentleman, and he turned away his head with a motion of sovereign contempt.

" Come, come, sirs," Colonel Beverley cried, " remember the sacred law of hospitality. You are all my guests, and you have a lady here, whose bright eyes should be a balm for controversies."

The Governor had sat with his lips closed and his eyes roving the table. He dearly loved a quarrel, and was minded to use me to bait those whom he liked little.

" What is all this talk about gentility ? " he said. " A man is as good as his brains and his right arm, and no better. I am of the creed of the Levellers, who would have a man stand stark before his Maker."

He could not have spoken words better calculated to set the company against me. My host looked glum and disapproving, and all the silken gentlemen murmured. The Virginian cavalier had as pretty a notion of the worth of descent as any Highland land-louper. Indeed, to be honest I would have controverted the Governor myself, for I have ever held that good blood is a potent advantage to its possessor.

Suddenly the grave man who sat by Miss Elspeth's side spoke up. By this time I had remembered that he was Doctor James Blair, the lately come commissary of the diocese of London, who represented all that Virginia had in the way of a bishop. He had a shrewd, kind face, like a Scots dominie, and a mouth that shut as tight as the Governor's.

"Your tongue proclaims you my countryman, sir," he said. "Did I hear right that your name was Garvald?"

"Of Auchencairn?" he asked, when I had assented.

"Of Auchencairn, or what is left of it," I said.

"Then, gentlemen," he said, addressing the company, "I can settle the dispute on the facts, without questioning his Excellency's dogma. Mr. Garvald is of as good blood as any in Scotland. And that," said he firmly, "means that in the matter of birth he can hold up his head in any company in any Christian land."

I do not think this speech made any man there look on me with greater favour, but it enormously increased my own comfort. I have never felt such a glow of gratitude as then filled my heart to the staid cleric. That he was of near kin to Miss Elspeth made it tenfold sweeter. I forgot my old clothes and my uncouth looks; I forgot, too, my irritation with the brocaded gentleman. If her kin thought me worthy, I cared not a bodle for the rest of mankind.

Presently we rose from table, and Colonel Beverley summoned us to the Green Parlour, where Miss Elspeth was brewing a dish of chocolate, then a new-fangled luxury in the dominion. I would fain have made my escape, for if my appearance was unfit for a dining-hall, it was an outrage in a lady's withdrawing-room. But Doctor Blair came forward to me and shook me warmly by the hand, and was full of gossip about Clydesdale, from which apparently he had been absent these twenty years. "My niece bade me bring you to her," he said. "She, poor child, is a happy exile, but she has now and then an exile's longings. A Scots tongue is pleasant in her ear."

So I perforce had to follow him into a fine room with an oaken floor, whereon lay rich Smyrna rugs and the skins of wild beasts from the wood. There was a prodigious number of soft couches of flowered damask, and little tables inlaid with foreign woods and jeweller's work. 'Twas well enough for your fine gentleman in his buckled shoes and silk stockings to enter such a place, but for myself, in my coarse boots, I seemed like a colt in a flower garden. The girl sat by a brazier of charcoal, with the scarlet-coated negro at hand doing her commands. She was so busy at the chocolate making that when her uncle said, " Elspeth, I have brought you Mr. Garvald," she had no hand to give me. She looked up and smiled, and went on with the business, while I stood awkwardly by, the scorn of the assured gentlemen around me.

By and by she spoke : " You and I seem fated to meet in odd places. First it was at Carnwath in the rain, and then at the Cauldstaneslap in a motley company. Then I think it was in the Tolbooth, Mr. Garvald, when you were very gruff to your deliverer. And now we are both exiles, and once more you step in like a bogle out of the night. Will you taste my chocolate ? "

She served me first, and I could see how little the favour was to the liking of her little retinue of courtiers. My silken gentleman, whose name was Grey, broke in on us abruptly.

" What is this story, sir, of Indian dangers ? You are new to the country, or you would know that it is the old cry of the landless and the lawless. Every out-at-elbows republican makes it a stick to beat His Majesty."

" Are you a republican, Mr. Garvald ? " she asked. " Now that I remember, I have seen you in Whiggamore company."

" Why, no," I said. " I do not meddle with politics. I am a merchant, and am well content with any Government that will protect my trade and my person."

A sudden perversity had taken me to show

myself at my most prosaic and unromantic. I think it was the contrast with the glamour of those fine gentlemen. I had neither claim nor desire to be of their company, and to her I could make no pretence.

He laughed scornfully. "Yours is a noble cause," he said. "But you may sleep peacefully in your bed, sir. Be assured that there are a thousand gentlemen of Virginia whose swords will leap from their scabbards at a breath of peril, on behalf of their women and their homes. And these," he added, taking snuff from a gold box, "are perhaps as potent spurs to action as the whims of a busybody or the gains of a house-keeping trader."

I was determined not to be provoked, so I answered nothing. But Miss Elspeth opened her eyes and smiled sweetly upon the speaker.

"La, Mr. Grey, I protest you are too severe. Busybody—well, it may be. I have found Mr. Garvald very busy in other folks' affairs. But I do assure you he is no house-keeper. I have seen him in desperate conflict with savage men, and even with His Majesty's redcoats. If trouble ever comes to Virginia, you will find him, I doubt not, a very bold moss-trooper."

It was the light, laughing tone I remembered well, but now it did not vex me. Nothing that she could say or do could break the spell that had fallen on my heart. "I pray it may be so," said Mr. Grey as he turned aside.

By this time the Governor had come forward,

and I saw that my presence was no longer desired. I wanted to get back to Shalah and solitude. The cold bed on the shore would be warmed for me by happy dreams. So I found my host, and thanked him for my entertainment. He gave me good-evening hastily, as if he were glad to be rid of me.

At the hall door some one tapped me on the shoulder, and I turned to find my silken cavalier.

"It seems you are a gentleman, sir," he said, "so I desire a word with you. Your manners at table deserved a whipping, but I will conde-scend to forget them. But a second offence shall be duly punished." He spoke in a high, lisping voice, which was the latest London importation.

I looked him square in the eyes. He was maybe an inch taller than me, a handsome fellow, with a flushed, petulant face and an overweening pride in his arched brows.

"By all means let us understand each other," I said. "I have no wish to quarrel with you. Go your way and I will go mine, and there need be no trouble."

"That is precisely the point," said he. "I do not choose that your way should take you again to the side of Miss Elspeth Blair. If it does, we shall quarrel."

It was the height of flattery. At last I had found a fine gentleman who did me the honour to regard me with jealous eyes. I laughed loudly with delight.

He turned and strolled back to the company. Still laughing, I passed from the house, lit my lantern, and plunged into the woods.

CHAPTER XI

GRAVITY OUT OF BED

A WEEK later I had a visit from old Mercer. He came to my house in the evening just after the closing of the store. First of all, he paid out to me the gold I had lost from my ship at Accomac, with all the gravity in the world, as if it had been an ordinary merchant's bargain. Then he produced some papers, and putting on big horn spectacles, proceeded to instruct me in them. They were lists, fuller than those I had already got, of men up and down the country whom Lawrence trusted. Some I had met, many I knew of, but two or three gave me a start. There was a planter in Henricus who had treated me like dirt, and some names from Essex county that I did not expect. Especially there were several in James Town itself—one a lawyer body I had thought the obedient serf of the London merchants, one the schoolmaster, and another a drunken skipper of a river boat. But what struck me most was the name of Colonel Beverley.

"Are you sure of all these?" I asked.

" Sure as death," he said. " I'm not saying
that they're all friends of yours, Mr. Garvald.
Ye've trampled on a good wheen toes since you
came to these parts. But they're all men to ride
the ford with, if that should come which we
ken of."

Some of the men on the list were poor settlers,
and it was our business to equip them with horse
and gun. That was to be my special duty—that
and the establishing of means by which they could
be summoned quickly. With the first Mercer
could help me, for he had his hand on all the lines
of the smuggling business, and there were a dozen
ports on the coast where he could land arms.
Horses were an easy matter, requiring only the
doling out of money. But the summoning business
was to be my particular care. I could go about
the country in my ordinary way of trade without
exciting suspicion, and my house was to be the
rendezvous of every man on the list who wanted
news or guidance.

" Can ye trust your men ? " Mercer asked, and
I replied that Faulkner was as staunch as cold
steel, and that he had picked the others.

" Well, let's see your accommodation," and
the old fellow hopped to his feet, and was out
of doors before I could get the lantern.

Mercer on a matter of this sort was a different
being from the decayed landlord of the water-
side tavern. His spectacled eyes peered everywhere, and his shrewd sense judged instantly of
a thing's value. He approved of the tobacco-

shed as a store for arms, for he could reach it from the river by a little-used road through the woods. It was easy so to arrange the contents that a passing visitor would guess nothing, and no one ever penetrated to its recesses but Faulkner and myself. I summoned Faulkner to the conference, and told him his duties, which he undertook with sober interest. He was a dry stick from Fife, who spoke seldom and wrought mightily.

Faulkner attended to Mercer's consignments, and I took once more to the road. I had to arrange that arms from the coast or the riversides could be sent inland, and for this purpose I had a regiment of pack horses that delivered my own stores as well. I had to visit all the men on the list whom I did not know, and a weary job it was. I repeated again my toil of the first year, and in the hot Virginian summer rode the length and breadth of the land. My own business prospered hugely, and I bought on credit such a stock of tobacco as made me write my uncle for a fourth ship at the harvest sailing. It seemed a strange thing, I remember, to be bargaining for stuff which might never be delivered, for by the autumn the dominion might be at death grips.

In those weeks I discovered what kind of force Lawrence leaned on. He who only knew James Town and the rich planters knew little of the true Virginia. There were old men who had long memories of Indian fights, and men in their prime who had risen with Bacon, and young men who had their eyes turned to the unknown West.

There were new-comers from Scotland and North Ireland, and a stout band of French Protestants, most of them gently born, who had sought freedom for their faith beyond the sway of King Louis. You cannot picture a hardier or more spirited race than the fellows I thus recruited. The forest settler who swung an axe all day for his livelihood could have felled the ordinary fine gentleman with one blow of his fist. And they could shoot too, with their rusty matchlocks or clumsy snapchances. In some few the motive was fear, for they had seen or heard of the tender mercies of the savages. But in most, I think, it was a love of bold adventure, and especially the craving to push the white man's province beyond the narrow borders of the Tidewater. If you say that this was something more than defence, I claim that the only way to protect a country is to make sure of its environs. What hope is there of peace if your frontier is the rim of an unknown forest ?

My hardest task was to establish some method of sending news to the outland dwellers. For this purpose I had to consort with queer folk. Shalah, who had become my second shadow, found here and there little Indian camps, from which he chose young men as messengers. In one place I would get a settler with a canoe, in another a woodman with a fast horse, and in a third some lad who prided himself on his legs. The rare country taverns were a help, for most of their owners were in the secret. The Tidewater is a flat forest region,

so we could not light beacons as in a hilly land.
But by the aid of Shalah's woodcraft I concocted
a set of marks on trees and dwellings which would
speak a language to any initiate traveller. The
Indians, too, had their own silent tongue, by which
they could send messages over many leagues in a
short space. I never learned the trick of it, though
I tried hard with Shalah as interpreter ; for that
you must have been suckled in a wigwam.

When I got back to James Town, Faulkner
would report on his visitors, and he seems to
have had many. Rough fellows would ride up
at the darkening, bringing a line from Mercer, or
more often an agreed password, and he had to
satisfy their wants and remember their news. So
far I had had no word from Lawrence, though
Mercer reported that Ringan was still sending
arms. That tobacco-shed of mine would have
made a brave explosion if some one had kindled
it, and, indeed, the thing more than once was near
happening through a negro's foolishness. I spent
all my evenings, when at home, in making a map
of the country. I had got a rough chart from the
Surveyor-General, and filled up such parts as I
knew, and over all I spread a network of lines
which meant my ways of sending news. For in-
stance, to get to a man in Essex county, the word
would be passed by Middle Plantation to York
Ferry. Thence in an Indian's canoe it would be
carried to Aird's store on the Mattaponey, from
which a woodman would take it across the swamps
to a clump of hemlocks. There he would make

certain marks, and a long-legged lad from the
Rappahannock, riding by daily to school, would
carry the tidings to the man I wanted. And so
forth over the habitable dominion. I calculated
that there were not more than a dozen of Lawrence's men who within three days could not get
the summons and within five be at the proper
rendezvous.

One evening I was surprised by a visit from
Colonel Beverley. He came openly on a fine bay
horse with two mounted negroes as attendants.
I had parted from him dryly, and had been surprised to find that he was one of us ; but when I
had talked with him a little, it appeared that he
had had a big share in planning the whole business. We mentioned no names, but I gathered
that he knew Lawrence, and was at least aware
of Ringan. He warned me, I remember, to be on
my guard against some of the young bloods, who
might visit me to make mischief. " It's not that
they know anything of our affairs," he said, " but
that they have got a prejudice against yourself,
Mr. Garvald. They are foolish, hot-headed lads,
very puffed up by their pride of gentrice, and I do
not like the notion of their playing pranks in that
tobacco-shed."

I asked him a question which had long puzzled
me, why the natural defence of a country should
be kept so secret. " The Governor, at any rate,"
I said, " would approve, and we are not asking
the burgesses for a single guinea."

" Yes, but the Governor would play a wild

hand," was the answer. "He would never permit the thing to go on quietly, but would want to ride at the head of the men, and the whole fat would be in the fire. You must know, Mr. Garvald, that politics run high in our Virginia. There are scores of men who would see in our enterprise a second attempt like Bacon's, and, though they might approve of our aims, would never hear of one of Bacon's folk serving with us. I was never a Bacon's man, for I was with Berkeley in Accomac and at the taking of James Town, but I know the quality of the rough fellows that Bacon led, and I want them all for this venture. Besides, who can deny that there is more in our plans than a defence against Indians ? There are many who feel with me that Virginia can never grow to the fullness of a nation so long as she is cooped up in the Tidewater. New-comers arrive by every ship from England, and press on into the wilderness. But there can be no conquest of the wilderness till we have broken the Indian menace, and pushed our frontier up to the hills—ay, and beyond them. But tell that to the ordinary planter, and he will consign you to the devil. He fears these new-comers, who are simple fellows that do not respect his grandeur. He fears that some day they may control the assembly by their votes. He wants the Tidewater to be his castle, with porters and guards to hound away strangers. Man alive, if you had tried to put reason into some of their heads, you would despair of human nature. Let them get a hint of our preparations, and there will be petitions to Council and a howling about treason, and in a week you will be in gaol, Mr. Garvald. So we must move cannily, as you Scots say."

That conversation made me wary, and I got Faulkner to keep a special guard on the place when I was absent. At the worst, he could summon Mercer, who would bring a rough crew from the water-side to his aid. Then once more I disappeared into the woods.

In these days a new Shalah revealed himself. I think he had been watching me closely for the past months, and slowly I had won his approval. He showed it by beginning to talk as he loped by my side in our forest wanderings. The man was like no Indian I have ever seen. He was a Senecan, and so should have been on the side of the Long House; but it was plain that he was an outcast from his tribe, and, indeed, from the whole Indian brotherhood. I could not fathom him, for he seemed among savages to be held in deep respect, and yet here he was, the ally of the white man against his race. His lean, supple figure, his passionless face, and his high, masterful air had a singular nobility in them. To me he was never the servant, scarcely even the companion, for he seemed like a being from another world, who had a knowledge of things hid from human ken. In woodcraft he was a master beyond all thought of rivalry. Often, when time did not press, he would lead me, clumsy as I was, so that I could almost touch the muzzle of a crouching deer, or lay a

hand on a yellow panther, before it slipped like a
live streak of light into the gloom. He was an
eerie fellow, too. Once I found him on a high
river-bank at sunset watching the red glow behind
the blue shadowy forest.

" There is blood in the West," he said, pointing
like a prophet with his long arm. " There is blood
in the hills, which is flowing to the waters. At
the Moon of Stags it will flow, and by the Moon
of Wildfowl it will have stained the sea."

He had always the hills at the back of his head.
Once, when we caught a glimpse of them from a
place far up the James River, he stood like a statue
gazing at the thin line which hung like a cloud in
the west. I am upland bred, and to me, too, the
sight was a comfort as I stood beside him.

" The *Manitou* in the hills is calling," he said
abruptly. " I wait a little, but not long. You
too will follow, brother, to where the hawks wheel
and the streams fall in vapour. There we shall
find death or love, I know not which, but it will
be a great finding. The gods have written it on
my heart."

Then he turned and strode away, and I did not
dare to question him. There was that about him
which stirred my prosaic soul into a wild poetry,
till for the moment I saw with his eyes, and heard
strange voices in the trees.

Apart from these uncanny moods he was the
most faithful helper in my task. Without him I
must have been a mere child. I could not read
the lore of the forest ; I could not have found my

way as he found it through pathless places.   From
him, too, I learned that we were not to make our
preparations unwatched.

Once, as we were coming from the Rappahannock to the York, he darted suddenly into the
undergrowth below the chestnuts.   My eye could
see no clue on the path, and, suspecting nothing,
I waited on him to return.   Presently he came,
and beckoned me to follow.   Thirty yards into
the coppice we found a man lying dead, with a
sharp stake holding him to the ground, and a raw,
red mass where had been once his head.

" That was your messenger, brother," he whispered, " the one who was to carry word from the
Mattaponey to the north.   See, he has been dead
for two suns."

He was one of the tame Algonquins who dwelt
by Aird's store.

" Who did it ? " I asked, with a very sick
stomach.

" A Cherokee.   Some cunning one, and he left
a sign to guide us."

He showed me a fir-cone he had picked up from
the path, with the sharp end cut short and a thorn
stuck in the middle.

The thing disquieted me horribly, for we had
heard no word yet of any movement from the
West.   And yet it seemed that our enemy's scouts
had come far down into the Tidewater, and knew
enough to single out for death a man we had en-
rolled for service.   Shalah slipped off without a
word, and I was left to continue my journey alone.

I will not pretend that I liked the business. I saw an Indian in every patch of shadow, and looked pretty often to my pistols before I reached the security of Aird's house.

Four days later Shalah appeared at James Town. "They were three," he said simply. "They came from the hills a moon ago, and have been making bad trouble on the Rappahannock. I found them at the place above the beaver traps of the Ooniche. They return no more to their people."

After that we sent out warnings, and kept a close eye on the different lodges of the Algonquins. But nothing happened till weeks later, when the tragedy on the Rapidan fell on us like a thunder-clap.

All this time I had been too busy to go near the town or the horse-racings and holiday meetings where I might have seen Elspeth. But I do not think she was ever many minutes out of my mind. Indeed, I was almost afraid of a meeting, lest it should shatter the bright picture which comforted my solitude. But one evening in June, as I jogged home from Middle Plantation through the groves of walnuts, I came suddenly at the turn of the road on a party. Doctor James Blair, mounted on a stout Flanders cob, held the middle of the path, and at his side rode the girl, while two servants followed with travelling valises. I was upon them before I could rein up, and the Doctor cried a hearty good-day. So I took my place by Elspeth, and, with my heart beating wildly, accom-

panied them through the leafy avenues and by the
green melon-beds in the clearings till we came out
on the prospect of the river.

The Doctor had a kindness for me, and was
eager to talk of his doings. He was almost as
great a moss-trooper as myself, and, with Elspeth
for company, had visited near every settlement in
the dominion. Education and Christian privileges
were his care, and he deplored the backward state
of the land. I remember that even then he was
full of his scheme for a Virginian college to be
established at Middle Plantation, and he wrote
weekly letters to his English friends soliciting
countenance and funds. Of the happy issue of
these hopes, and the great college which now
stands at Williamsburg, there is no need to remind this generation.

But in that hour I thought little of education.
The Doctor boomed away in his deep voice, and
I gave him heedless answers. My eyes were ever
wandering to the slim figure at my side. She
wore a broad hat of straw, I remember, and her
skirt and kirtle were of green, the fairies' colour.
I think she was wearied with the sun, for she
spoke little; but her eyes when they met mine
were kind. That day I was not ashamed of my
plain clothes or my homely face, for they suited
well with the road. My great boots of untanned
buckskin were red with dust, I was bronzed like
an Indian, and the sun had taken the colour out
of my old blue coat. But I smacked of travel and
enterprise, which to an honest heart are dearer

than brocade. Also I had a notion that my very homeliness revived in her the memories of our common motherland. I had nothing to say, having acquired the woodland habit of silence, and perhaps it was well. My clumsy tongue would have only broken the spell which the sunlit forests had woven around us.

As we reached my house a cavalier rode up with a bow and a splendid sweep of his hat. 'Twas my acquaintance, Mr. Grey, come to greet the travellers. Elspeth gave me her hand at parting, and I had from the cavalier the finest glance of hate and jealousy which ever comforted the heart of a backward lover.

CHAPTER XII

THE next Sunday I was fool enough to go to church, for Doctor Blair was announced to preach the sermon. Now I knew very well what treatment I should get, and that it takes a stout fellow to front a conspiracy of scorn. But I had got new courage from my travels, so I put on my best suit of murrey-coloured cloth, my stockings of cherry silk, the gold buckles which had been my father's, my silk-embroidered waistcoat, freshly-ironed ruffles, and a new hat which had cost forty shillings in London town. I wore my own hair, for I never saw the sense of a wig save for a bald man, but I had it deftly tied. I would have cut a great figure had there not been my bronzed and rugged face to give the lie to my finery.

It was a day of blistering heat. The river lay still as a lagoon, and the dusty red roads of the town blazed like a furnace. Before I had got to the church door I was in a great sweat, and stopped in the porch to fan myself. Inside 'twas cool enough, with a pleasant smell from the cedar pews, but there was such a press of a congregation that many were left standing. I had a good place just below the choir, where I saw the Governor's carved chair, with the Governor's self before it on his kneeling-cushion making pretence to pray. Round the choir rail and below the pulpit clustered many young exquisites, for this was a sovereign place from which to show off their finery. I could not get a sight of Elspeth.

Doctor Blair preached us a fine sermon from the text, "*My people shall dwell in a pleasant habitation, and in sure dwellings, and in quiet resting-places,*" but his hearers were much disturbed by the continual chatter of the fools about the choir rail. Before he had got to the Prayer of Chrysostom the exquisites were whispering like pigeons in a dovecot, exchanging snuff-boxes, and ogling the women. So intolerable it grew that the Doctor paused in his discourse and sternly rebuked them, speaking of the laughter of fools which is as the crackling of thorns under a pot. This silenced them for a little, but the noise broke out during the last prayer, and with the final word of the Benediction my gentlemen thrust their way through the congregation, that they might be the first at the church door. I have never seen so unseemly a sight, and for a moment I thought that Governor Nicholson would call the halberdiers and set them in the pillory. He refrained, though his face was dark with wrath, and I judged that there would be some hard words said before the matter was finished.

I must tell you that during the last week I had been coming more into favour with the prosperous families of the colony. Some one may have spoken well of me, perhaps the Doctor, or they may have seen the justice of my way of trading. Anyhow, I had a civil greeting from several of the planters, and a bow from their dames. But no sooner was I in the porch than I saw that trouble was afoot with the young bloods. They were drawn up on both sides the path, bent on quizzing me. I sternly resolved to keep my temper, but I foresaw that it would not be easy.

"Behold the shopman in his Sunday best," said one.

"I thought that Sawney wore bare knees on his dirty hills," said another.

One pointed to my buckles. "Pinchbeck out of the store," he says.

"Ho, ho, such finery!" cried another. "See how he struts like a gamecock."

"There's much ado when beggars ride," said a third, quoting the proverb.

It was all so pitifully childish that it failed to provoke me. I marched down the path with a smile on my face, which succeeded in angering them. One young fool, a Norton from Malreward, would have hustled me, but I saw Mr. Grey hold him back. "No brawling here, Austin," said my rival.

They were not all so discreet. One of the Kents of Gracedieu tried to trip me by thrusting his cane between my legs. But I was ready for him, and, pulling up quick and bracing my knees, I snapped the thing short, so that he was left to dangle the ivory top.

Then he did a wild thing. He flung the remnant at my face, so that the ragged end scratched my cheek. When I turned wrathfully I found a circle of grinning faces.

It is queer how a wound, however slight, breaks a man's temper and upsets his calm resolves. I think that then and there I would have been involved in a mellay, had not a voice spoke behind me.

" Mr. Garvald," it said, " will you give me the favour of your arm ? We dine to-day with his Excellency."

I turned to find Elspeth, and close behind her Doctor Blair and Governor Nicholson.

All my heat left me, and I had not another thought for my tormentors. In that torrid noon she looked as cool and fragrant as a flower. Her clothes were simple compared with the planters' dames, but of a far more dainty fashion. She wore, I remember, a gown of pale sprigged muslin, with a blue kerchief about her shoulders and blue ribbons in her wide hat. As her hand lay lightly on my arm I did not think of my triumph, being wholly taken up with the admiration of her grace. The walk was all too short, for the Governor's lodging was but a stone's-throw distant. When we parted at the door I hoped to find some of my mockers still lingering, for in that hour I think I could have flung any three of them into the river.

None were left, however, and as I walked homewards I reflected very seriously that the baiting of Andrew Garvald could not endure for long. Pretty soon I must read these young gentry a lesson, little though I wanted to embroil myself in quarrels. I called them "young" in scorn, but few of them, I fancy, were younger than myself.

Next day, as it happened, I had business with Mercer at the water-side, and as I returned along the harbour front I fell in with the Receiver of Customs, who was generally called the Captain of the Castle, from his station at Point Comfort. He was an elderly fellow who had once been a Puritan, and still cherished a trace of the Puritan modes of speech. I had often had dealings with him, and had found him honest, though a thought truculent in manner. He had a passion against all smugglers and buccaneers, and, in days to come, was to do good service in ridding Accomac of these scourges. He feared God, and did not greatly fear much else.

He was sitting on the low wall smoking a pipe, and had by him a very singular gentleman. Never have I set eyes on a more decorous merchant. He was habited neatly and soberly in black, with a fine white cravat and starched shirt-bands. He wore a plain bob-wig below a huge flat-brimmed hat, and big blue spectacles shaded his eyes. His mouth was as precise as a lawyer's, and altogether he was a very whimsical, dry fellow to find at a Virginian port.

The Receiver called me to him and asked after

a matter which we had spoken of before. Then he made me known to his companion, who was a Mr. Fairweather, a merchant out of Boston.

"The Lord hath given thee a pleasant dwelling, friend," said the stranger, snuffling a little through his nose.

From his speech I knew that Mr. Fairweather was of the sect of the Quakers, a peaceable race that Virginia had long ill-treated.

"The land is none so bad," said the Receiver, "but the people are a perverse generation. Their hearts are set on vanity, and puffed up with pride. I could wish, Mr. Fairweather, that my lines had fallen among your folk in the north, where, I am told, true religion yet flourisheth. Here we have nothing but the cold harangues of the Commissary, who seeketh after the knowledge that perisheth rather than the wisdom which is eternal life."

"Patience, friend," said the stranger. "Thee is not alone in thy crosses. The Lord hath many people up Boston way, but they are sore beset by the tribulations of Zion. On land there is war and rumour of war, and on the sea the ships of the godly are snatched by every manner of ocean thief. Likewise we have dissension among ourselves, and a constant strife with the froward human heart. Still is Jerusalem troubled, and there is no peace within her bulwarks."

"Do the pirates afflict you much in the north?" asked the Receiver with keen interest.

The stranger turned his large spectacles upon him, and then looked blandly at me. Suddenly

I had a notion that I had seen that turn of the neck and poise of the head before.

"Woe is me," he cried in a stricken voice. "The French have two fair vessels of mine since March, and a third is missing. Some say it ran for a Virginian port, and I am here to seek it. Heard thee ever, friend, of a strange ship in the James or the Potomac?"

"There be many strange ships," said the Receiver, "for this dominion is the goal for all the wandering merchantmen of the earth. What was the name of yours?"

"A square-rigged schooner out of Bristol, painted green, with a white figurehead of a winged heathen god."

"And the name?"

"The name is a strange one. It is called *The Horn of Diarmaid*, but I seek to prevail on the captain to change it to *The Horn of Mercy*."

"No such name is known to me," and the Receiver shook his head. "But I will remember it, and send you news."

I hope I did not betray my surprise, but for all that it was staggering. Of all disguises and of all companies this was the most comic and the most hazardous. I stared across the river till I had mastered my countenance, and when I looked again at the two they were soberly discussing the harbour dues of Boston.

Presently the Receiver's sloop arrived to carry him to Point Comfort. He nodded to me, and took an affectionate farewell of the Boston man.

I heard some good mouth-filling texts exchanged between them.

Then, when we were alone, the Quaker turned to me, " Man, Andrew," he said, "it was a good thing that I had a Bible upbringing. I can manage the part fine, but I flounder among the ' thees ' and ' thous.' I would be the better of a drink to wash my mouth of the accursed pronouns. Will you be alone to-night about the darkening ? Then I'll call in to see you, for I've much to tell you."

That evening about nine the Quaker slipped into my room.

" How about that tobacco-shed ? " he asked. " Is it well guarded ? "

" Faulkner and one of the men sleep above it, and there are a couple of fierce dogs chained at the door. Unless they know the stranger, he will be apt to lose the seat of his breeches."

The Quaker nodded, well pleased. " That is well, for I heard word in the town that to-night you might have a visitor or two." Then he walked to a stand of arms on the wall and took down a small sword, which he handled lovingly. "A fair weapon, Andrew," said he. " My new sect forbids me to wear a blade, but I think I'll keep this handy beside me in the chimney corner."

Then he gave me the news. Lawrence had been far inland with the Monacans, and had brought back disquieting tales. The whole nation of the Cherokees along the line of the mountains was unquiet. Old family feuds had been patched up, and there was a coming and going of messengers from Chickamauga to the Potomac.

"Well, we're ready for them," I said, and I told him the full story of our preparations.

"Ay, but that is not all. I would not give much for what the Cherokees and the Tuscaroras could do. There might be some blood shed and a good few blazing roof-trees in the back country, but no Indian raid would stand against our lads. But I have a notion—maybe it's only a notion, though Lawrence is half inclined to it himself—that there's more in this business than a raid from the hills. There's something stirring in the West, away in the parts that no white man has ever travelled. From what I learn there's a bigger brain than an Indian's behind it."

"The French ? " I asked.

"Maybe, but maybe not. What's to hinder a blackguard like Cosh, with ten times Cosh's mind, from getting into the Indian councils, and turning the whole West loose on the Tidewater ? "

"Have you any proof ? " I asked, much alarmed.

"Little at present. But one thing I know. There's a man among the tribes that speaks English."

"Great God, what a villain ! " I cried. "But how do you know ? "

"Just this way. The Monacans put an arrow through the neck of a young brave, and they found this in his belt."

He laid before me a bit of a printed Bible leaf. About half was blank paper, for it came at the end of the Book of Revelation. On the blank part some signs had been made in rude ink which I could not understand.

"But this is no proof," I said. "It's only a relic from some plundered settlement. Can you read those marks ? "

"I cannot, nor could the Monacans. But look at the printed part."

I looked again, and saw that some one had very carefully underlined certain words. These made a sentence, and read, "*John, servant of the prophecy, is at hand.*"

"The underlining may have been done long ago," I hazarded.

"No, the ink is not a month old," he said, and I could do nothing but gape.

"Well, what's your plan ? " I said at last.

"None, but I would give my right hand to know what is behind the hills. That's our weakness, Andrew. We have to wait here, and since we do not know the full peril, we cannot fully prepare. There may be mischief afoot which would rouse every sleepy planter out of bed, and turn the Tidewater into an armed camp. But we know nothing. If we had only a scout——"

"What about Shalah ? " I asked.

"Can you spare him ? " he replied; and I knew I could not.

"I see nothing for it," I said, "but to wait till we are ready, and then to make a reconnais-

sance, trusting to be in time. This is the first
week of July. In another fortnight every man on
our list will be armed, and every line of communi-
cation laid. Then is our chance to make a bid
for news."

He nodded, and at that moment came the
growling of dogs from the sheds. Instantly his
face lost its heavy preoccupation, and under his
Quaker's mask became the mischievous countenance of a boy. " That's your friends," he said.
" Now for a merry meeting."

In the sultry weather I had left open window
and door, and every sound came clear from the
outside. I heard the scuffling of feet, and some
confused talk, and presently there stumbled
into my house half a dozen wild-looking figures.
They blinked in the lamplight, and one begged
to know if " Mr. Garbled " were at home. All
had decked themselves for this play in what they
fancied was the dress of pirates—scarlet sashes,
and napkins or turbans round their heads, big
boots, and masks over their eyes. I did not recognize a face, but I was pretty clear that Mr. Grey
was not of the number, and I was glad, for the
matter between him and me was too serious for
this tomfoolery. All had been drinking, and one
at least was very drunk. He stumbled across
the floor, and all but fell on Ringan in his
chair.

" Hullo, old Square-Toes," he hiccupped ;
" what the devil are you ? "

" Friend, thee is shaky on thy legs," said

Ringan, in a mild voice. " It were well for thee to be in bed."

" Bed," cried the roysterer ; " no bed for me this night ! Where is that damnable Scots pack-man ? "

I rose very quietly and lit another lamp. Then I shut the window, and closed the shutters. " Here I am," I said, " very much at your service, gentle-men."

One or two of the sober ones looked a little embarrassed, but the leader, who I guessed was the youth from Gracedieu, was brave enough.

" The gentlemen of Virginia," he said loudly, " being resolved that the man Garvald is an offence to the dominion, have summoned the Free Companions to give him a lesson. If he will sign a bond to leave the country within a month, we are instructed to be merciful. If not, we have here tar and feathers and sundry other adornments, and to-morrow's morn will behold a pretty sight. Choose, you Scotch swine." In the excess of his zeal, he smashed with the handle of his sword a clock I had but lately got from Glasgow.

Ringan signed to me to keep my temper. He pretended to be in a great taking.

" I am a man of peace," he cried, " but I can-not endure to see my friend outraged. Prithee, good folk, go away. See, I will give thee a guinea each to leave us alone."

This had the desired effect of angering them. " Curse your money," one cried. " You damned

traders think that you can buy a gentleman.
Take that for your insult." And he aimed a
blow with the flat of his sword, which Ringan
easily parried.

"I had thought thee a pirate," said the mild
Quaker, "but thee tells me thee is a gentleman."

"Hold your peace, Square-Toes," cried the
leader, "and let's get to business."

"But if ye be gentlefolk," pleaded Ringan,
"ye will grant a fair field. I am no fighter, but
I will stand by my friend."

I, who had said nothing, now broke in. "It
is a warm evening for sword-play, but if it is
your humour, so be it."

This seemed to them hugely comic. "La!"
cried one, "Sawney with a sword!" And he
plucked forth his own blade, and bent it on the
floor.

Ringan smiled gently. "Thee must grant me
the first favour," he said, "for I am the chal-
lenger, if that be the right word of the carnally
minded." And standing up, he picked up the
blade from beside him, and bowed to the leader
from Gracedieu.

Nothing loath he engaged, and the others
stood back expecting a high fiasco. They saw it.
Ringan's sword played like lightning round the
wretched youth, it twitched the blade from his
grasp, and forced him back with a very white
face to the door. In less than a minute, it seemed,
he was there, and as he yielded so did the door,
and he disappeared into the night. He did not

return, so I knew that Ringan must have spoke a word to Faulkner.

"Now for the next bloody-minded pirate," cried Ringan, and the next with a very wry face stood up. One of the others would have joined in, but, crying, "For shame, a fair field," I beat down his sword.

The next took about the same time to reach the door, and disappeared into the darkness, and the third about half as long. Of the remaining three, one sulkily declined to draw, and the other two were over drunk for anything. They sat on the floor and sang a loose song.

"It seems, friends," said the Quaker, "that ye be more ready with words than with deeds. I pray thee"—this to the sober one—"take off these garments of sin. We be peaceful traders, and cannot abide the thought of pirates."

He took them off, sash, breeches, jerkin, turban and all, and stood up in his shirt. The other two I stripped myself, and so drunk were they that they entered into the spirit of the thing, and themselves tore at the buttons. Then with Ringan's sword behind them, the three marched out of doors.

There we found their companions stripped and sullen, with Faulkner and the men to guard them. We made up neat parcels of their clothes, and I extorted their names, all except one who was too far gone in drink.

"To-morrow, gentlemen," I said, "I will send back your belongings, together with the tar and feathers, which you may find useful some other day. The night is mild, and a gentle trot will keep you from taking chills. I should recommend hurry, for in five minutes the dogs will be loosed. A pleasant journey to you."

They moved off, and then halted and apparently were for returning. But they thought better of it, and presently they were all six of them racing and stumbling down the hill in their shirts.

The Quaker stretched his legs and lit a pipe. " Was it not a scurvy trick of fate," he observed to the ceiling, " that these poor lads should come here for a night's fooling, and find the best sword in the Five Seas ? "

CHAPTER XIII

I STUMBLE INTO A GREAT FOLLY

I NEVER breathed a word about the night's doings, nor for divers reasons did Ringan; but the story got about, and the young fools were the laughing-stock of the place. But there was a good deal of wrath, too, that a trader should have presumed so far, and I felt that things were gathering to a crisis with me. Unless I was to suffer endlessly these petty vexations, I must find a bold stroke to end them. It annoyed me that when so many grave issues were in the balance I should have these troubles, as if a man should be devoured by midges when waiting on a desperate combat.

The crisis came sooner than I looked for. There was to be a great horse-racing at Middle Plantation the next Monday, which I had half a mind to attend, for, though I cared nothing for the sport, it would give me a chance of seeing some of our fellows from the York River. One morning I met Elspeth in the street of James Town, and she cried laughingly that she looked to see me at the races. After that I had no choice but go ; so on the Monday morning I dressed myself with care, mounted my best horse, and rode to the gathering.

'Twas a pretty sight to see the spacious green meadow, now a little yellowing with the summer heat, set in the girdle of dark and leafy forest. I counted over forty chariots which had brought the rank of the countryside, each with its liveried servant and its complement of out-riders. The fringe of the course blazed with ladies' finery, and a tent had been set up with a wide awning from which the fashionables could watch the sport. On the edge of the woods a multitude of horses were picketed, and there were booths that sold food and drink, merry-go-rounds and fiddlers, and an immense concourse of every condition of folk, black slaves and water-side Indians, squatters from the woods, farmers from all the valleys, and the scum and ruck of the plantations. I found some of my friends, and settled my business with them, but my eyes were always straying to the green awning where I knew that Elspeth sat.

I am no judge of racing, but I love the aspect of sleek, slim horses, and I could applaud a skill in which I had no share. I can keep my seat on most four-legged beasts, but my horsemanship is a clumsy, rough-and-ready affair, very different from the effortless grace of your true cavalier. Mr. Grey's prowess, especially, filled me with awe. He would leap an ugly fence without moving an inch in his saddle, and both in skill and the quality of his mounts he was an easy victor. The sight of such accomplishments depressed my pride, and I do not think I would have ventured near the tent had it not been for the Governor.

He saw me on the fringe of the crowd, and called me to him. " What bashfulness has taken you to-day, sir ? " he cried. " That is not like your usual. There are twenty pretty dames here who pine for a word from you."

I saw his purpose well 'enough. He loved to make mischief, and knew that the sight of me among the Virginian gentry would infuriate my unfriends. But I took him at his word and elbowed my way into the enclosure.

Then I wished to Heaven I had stayed at home. I got insolent glances from the youths, and the cold shoulder from the ladies. Elspeth smiled when she saw me, but turned the next second to gossip with her little court. She was a devout lover of horses, and had eyes for nothing but the racing. Her cheeks were flushed, and it was pretty to watch her excitement ; how she hung breathless on the movements of the field, and clapped her hands at a brave finish. Pretty, indeed, but exasperating to one who had no part in that pleasant company.

I stood gloomily by the rail at the edge of the ladies' awning, acutely conscious of my loneliness. Presently Mr. Grey, whose racing was over, came to us, and had a favour pinned in his coat by Elspeth's fingers. He was evidently high in her good graces, for he sat down by her and talked gleefully. I could not but admire his handsome, eager face, and admit with a bitter grudge that you would look long to find a comelier pair.

All this did not soothe my temper, and after an hour of it I was in desperate ill-humour with the world. I had just reached the conclusion that I had had as much as I wanted, when I heard Elspeth's voice calling me.

"Come hither, Mr. Garvald," she said. "We have a dispute which a third must settle. I favour the cherry, and Mr. Grey fancies the blue ; but I maintain that blue crowds cherry unfairly at the corners. Use your eyes, sir, at the next turning."

I used my eyes, which are very sharp, and had no doubt of it.

"That is a matter for the Master of the Course," said Mr. Grey. "Will you uphold your view before him, sir ? "

I said that I knew too little of the sport to be of much weight as a witness. To this he said nothing, but offered to wager with me on the result of the race, which was now all but ending. "Or no," said he, "I should not ask you that. A trader is careful of his guineas."

Elspeth did not hear, being intent on other things, and I merely shrugged my shoulders, though my fingers itched for the gentleman's ears.

In a little the racing ceased, and the ladies made ready to leave. Doctor Blair appeared, protesting that the place was not for his cloth, and gave Elspeth his arm to escort her to his coach. She cried a merry good-day to us, and reminded Mr. Grey that he had promised to sup with them on the morrow. When she had gone I spied a lace scarf which she had forgotten, and picked it up to restore it.

This did not please the other. He snatched it from me, and when I proposed to follow, tripped me deftly, and sent me sprawling among the stools. As I picked myself up, I saw him running to overtake the Blairs.

This time there was no discreet girl to turn the edge of my fury. All the gibes and annoyances of the past months rushed into my mind, and set my head throbbing. I was angry, but very cool with it all, for I saw that the matter had now gone too far for tolerance. Unless I were to be the butt of Virginia, I must assert my manhood.

I flicked the dust from my coat, and walked quietly to where Mr. Grey was standing amid a knot of his friends, who talked of the races and their losses and gains. He saw me coming, and said something which made them form a staring alley, down which I strolled. He kept regarding me with bright, watchful eyes.

" I have been very patient, sir," I said, " but there is a limit to what a man may endure from a mannerless fool." And I gave him a hearty slap on the face.

Instantly there was a dead silence, in which the sound seemed to linger intolerably. He had grown very white, and his eyes were wicked.

"I am obliged to you, sir," he said. "You are some kind of ragged gentleman, so no doubt you will give me satisfaction."

"When and where you please," I said sedately.

"Will you name your friend now ¿ " he asked. "These matters demand quick settlement."

To whom was I to turn ? I knew nobody of the better class who would act for me. For a moment I thought of Colonel Beverley, but his age and dignity were too great to bring him into this squabble of youth. Then a notion struck me.

"If you will send your friend to my man, John Faulkner, he will make all arrangements. He is to be found any day in my shop."

With this defiance, I walked nonchalantly out of the dumbfoundered group, found my horse, and rode homewards.

My coolness did not last many minutes, and long ere I had reached James Town I was a prey to dark forebodings. Here was I, a peaceful trader, who desired nothing more than to live in amity with all men, involved in a bloody strife. I had sought it, and yet it had been none of my seeking. I had graver thoughts to occupy my mind than the punctilios of idle youth, and yet I did not see how the thing could have been shunned. It was my hard fate to come athwart an obstacle which could not be circumvented, but must be broken. No friend could help me in the business, not Ringan, nor the Governor, nor Colonel Beverley. It was my own affair, which I must go through with alone. I felt as solitary as a pelican.

Remember, I was not fighting for any whimsy about honour, nor even for the love of Elspeth. I had openly provoked Grey because the hostility of the young gentry had become an intolerable nuisance in my daily life. So, with such pedestrian reasons in my mind, I could have none of the heady enthusiasm of passion. I wanted him and his kind cleared out of my way, like a noisome insect, but I had no flaming hatred of him to give me heart.

The consequence was that I became a prey to dismal fear. That bravery which knows no ebb was never mine. Indeed, I am by nature timorous, for my fancy is quick, and I see with horrid clearness the incidents of a peril. Only a shamefaced conscience holds me true, so that, though I have often done temerarious deeds, it has always been because I feared shame more than the risk, and my knees have ever been knocking together and my lips dry with fright. I tried to think soberly over the future, but could get no conclusion save that I would not do murder. My conscience was pretty bad about the whole business. I was engaged in the kind of silly conflict which I had been bred to abhor ; I had none of the common gentleman's notions about honour ; and I knew that if by any miracle I slew Grey I should be guilty in my own eyes of murder. I would not risk the guilt. If God had determined that I should perish before my time, then perish I must.

This despair brought me a miserable kind of

comfort. When I reached home I went straight
to Faulkner.

"I have quarrelled to-day with a gentleman,
John, and have promised him satisfaction. You
must act for me in the affair. Some one will
come to see you this evening, and the meeting
had better be at dawn to-morrow."

He opened his eyes very wide. "Who is it,
then ? " he asked.

"Mr. Charles Grey of Grey's Hundred," I
replied.

This made him whistle low. "He's a fine
swordsman," he said. "I never heard there
was any better in the dominion. You'll be to
fight with swords ? "

I thought hard for a minute. I was the chal-
lenged, and so had the choice of weapons. "No,"
said I, "you are to appoint pistols, for it is my
right."

At this Faulkner slowly grinned. "It's a
new weapon for these affairs. What if they'll
not accept ? But it's no business of mine, and
I'll remember your wishes." And the strange
fellow turned again to his accounts.

I spent the evening looking over my papers and
making various appointments in case I did not
survive the morrow. Happily the work I had
undertaken for Lawrence was all but finished,
and of my ordinary business Faulkner knew as
much as myself. I wrote a letter to Uncle Andrew,
telling him frankly the situation, that he might
know how little choice I had. It was a cold-

blooded job making these dispositions, and I hope never to have the like to do again. Presently I heard voices outside, and Faulkner came to the door with Mr. George Mason, the younger, of Thornby, who passed for the chief buck in Virginia. He gave me a cold bow.

" I have settled everything with this gentleman, but I would beg of you, sir, to reconsider your choice of arms. My friend will doubtless be ready enough to humour you, but you have picked a barbarous weapon for Christian use."

" It's my only means of defence," I said.

" Then you stick to your decision ? "

" Assuredly," said I, and, with a shrug of the shoulders, he departed.

I did not attempt to sleep. Faulkner told me that we were to meet the next morning half an hour after sunrise at a place in the forest a mile distant. Each man was to fire one shot, but two pistols were allowed in case of a misfire. All that night by the light of a lamp I got my weapons ready. I summoned to my recollection all the knowledge I had acquired, and made sure that nothing should be lacking so far as human skill would go. I had another pistol besides the one I called " Elspeth," also made in Glasgow, but a thought longer in the barrel. For this occasion I neglected cartouches, and loaded in the old way. I tested my bullets time and again, and weighed out the powder as if it had been gold dust. It was short range, so I made my charges small. I tried my old device of wrapping each bullet in soft wool smeared with beeswax. All this passed the midnight hours, and then I lay down for a little rest, but not for sleep.

I was glad when Faulkner summoned me half an hour before sunrise. I remember that I bathed head and shoulders in cold water, and very carefully dressed myself in my best clothes. My pistols lay in the box which Faulkner carried. I drank a glass of wine, and as we left I took a long look at the place I had created, and the river now lit with the first shafts of morning. I wondered incuriously if I should ever see it again.

My tremors had all gone by now, and I was in a mood of cold, thoughtless despair. The earth had never looked so bright as we rode through the green aisles all filled with the happy song of birds. Often on such a morning I had started on a journey, with my heart grateful for the goodness of the world. Were I to keep the road, I should come in time to the swampy bank of the York ; and then would follow the chestnut forest and the wide marshes towards the Rappahannock ; and everywhere I should meet friendly human faces, and then at night I should eat a hunter's meal below the stars. But that was all past, and I was moving towards death in a foolish strife in which I had no heart, and where I could find no honour. I think I laughed aloud at my exceeding folly.

We turned from the path into an alley which led to an open space on the edge of a derelict clearing. There, to my surprise, I found a considerable company assembled. Grey was there with his second, and a dozen or more of his companions stood back in the shadow of the trees. The young blood of Virginia had come out to see the trader punished.

During the few minutes while the seconds were busy pacing the course and arranging for the signal, I had no cognizance of the world around me. I stood with abstracted eyes watching a grey squirrel in one of the branches, and trying to recall a line I had forgotten in a song. There seemed to be two Andrew Garvalds that morning, one filled with an immense careless peace, and the other a weak creature who had lived so long ago as to be forgotten. I started when Faulkner came to place me, and followed him without a word. But as I stood up and saw Grey twenty paces off, turning up his wristbands and tossing his coat to a friend, I realized the business I had come on. A great flood of light was rolling down the forest aisles, but it was so clear and pure that it did not dazzle. I remember thinking in that moment how intolerable had become the singing of birds.

I deadened my heart to memories, took my courage in both hands, and forced myself to the ordeal. For it is an ordeal to face powder if you have not a dreg of passion in you, and are resolved to make no return. I am left-handed, and so, in fronting my opponent, I exposed my heart. If Grey were the marksman I thought him, now was his chance for revenge.

My wits were calm now, and my senses very clear. I heard a man say slowly that he would count three and then drop his kerchief, and at the dropping we should fire. Our eyes were on him as he lifted his hand and slowly began,—

" One—two——"

Then I looked away, for the signal mattered nothing to me. I suddenly caught Grey's eyes, and something whistled past my ear, cutting the lobe and shearing off a lock of hair. I did not heed it. What filled my mind was the sight of my enemy, very white and drawn in the face, holding a smoking pistol and staring at me.

I emptied my pistol among the tree-tops.

No one moved. Grey continued to stare, leaning a little forward, with his lips working.

Then I took from Faulkner my second pistol. My voice came out of my throat, funnily cracked as if from long disuse.

" Mr. Grey," I cried, " I would not have you think that I cannot shoot."

Forty yards from me on the edge of the covert a turkey stood, with its foolish, inquisitive head. The sound of the shots had brought the bird out to see what was going on. It stood motionless, blinking its eyes, the very mark I desired.

I pointed to it with my right hand, flung forward my pistol, and fired. It rolled over as dead as stone, and Faulkner walked to pick it up. He put back my pistols in the box, and we turned to seek the horses. . . .

Then Grey came up to me. His mouth was hard-set, but the lines were not of pride. I saw that he too had been desperately afraid, and I rejoiced that others besides me had been at breaking-point.

"Our quarrel is at an end, sir ? " he said, and his voice was hesitating.

"Why, yes," I said. "It was never my seeking, though I gave the offence."

"I have behaved like a cub, sir," and he spoke loud, so that all could hear. "You have taught me a lesson in gentility. Will you give me your hand ? "

I could find no words, and dumbly held out my right hand.

"Nay, sir," he said, "the other, the one that held the trigger. I count it a privilege to hold the hand of a brave man."

I had been tried too hard, and was all but proving my bravery by weeping like a bairn.

CHAPTER XIV

A WILD WAGER

THAT July morning in the forest gave me, if not popularity, at any rate peace. I had made good my position. Henceforth the word went out that I was to be let alone. Some of the young men, indeed, showed signs of affecting my society, including that Mr. Kent of Gracedieu who had been stripped by Ringan. The others treated me with courtesy, and I replied with my best manners. Most of them were of a different world to mine, and we could not mix, so 'twas right that our deportment should be that of two dissimilar but amiable nations bowing to each other across a frontier.

All this was a great ease, but it brought one rueful consequence. Elspeth grew cold to me. Women, I suppose, have to condescend, and protect, and pity. When I was an outcast she was ready to shelter me; but now that I was in some degree of favour with others the need for this was gone, and she saw me without illusion in all my angularity and roughness. She must have heard of the duel, and jumped to the conclusion that the quarrel had been about herself, which was not the truth. The notion irked her pride, that her name should ever be brought into the brawls of men. When I passed her in the streets she greeted me coldly, and all friendliness had gone out of her eyes.

My days were so busy that I had little leisure for brooding, but at odd moments I would fall into a deep melancholy. She had lived so constantly in my thoughts that without her no project charmed me. What mattered wealth or fame, I thought, if she did not approve ? What availed my striving, if she were not to share in the reward ? I was in this mood when I was bidden by Doctor Blair to sup at his house.

I went thither in much trepidation, for I feared a great company, in which I might have no chance of a word from her. But I found only the Governor, who was in a black humour, and disputed every word that fell from the Doctor's mouth. This turned the meal into one long wrangle, in which the high fundamentals of government in Church and State were debated by two choleric gentlemen. The girl and I had no share in the conversation ; indeed, we were clearly out of place : so she could not refuse when I proposed a walk in the garden. The place was all cool and dewy after the scorching day, and the bells of the flowers made the air heavy with fragrance. Somewhere near a man was playing on the flageolet, a light, pretty tune which set her feet tripping.

I asked her bluntly wherein I had offended.

"Offended!" she cried. "Why should I take offence? I see you once in a blue moon. You flatter yourself strangely, Mr. Garvald, if you think you are ever in my thoughts."

"You are never out of mine," I said dismally.

At this she laughed, something of the old elfin laughter which I had heard on the wet moors.

"A compliment!" she cried. "To be mixed up eternally with the weights of tobacco and the prices of Flemish lace. You are growing a very pretty courtier, sir."

"I am no courtier," I said. "I think brave things of you, though I have not the words to fit them. But one thing I will say to you. Since ever you sang to the boy that once was me your spell has been on my soul. And when I saw you again three months back that spell was changed from the whim of youth to what men call love. Oh, I know well there is no hope for me. I am not fit to tie your shoe-latch. But you have made a fire in my cold life, and you will pardon me if I dare warm my hands. The sun is brighter because of you, and the flowers fairer, and the birds' song sweeter. Grant me this little boon, that I may think of you. Have no fears that I will pester you with attentions. No priest ever served his goddess with a remoter reverence than mine for you."

She stopped in an alley of roses and looked me in the face. In the dusk I could not see her eyes.

"Fine words," she said. "Yet I hear that you

have been wrangling over me with Mr. Charles
Grey, and exchanging pistol shots. Is that your
reverence ? "

In a sentence I told her the truth. " They
forced my back to the wall," I said, " and there
was no other way. I have never uttered your
name to a living soul."

Was it my fancy that when she spoke again
there was a faint accent of disappointment ?

" You are an uncomfortable being, Mr. Garvald.
It seems you are predestined to keep Virginia from
sloth. For myself I am for the roses and the old
quiet ways."

She plucked two flowers, one white and one of
deepest crimson.

" I pardon you," she said, " and for token I
will give you a rose. It is red, for that is your
turbulent colour. The white flower of peace shall
be mine."

I took the gift, and laid it in my bosom.

Two days later, it being a Monday, I dined with
his Excellency at the Governor's house at Middle
Plantation. The place had been built new for my
lord Culpepper, since the old mansion at James
Town had been burned in Bacon's rising. The
company was mainly of young men, but three
ladies—the mistresses of Arlington and Cobwell
Manors, and Elspeth in a new saffron gown—
varied with their laces the rich coats of the men.
I was pleasantly welcomed by everybody. Grey
came forward and greeted me, very quiet and civil,

and I sat by him throughout the meal. The
Governor was in high good humour, and presently
had the whole company in the same mood. Of
them all, Elspeth was the merriest. She had the
quickest wit and the deftest skill in mimicry, and
there was that in her laughter which would infect
the glummest.

That very day I had finished my preparations.
The train was now laid, and the men were ready,
and a word from Lawrence would line the West
with muskets. But I had none of the satisfaction
of a completed work. It was borne in upon me
that our task was scarcely begun, and that the
peril that threatened us was far darker than we
had dreamed. Ringan's tale of a white leader
among the tribes was always in my head. The
hall where we sat was lined with portraits of men
who had borne rule in Virginia. There was Captain John Smith, trim-bearded and bronzed ; and
Argall and Dale, grave and soldierly ; there was
Francis Wyat, with the scar got in Indian wars ;
there hung the mean and sallow countenance of
Sir John Harvey. There, too, was Berkeley, with
his high complexion and his love-locks, the great
gentleman of a vanished age ; and the gross ro-
tundity of Culpepper ; and the furtive eye of my
lord Howard, who was even now the reigning
Governor. There was a noble picture of King
Charles the Second, who alone of monarchs was
represented. Soft-footed lackeys carried viands
and wines, and the table was a mingling of silver
and roses. The afternoon light came soft through

the trellis, and you could not have looked for a fairer picture of settled ease. Yet I had that in my mind which shattered the picture. We were feasting like the old citizens of buried Pompeii, with the lava even now, perhaps, flowing hot from the mountains. I looked at the painted faces on the walls, and wondered which I would summon to our aid if I could call men from the dead. Smith, I thought, would be best; but I reflected uneasily that Smith would never have let things come to such a pass. At the first hint of danger he would have been off to the West to scotch it in the egg.

I was so filled with sober reflections that I talked little; but there was no need of me. Youth and beauty reigned, and the Governor was as gay as the youngest. Many asked me to take wine with them, and the compliment pleased me. There was singing, likewise—Sir William Davenant's song to his mistress, and a Cavalier rant or two, and a throaty ditty of the seas; and Elspeth sang very sweetly the old air of " Greensleeves." We drank all the toasts of fashion—His Majesty of England, confusion to the French, the health of Virginia, rich harvests, full cellars, and pretty dames. Presently when we had waxed very cheerful, and wine had risen to several young heads, the Governor called on us to brim our glasses.

" Be it known, gentlemen, and you, fair ladies," he cried, " that to-day is a more auspicious occasion than any Royal festival or Christian holy day. To-day is Dulcinea's birthday. I summon you to drink to the flower of the West, the brightest gem in Virginia's coronal."

At that we were all on our feet. The gentlemen snapped the stems of their glasses to honour the sacredness of the toast, and there was such a shouting and pledging as might well have turned a girl's head. Elspeth sat still and smiling. The mockery had gone out of her eyes, and I thought they were wet. No queen had ever a nobler salutation, and my heart warmed to the generous company. Whatever its faults, it did due homage to beauty and youth.

Governor Francis was again on his feet.

" I have a birthday gift for the fair one. You must know that once at Whitehall I played at cartes with my lord Culpepper, and the stake on his part was one-sixth portion of that Virginian territory which is his freehold. I won, and my lord conveyed the grant to me in a deed properly attested by the attorneys. We call the place the Northern Neck, and 'tis all the land between the Rappahannock and the Potomac as far west as the sunset. It is undivided, but my lord stipulated that my portion should lie from the mountains westward. What good is such an estate to an ageing bachelor like me, who can never visit it ? But 'tis a fine inheritance for youth, and I propose to convey it to Dulcinea as a birthday gift. Some day, I doubt not, 'twill be the Eden of America."

At this there was a great crying out and some laughter, which died away when it appeared that the Governor spoke in all seriousness.

" I make one condition," he went on. " Twenty years back there was an old hunter, called Studd, who penetrated the mountains. He travelled to the head-waters of the Rapidan, and pierced the hills by a pass which he christened Clearwater Gap. He climbed the highest mountain in those parts, and built a cairn on the summit, in which he hid a powder-horn with a writing within. He was the first to make the journey, and none have followed him. The man is dead now, but he told me the tale, and I will pledge my honour that it is true. It is for Dulcinea to choose a champion to follow Studd's path and bring back his powder-horn. On the day I receive it she takes sasine of her heritage. Which of you gallants offers for the venture ? "

To this day I do not know what were Francis Nicholson's motives. He wished the mountains crossed, but he cannot have expected to meet a pathfinder among the youth of the Tidewater. I think it was the whim of the moment. He would endow Elspeth, and at the same time test her cavaliers. To the ordinary man it seemed the craziest folly. Studd had been a wild fellow, half Indian in blood and wholly Indian in habits, and for another to travel fifty miles into the heart of the desert was to embrace destruction. The company sat very silent. Elspeth, with a blushing cheek, turned troubled eyes on the speaker.

As for me, I had found the chance I wanted. I was on my feet in a second. " I will go," I said ;

and I had hardly spoken when Grey was beside me, crying, " And I."

Still the company sat silent. 'Twas as if the shadow of a sterner life had come over their young gaiety. Elspeth did not look at me, but sat with cast-down eyes, plucking feverishly at a rose. The Governor laughed out loud.

" Brave hearts ! " he cried. " Will you travel together ? "

I looked at Grey. " That can hardly be," he said.

"Well, we must spin for it," said Nicholson, taking a guinea from his pocket. " Royals for Mr. Garvald, quarters for Mr. Grey," he cried as he spun it.

It fell Royals. We had both been standing, and Grey now bowed to me and sat down. His face was very pale and his lips tightly shut.

The Governor gave a last toast. " Let us drink," he called, " to Dulcinea's champion and the fortunes of his journey." At that there was such applause you might have thought me the best-liked man in the dominion. I looked at Elspeth, but she averted her eyes.

As we left the table I stepped beside Grey. " You must come with me," I whispered. " Nay, do not refuse. When you know all you will come gladly." And I appointed a meeting on the next day at the Half-way Tavern.

I got to my house at the darkening, and found Ringan waiting for me.

This time he had not sought a disguise, but he kept his fiery head covered with a broad hat, and the collar of his seaman's coat enveloped his lower face. To a passer-by in the dusk he must have seemed an ordinary ship's captain stretching his legs on land.

He asked for food and drink, and I observed that his manner was very grave.

" Are things in train, Andrew ? " he asked.

I told him " to the last stirrup buckle."

" It's as well," said he, " for the trouble has begun."

Then he told me a horrid tale. The Rapidan is a stream in the north of the dominion, flowing into the Rappahannock on its south bank. Two years past a family of French folk—D'Aubigny was their name—had made a home in a meadow by that stream and built a house and a strong stockade, for they were in dangerous nearness to the hills, and had no neighbours within forty miles. They were gentlefolk of some substance, and had carved out of the wilderness a very pretty manor with orchards and flower gardens. I had never been to the place, but I had heard the praise of it from dwellers on the Rappahannock. No Indians came near them, and there they abode, happy in their solitude—a husband and wife, three little children, two French servants, and a dozen negroes.

A week ago tragedy had come like a thunderbolt. At night the stockade was broke, and the family woke from sleep to hear the war-whoop and see by the light of their blazing byres a band of painted savages. It seems that no resistance was possible, and they were butchered like sheep. The babes were pierced with stakes, the grown folk were scalped and tortured, and by sunrise in that peaceful clearing there was nothing but blood-stained ashes.

Word had come down the Rappahannock. Ringan said he had heard it in Accomac, and had sailed to Sabine to make sure. Men had ridden out from Stafford county, and found no more than a child's toy and some bloody garments.

" Who did it ? " I asked, with fury rising in my heart.

" It's Cherokee work. There's nothing strange in it, except that such a deed should have been dared. But it means the beginning of our business. D'you think the Stafford folk will sleep in their beds after that ? And that's precisely what perplexes me. The Governor will be bound to send an expedition against the murderers, and they'll not be easy found. But while the militia are routing about on the Rapidan, what hinders the big invasion to come down the James or the Chickahominy or the Pamunkey or the Mattaponey and find a defenceless Tidewater ? As I see it, there's deep guile in this business. A Cherokee murder is nothing out of the way, but these blackguards were not killing for mere pleasure. As I've said before, I would give my right hand to have better information. It's this land business that fickles one. If it were a matter of islands and ocean bays, I would have long ago riddled out the heart of it."

"We're on the way to get news," I said, and I told him of my wager that evening.

"Man, Andrew!" he cried, "it's providential. There's nothing to hinder you and me and a few others to ride clear into the hills, with the Tidewater thinking it no more than a play of daft young men. You must see Nicholson, and get him to hold his hand till we send him word. In two days Lawrence will be here, and we can post our lads on each of the rivers, for it's likely any Indian raid will take one of the valleys. You must see that Governor of yours first thing in the morning, and get him to promise to wait on your news. Then he can get out his militia, and stir up the Tidewater. Will he do it, think you?"

I said I thought he would.

"And there's one other thing. Would he agree to turning a blind eye to Lawrence, if he comes back? He'll not trouble them in James Town, but he's the only man alive to direct our own lads."

I said I would try, but I was far from certain. It was hard to forecast the mind of Governor Francis.

"Well, Lawrence will come whether or no. You can sound the man, and if he's dour let the matter be. Lawrence is now on the Roanoke, and his plan is to send out the word to-morrow, and gather in the posts. He'll come to Frew's place on the South Fork River, which is about the middle of

the frontier line. To-day is Monday, to-morrow
the word will go out, by Friday the men will be
ready, and Lawrence will be in Virginia. The
sooner you're off the better, Andrew. What do
you say to Wednesday ? "

"That day will suit me fine," I said ; " but
what about my company ? "

"The fewer the better. Who were you thinking of ? "

"You for one," I said, "and Shalah for a
second."

He nodded.

"I want two men from the Rappahannock—a
hunter of the name of Donaldson and the Frenchman Bertrand."

"That makes five. Would you like to even the
number ? "

"Yes," I said. "There's a gentleman of the
Tidewater, Mr. Charles Grey, that I've bidden to
the venture."

Ringan whistled. "Are you sure that's wise ?
There'll be little use for braw clothes and fine
manners in the hills."

"All the same there'll be a use for Mr. Grey.
When will you join us ? "

"I've a bit of business to do hereaways, but I'll
catch you up. Look for me at Aird's store on
Thursday morning."

CHAPTER XV

I WAS at the Governor's house next day before
he had breakfasted. He greeted me laughingly.

"Has the champion come to cry forfeit ?" he
asked. "It is a long, sore road to the hills, Mr.
Garvald."

"I've come to make confession," I said, and I
plunged into my story of the work of the last
months.

He heard me with lowering brows. "Who the
devil made you Governor of this dominion, sir ?
You have been levying troops without His Majesty's permission. Your offence is no less than
high treason. I've a pretty mind to send you to
the guard-house."

"I implore you to hear me patiently," I cried.
Then I told him what I had learned in the Carolinas and at the outland farms. "You yourself
told me it was hopeless to look for a guinea from
the Council. I was but carrying out your desires.
Can you blame me if I've toiled for the public
weal and neglected my own fortunes ?"

He was scarcely appeased. "You're a damnable kind of busybody, sir, the breed of fellow that plunges states into revolutions. Why, in Heaven's name, did you not consult me?"

"Because it was wiser not to," I said stoutly. "Half my recruits are old soldiers of Bacon. If the trouble blows past, they go back to their steadings and nothing more is heard of it. If trouble comes, who are such natural defenders of the dominion as the frontier dwellers? All I have done is to give them the sinews of war. But if Governor Nicholson had taken up the business, and it were known that he had leaned on old rebels, what would the Council say? What would have been the view of my lord Howard and the wiseacres in London?"

He said nothing, but knit his brows. My words were too much in tune with his declared opinions for him to gainsay them.

"It comes to this, then," he said at length. "You have raised a body of men who are waiting marching orders. What next, Mr. Garvald?"

"The next thing is to march. After what befell on the Rapidan, we cannot sit still."

He started. "I have heard nothing of it."

Then I told him the horrid tale. He got to his feet and strode up and down the room, with his dark face working.

"God's mercy, what a calamity! I knew the folk. They came here with letters from his Grace of Shrewsbury. Are you certain your news is true?"

"Alas! there is no doubt. Stafford county is in a ferment, and the next post from the York will bring you word."

"Then, by God, it is for me to move. No Council or Assembly will dare gainsay me. I can order a levy by virtue of His Majesty's commission."

"I have come to pray you to hold your hand till I send you better intelligence," I said.

His brows knit again. "But this is too much. Am I to refrain from doing my duty till I get your gracious consent, sir?"

"Nay, nay," I cried. "Do not misunderstand me. This thing is far graver than you think, sir. If you send your levies to the Rapidan, you leave the Tidewater defenceless, and while you are hunting a Cherokee party in the north, the enemy will be hammering at your gates."

"What enemy?" he asked.

"I do not know, and that is what I go to find out." Then I told him all I had gathered about the unknown force in the hills, and the apparent strategy of a campaign which was beyond an Indian's wits. "There is a white man at the back of it," I said, "a white man who talks in Bible words and is mad for devastation."

His face had grown very solemn. He went to a bureau, unlocked it, and took from a drawer a bit of paper, which he tossed to me.

"I had that a week past to-morrow. My servant got it from an Indian in the woods."

It was a dirty scrap, folded like a letter, and bearing the superscription, " *To the man Francis Nicholson, presently Governor in Virginia.*" I opened it and read :—

" *Thou comest to me with a sword and with a spear and with a shield : but I come to thee in the name of the Lord of Hosts, the God of the armies of Israel, whom thou hast defied.*"

" There," I cried, " there is proof of my fears. What kind of Indian sends a message like that ? Trust me, sir, there is a far more hellish mischief brewing than any man wots of."

" It looks not unlike it," he said grimly. " Now let's hear what you propose."

" I can have my men at their posts by the week end. We will string them out along the frontier, and hold especially the river valleys. If invasion comes, then at any rate the Tide-water will get early news of it. Meantime I and my friends, looking for Studd's powder-horn, with a mind to confirm your birthday gift to Miss Elspeth Blair, will push on to the hills and learn what is to be learned there."

" You will never come back," he said tartly. " An Indian stake and a bloody head will be the end of all of you."

" Maybe," I said, " though I have men with me that can play the Indian game. But if in ten days' time from now you get no word, then you can fear the worst, and set your militia going. I have a service of posts which will carry news to you as quick as a carrier pigeon. Whatever we learn you shall hear of without delay, and you can make your dispositions accordingly. If the devils find us first, then get in touch with my men at Frew's homestead on the South Fork River, for that will be the headquarters of the frontier army."

"Who will be in command there when you are gallivanting in the hills ? " he asked.

"One whose name had better not be spoken. He lies under sentence of death by Virginian law ; but, believe me, he is an honest soul and a good patriot, and he is the one man born to lead these outland troops."

He smiled. "His Christian name is Richard, maybe ? I think I know your outlaw. But let it pass. I ask no names. In these bad times we cannot afford to despise any man's aid."

He pulled out a chart of Virginia, and I marked for him our posts, and indicated the line of my own journey.

"Have you ever been in the wars, Mr. Garvald ? " he asked.

I told him no.

"Well, you have a very pretty natural gift for the military art. Your men will screen the frontier line, and behind that screen I will get our militia force in order, while meantime you are reconnoitring the enemy. It's a very fair piece of strategy. But I am mortally certain you yourself will never come back."

The odd thing was that at that moment I did not fear for myself. I had lived so long with my scheme that I had come to look upon it almost like a trading venture, in which one calculates risks and gains on paper, and thinks no more of it. I had none of the black fright which I had suffered before my meeting with Grey. Happily though a young man's thoughts may be long, his fancy takes short views. I was far more concerned with what might happen in my absence in the Tidewater than with our fate in the hills.

"It is a gamble," I said, "but the stakes are noble, and I have a private pride in its success."

"Also the goad of certain bright eyes," he said, smiling. "Little I thought, when I made that offer last night, I was setting so desperate a business in train. There was a good Providence in that. For now we can give out that you are gone on a madcap ploy, and there will be no sleepless nights in the Tidewater. I must keep their souls easy, for once they are scared there will be such a spate of letters to New York as will weaken the courage of our Northern brethren. For the militia I will give the excuse of the French menace. The good folk will laugh at me for it, but they will not take fright. God's truth, but it is a devilish tangle. I could wish I had your part, sir, and be free to ride out on a gallant venture. Here I have none of the zest of war, but only a thousand cares and the carking task of soothing fools."

We spoke of many things, and I gave him a full account of the composition and strength of our levies. When I left he paid me a compliment, which, coming from so sardonic a soul, gave me peculiar comfort.

"I have seen something of men and cities, sir," he said, "and I know well the foibles and the strength of my countrymen; but I have never met your equal for cold persistence. You are a trader, and have turned war into a trading venture. I do believe that when you are at your last gasp you will be found calmly casting up your accounts with life. And I think you will find a balance on the right side. God speed you, Mr. Garvald. I love your sober folly."

I had scarcely left him when I met a servant of the Blairs, who handed me a letter. 'Twas from Elspeth—the first she had ever written me. I tore it open, and found a very disquieting epistle. Clearly she had written it in a white heat of feeling. "*You spoke finely of reverence,*" she wrote, "*and how you had never named my name to a mortal soul. But to-night you have put me to open shame. You have offered yourself for a service which I did not seek. What care I for his Excellency's gifts? Shall it be said that I was the means of sending a man into deadly danger to secure me a foolish estate? You have offended me grossly, and I pray you spare me further offence. I command you to give up this journey. I will not have my name bandied about in this land as a wanton who sets silly youth by the ears to gratify her pride. If you desire to retain a shred of my friendship, go to his Excellency and tell him that by my orders you withdraw from the wager.*"

This letter did not cloud my spirits as it should.

For one thing, she signed it " Elspeth," and for
another, I had the conceited notion that what
moved her most was the thought that I was running into danger. I longed to have speech with
her, but I found from the servant that Doctor
Blair had left that morning on a journey of pas-
toral visitation, and had taken her with him. The
man did not know their destination, but believed
it to be somewhere in the north. The thought
vaguely disquieted me. In these perilous times
I wished to think of her as safe in the coastlands,
where a ship would give a sure refuge.

I met Grey that afternoon at the Half-way
Tavern. In the last week he seemed to have
aged and grown graver. There was now no hint
of the light arrogance of old. He regarded me
curiously, but without hostility.

" We have been enemies," I said, " and now,
though there may be no friendship, at any rate
there is a truce to strife. Last night I begged
of you to come with me on this matter of the
Governor's wager, but 'twas not the wager I
thought of."

Then I told him the whole tale. " The stake
is the safety of this land, of which you are a notable
citizen. I ask you, because I know you are a
brave man. Will you leave your comfort and
your games for a season, and play for higher stakes
at a more desperate hazard ? "

I told him everything, even down to my talk
with the Governor. I did not lessen the risks

and hardships, and I gave him to know that his companions would be rough folk, whom he may well have despised. He heard me out with his eyes fixed on the ground. Then suddenly he raised a shining face.

" You are a generous enemy, Mr. Garvald. I behaved to you like a peevish child, and you retaliate by offering me the bravest venture that man ever conceived. I am with you with all my heart. By God, sir, I am sick of my cushioned life. This is what I have been longing for in my soul since I was born. . . ."

That night I spent making ready. I took no servant, and in my saddle-bags was stored the little I needed. Of powder and shot I had plenty, and my two pistols and my hunting musket. I gave Faulkner instructions, and wrote a letter to my uncle to be sent if I did not return. Next morning at daybreak we took the road.

CHAPTER XVI

THE FORD OF THE RAPIDAN

'TWAS the same high summer weather through which I had ridden a fortnight ago with a dull heart on my way to the duel. Now Grey rode by my side, and my spirits were as light as a bird's. I had forgotten the grim part of the enterprise, the fate that might await me, the horrors we should certainly witness. I thought only of the joys of movement into new lands with tried companions. These last months I had borne a pretty heavy weight of cares. Now that was past. My dispositions completed, the thing was in the hands of God, and I was free to go my own road. Mocking-birds and thrushes cried in the thickets, squirrels flirted across the path, and now and then a shy deer fled before us. There come moments to every man when he is thankful to be alive, and every breath drawn is a delight; so at that hour I praised my Maker for His good earth, and for sparing me to rejoice in it.

Grey had met me with a certain shyness; but as the sun rose and the land grew bright he, too, lost his constraint, and fell into the same happy mood. Soon we were smiling at each other in the frankest comradeship, we two who but the other day had carried ourselves like game-cocks. He had forgotten his fine manners and his mincing London voice, and we spoke of the outland country of which he knew nothing, and of the hunting of game of which he knew much, exchanging our different knowledges, and willing to learn from each other. Long ere we had reached York Ferry I had found that there was much in common between the Scots trader and the Virginian cavalier, and the chief thing we shared was youth.

Mine, to be sure, was more in the heart, while Grey wore his open and fearless. He plucked the summer flowers and set them in his hat. He was full of catches and glees, so that he waked the echoes in the forest glades. Soon I, too, fell to singing in my tuneless voice, and I answered his " My lodging is on the cold ground " with some Scots ballad or a song of Davie Lindsay. I remember how sweetly he sang Colonel Lovelace's ode to Lucasta, writ when going to the wars :—

> " True, a new mistress now I chase,
>   The first foe in the field ;
> And with a stronger faith embrace
>   A sword, a horse, a shield.
>
> Yet this inconstancy is such
>   As thou too shalt adore :
> I could not love thee, dear, so much,
>   Loved I not Honour more."

I wondered if that were my case—if I rode out

for honour, and not for the pure pleasure of the riding. And I marvelled more to see the two of us, both lovers of one lady and vigilant rivals, burying for the nonce our feuds, and with the same hope serving the same cause.

We slept the night at Aird's store, and early the next morning found Ringan. A new Ringan indeed, as unlike the buccaneer I knew as he was unlike the Quaker. He was now the gentleman of Breadalbane, dressed for the part with all the care of an exquisite. He rode a noble roan, in his Spanish belt were stuck silver-hafted pistols, and a long sword swung at his side. When I presented Grey to him, he became at once the cavalier, as precise in his speech and polite in his deportment as any Whitehall courtier. They talked high and disposedly of genteel matters, and you would have thought that that red-haired pirate had lived his life among proud lords and high-heeled ladies. That is ever the way of the Highlander. He alters like a clear pool to every mood of the sky, so that the shallow observer knows not how deep the waters are.

Presently, when we had ridden into the chestnut forests of the Mattaponey, he began to forget his part. Grey, it appeared, was a student of campaigns, and he and Ringan were deep in a discussion of Condé's battles, in which both showed surprising knowledge. But the glory of the weather and of the woodlands, new as they were to a seafarer, set his thoughts wandering, and he fell to tales of his past which consorted ill with his

former decorum. There was a madcap zest in
his speech, something so merry and wild, that
Grey, who had fallen back into his Tidewater
manners, became once more the careless boy.
We stopped to eat in a glade by a slow stream,
and from his saddle-bags Ringan brought out
strange delicacies. There were sugared fruits
from the Main, and orange sirop from Jamaica,
and a kind of sweet punch made by the Hispaniola
Indians. As we ate and drank he would gossip
about the ways of the world; and though he
never mentioned his own doings, there was such
an air of mastery about him as made him seem
the centre figure of his tales. I could see that
Grey was mightily captivated, and all afternoon
he plied him with questions, and laughed joyously
at his answers. As we camped that night, while
Grey was minding his horse Ringan spoke of him
to me.

" I like the lad, Andrew. He has the makings
of a very proper gentleman, and he has the sense
to be young. What I complain of in you is that
you're desperate old. I wonder whiles if you ever
were a laddie. For me, though I'm ten years
the elder of the pair of you, I've no more years
than your friend, and I'm a century younger
than you. That's the Highland way. There's
that in our blood that keeps our eyes young though
we may be bent double. With us the heart is
aye leaping till Death grips us. To my mind it's
a lovable character that I fain would cherish. If
I couldn't sing on a spring morning or say a hearty

grace over a good dinner I'd be content to be put away in a graveyard."

And that, I think, is the truth. But at the time I was feeling pretty youthful, too, though my dour face and hard voice were a bad clue to my sentiments.

Next day on the Rappahannock we found Shalah, who had gone on to warn the two men I proposed to enlist. One of them, Donaldson, was a big, slow-spoken, middle-aged farmer, the same who had been with Bacon in the fight at Occaneechee Island. He just cried to his wife to expect him back when she saw him, slung on his back an old musket, cast a long leg over his little horse, and was ready to follow. The other, the Frenchman Bertrand, was a quiet, slim gentleman, who was some kin to the murdered D'Aubignys. I had long had my eye on him, for he was very wise in woodcraft, and had learned campaigning under old Turenne. He kissed his two children again and again, and his wife clung to his arms. There were tears in the honest fellow's eyes as he left, and I thought all the more of him, for he is the bravest man who has most to risk. I mind that Ringan consoled the lady in the French tongue, which I did not comprehend, and would not be hindered from getting out his saddle-bags and comforting the children with candied plums. He had near as grave a face as Bertrand when we rode off, and was always looking back to the homestead. He spoke long to the Frenchman in his own speech, and the sad face of the latter began to lighten.

I asked him what he said.

"Just that he was the happy man to have kind hearts to weep for him. A fine thing for a landless, childless fellow like me to say! But it's gospel truth, Andrew. I told him that his bairns would be great folks some day, and that their proudest boast would be that their father had ridden on this errand. Oh, and all the rest of the easy consolations. If it had been me, I would not have been muckle cheered. It's well I never married, for I would not have had the courage to leave my fireside."

We were now getting into a new and far lovelier country. The heavy forests and swamps which line the James and the York had gone, and instead we had rolling spaces of green meadowland, and little hills which stood out like sentinels of the great blue chain of mountains that hung in the west. Instead of the rich summer scents of the Tidewater, we had the clean, sharp smell of uplands, and cool winds relieved the noontide heat. By and by we struck the Rapidan, a water more like our Scots rivers, flowing in pools and currents, very different from the stagnant reaches of the Pamunkey. We were joined for a little bit by two men from Stafford county, who showed us the paths that horses could travel.

It was late in the afternoon that we reached a broad meadow hemmed in by noble cedars. I knew without telling that we were come to the scene of the tragedy, and with one accord we fell silent. The place had been well looked after, for a road had been made through the woods, and had been carried over marshy places on a platform of cedar piles. Presently we came to a log fence with a gate, which hung idly open. Within was a paddock, and beyond another fence, and beyond that a great pile of blackened timber. The place was so smiling and homelike under the westering sun that one looked to see a trim steading with the smoke of hearth fires ascending, and to hear the cheerful sounds of labour and of children's voices. Instead there was this grim, charred heap, with the light winds swirling the ashes.

Every man of us uncovered his head as he rode towards the melancholy place. I noticed a little rosary, which had been carefully tended, but horses had ridden through it, and the blossoms were trailing crushed on the ground. There was a flower garden too, much trampled, and in one corner a stream of water had been led into a pool fringed with forget-me-nots. A tiny water-wheel was turning in the fall, a children's toy, and the wheel still turned, though its owners had gone. The sight of that simple thing fairly brought my heart to my mouth.

That inspection was a gruesome business. One of the doorposts of the house still stood, and it was splashed with blood. On the edge of the ashes were some charred human bones. No one could tell whose they were, perhaps a negro's, perhaps the little mistress of the water-wheel. I looked at Ringan, and he was smiling, but his eyes were terrible. The Frenchman Bertrand was sobbing like a child.

We took the bones, and made a shallow grave for them in the rosary. We had no spades, but a stake did well enough to dig a resting-place for those few poor remains. I said over them the Twenty-third Psalm: " *Yea, though I walk through the valley of the shadow of death, I will fear no evil ; for Thou art with me ; Thy rod and Thy staff shall comfort me.*"

Then suddenly our mood changed. Nothing that we could do could help the poor souls whose bones lay among the ashes. But we could bring their murderers to book, and save others from a like fate.

We moved away from the shattered place to the ford in the river where the road ran north. There we looked back. A kind of fury seized me as I saw that cruel defacement. In a few hours we ourselves should be beyond the pale, among those human wolves who were so much more relentless than any beasts of the field. As I looked round our little company, I noted how deep the thing had bitten into our souls. Ringan's eyes still danced with that unholy blue light. Grey was very pale, and his jaw was set grimly. Bertrand had ceased from sobbing, and his face had the far-away wildness of the fanatic, such a look as his forbears may have worn at the news of St. Bartholomew. The big man Donaldson looked puzzled and sombre. Only Shalah stood impassive and aloof, with no trace of feeling on the bronze of his countenance.

"This is the place for an oath," I said. "We are six men against an army, but we fight for a holy cause. Let us swear to wipe out this deed of blood in the blood of its perpetrators. God has made us the executers of His judgments against horrid cruelty."

We swore, holding our hands high, that, when our duty to the dominion was done, we should hunt down the Cherokees who had done this deed till no one of them was left breathing. At that moment of tense nerves, no other purpose would have contented us.

"How will we find them?" quoth Ringan. "To sift a score of murderers out of a murderous nation will be like searching the ocean for a wave."

Then Shalah spoke.

"The trail is ten suns old, but I can follow it. The men were of the Meebaw tribe by this token." And he held up a goshawk's feather. "The bird that dropped that lives beyond the peaks of Shubash. The Meebaw are quick hunters and gross eaters, and travel slow. We will find them by the Tewawha."

"All in good time," I said. "Retribution must wait till we have finished our task. Can you find the Meebaw men again?"

"Yea," said Shalah, "though they took wings and flew over the seas I should find them."

Then we hastened away from that glade, none speaking to the other. We camped an hour's ride up the river, in a place secure against sur-prises in a crook of the stream with a great rock at our back. We were outside the pale now, and must needs adopt the precautions of a campaign ; so we split the night into watches. I did my two hours' sentry duty at that dead moment of the dark just before the little breeze which is the precursor of dawn, and I reflected very soberly on the slender chances of our returning from this strange wild world and its cruel mysteries.

CHAPTER XVII

I RETRACE MY STEPS

NEXT morning we passed through the foot-hills into an open meadow country. As I lifted up my eyes I saw for the first time the mountains near at hand. There they lay, not more than ten miles distant, woody almost to the summit, but with here and there a bold finger of rock pointing skywards. They looked infinitely high and rugged, far higher than any hills I had ever seen before, for my own Tinto or Cairntable would to these have been no more than a footstool. I made out a clear breach in the range, which I took to be old Studd's Clearwater Gap. The whole sight intoxicated me. I might dream of horrors in the low coast forests among their swampy creeks, but in that clear high world of the hills I believed lay safety. I could have gazed at them for hours, but Shalah would permit of no delay. He hurried us across the open meadows, and would not relax his pace till we were on a low wooded ridge with the young waters of the Rapidan running in a shallow vale beneath.

Here we halted in a thick clump of cedars, while he and Ringan went forward to spy out the land. In that green darkness, save by folk travelling along the ridge, we could not be detected, and I knew enough of Indian ways to believe that any large party would keep the stream sides. We lit a fire without fear, for the smoke was hid in the cedar branches, and some of us roasted corn-cakes. Our food in the saddle-bags would not last long, and I foresaw a ticklish business when it came to hunting for the pot. A gunshot in these narrow glens would reverberate like a cannon.

We dozed peacefully in the green shade, and smoked our pipes, waiting for the return of our envoys. They came towards sundown, slipping among us like ghosts.

Ringan signalled to me, and we put our coats over the horses' heads to prevent their whinnying. He stamped out the last few ashes of the fire, and Shalah motioned us all flat on our faces. Then I crawled to the edge of the ridge, and looked down through a tangle of vines on the little valley.

Our precautions had been none too soon, for a host was passing below, as stealthily as if it had been an army of the sheeted dead. Most were mounted, and it was marvellous to see the way in which they managed their horses, so that the beasts seemed part of the riders, and partook of their vigilance. Some were on foot, and moved with the long, loping, in-toed Indian stride. I guessed their number at three hundred, but what

awed me was their array. This was no ordinary
raid, but an invading army. My sight, as I think
I have said, is as keen as a hawk's, and I could
see that most of them carried muskets as well as
knives and tomahawks. The war-paint glistened
on each breast and forehead, and in the oiled hair
stood the crested feathers, dyed scarlet for battle.
My spirits sank as I reflected that now we were
cut off from the Tidewater.

When the last man had gone we crawled back
to the clump, now gloomy with the dusk of evening. I saw that Ringan was very weary, but
Shalah, after stretching his long limbs, seemed
fresh as ever. "Will you come with me, brother?"
he said. "We must warn the Rappahannock."

"Who are they?" I asked.

"Cherokees. More follow them. The assault
is clearly by the line of the Rappahannock. If
we hasten we may yet be in time."

I knew what Shalah's hastening meant. I
suppose I was the one of us best fitted for a hot-
foot march, and that that was the reason why the
Indian chose me. All the same my heart misgave
me. He ate a little food, while I stripped off the
garments I did not need, carrying only the one
pistol. I bade the others travel slowly towards
the mountains, scouting carefully ahead, and
promised that we should join them before the
next sundown. Then Shalah beckoned me, and
I plunged after him into the forest.

On our first visit to Ringan at the land-locked
Carolina harbour I had thought Shalah's pace

killing, but that was but a saunter to what he
now showed me. We seemed to be moving at
right angles to the Indian march. Once out of
the woods of the ridge we crossed the meadows,
mostly on our bellies, taking advantage of every
howe and crinkle. I followed him as obediently as
a child. When he ran so did I; when he crawled
my forehead was next his heel. After the grass-
lands came broken hillocks with little streams in
the bottoms. Through these we twisted, moving
with less care, and presently we had left the hills
and were looking over a wide, shadowy plain.

The moon was three-quarters full, and was
just beginning to climb the sky. Shalah sniffed
the wind, which blew from the south-west, and
set off at a sharp angle towards the north. We
were now among the woods again, and the tangled
undergrowth tried me sore. We had been going
for about three hours, and, though I was hard and
spare from much travel in the sun, my legs were
not used to this furious foot marching. My feet
grew leaden, and, to make matters worse, we dipped
presently into a big swamp, where we mired to
the knees and often to the middle. It would
have been no light labour at any time to cross
such a place, pulling oneself by the tangled shrubs
on to the rare patches of solid ground. But now,
when I was pretty weary, the toil was about the
limit of my strength. When we emerged on hard
land I was sobbing like a stricken deer. But
Shalah had no mercy. He took me through the
dark cedars at the same tireless pace, and in the

gloom I could see him flitting ahead of me, his
shoulders squared and his limbs as supple as a
racehorse's.   I remember I said over in my head
all the songs and verses I knew, to keep my mind
from my condition.   I had long ago got and lost
my second wind and whatever other winds there
be, and was moving less by bodily strength than
by sheer doggedness of spirit.   Weak tears were
running down my cheeks, my breath rasped in my
throat, but I was in the frame of mind that if
death had found me next moment my legs would
still have twitched in an effort to run.

At an open bit of the forest Shalah stopped
and looked at the sky.   I blundered into him,
and then from sheer weakness rolled on the ground.
He grunted and turned to me.   I felt his cool hand
passing over my brow and cheek, and his fingers
kneading the muscles of my forlorn legs.   'Twas
some Indian device, doubtless, but its power was
miraculous.   Under his hands my body seemed
to be rested and revived.   New strength stole
into my sinews, new vigour into my blood.   The
thing took maybe five minutes—not more ; but I
scrambled to my feet a man again.   Indeed I
was a better man than when I started, for this
Indian wizardry had given me an odd lightness
of head and heart.   When we took up the running, my body, instead of a leaden clog, seemed
to be a thing of air and feathers.

It was now hard on midnight, and the moon
was high in the heavens.   We bore somewhat
to the right, and I judged that our circuit was

completed, and that the time had come to steal
in front of the Indian route. The forest thinned,
and we traversed a marshy piece of country with
many single great trees. Often Shalah would
halt for a second, strain his ears, and sniff the light
wind like a dog. He seemed to find guidance,
but I got none, only the hoot of an owl or the
rooty smell of the woodland.

At last we struck a little stream, and followed
its course between high banks of pine. Suddenly
Shalah's movements became stealthy. Crouching in every patch of shade, and crossing open
spaces on our bellies, we turned from the stream,
surmounted a knoll, and came down on a wooded
valley. Shalah looked westwards, held up his
hand, and stood poised for a minute like a graven
image. Then he grunted, and spoke. " We are
safe," he said. " They are behind us, and are
camped for the night." How he knew that I
cannot tell ; but I seemed to catch on the breeze
a whiff of the rancid odour of Indian war-paint.

For another mile we continued our precautions,
and then moved more freely in the open. Now
that the chief peril was past, my fatigue came back
to me worse than ever. I think I was growing
leg-weary, like a horse, and from that ailment
there is no relief. My head buzzed like a beehive,
and when the moon set I had no power to pick
my steps, and stumbled and sprawled in the darkness. I had to ask Shalah for help, though it
was a sore hurt to my pride, and, leaning on his
arm, I made the rest of the journey.

I found myself splashing in a strong river. We crossed by a ford, so we had no need to swim, which was well for me, for I must have drowned. The chill of the water revived me somewhat, and I had the strength to climb the other bank. And then suddenly before me I saw a light, and a challenge rang out into the night.

The voice was a white man's, and brought me to my bearings. Weak as I was, I had the fierce satisfaction that our errand had not been idle. I replied with the password, and a big fellow strode out from a stockade.

"Mr. Garvald!" he said, staring. "What brings you here? Where are the rest of you?" He looked at Shalah and then at me, and finally took my arm and drew me inside.

There were a score in the place—Rappahannock farmers, a lean, watchful breed, each man with his musket. One of them, I mind, wore a rusty cuirass of chain armour, which must have been one of those sent out by the King in the first days of the dominion. They gave me a drink of rum and water, and in a little I had got over my worst weariness and could speak.

"The Cherokees are on us," I said, and I told them of the army we had followed.

"How many?" they asked.

"Three hundred for a vanguard, but more follow."

One man laughed, as if well pleased. "I'm in the humour for Cherokees just now. There's a score of scalps hanging outside, if you could see them, Mr. Garvald."

" What scalps ? " I asked, dumbfoundered.

" The Rapidan murderers. We got word of them in the woods yesterday, and six of us went hunting. It was pretty shooting. Two got away with some lead in them, the rest are in the Tewawha pools, all but their topknots. I've very little notion of Cherokees."

Somehow the news gave me intense joy. I thought nothing of the barbarity of it, or that white men should demean themselves to the Indian level. I remembered only the meadow by the Rapidan, and the little lonely water-wheel. Our vow was needless, for others had done our work.

" Would I had been with you ! " was all I said. " But now you have more than a gang of Meebaw raiders to deal with. There's an invasion coming down from the hills, and this is the first wave of it. I want word sent to Governor Nicholson at James Town. I was to tell him where the trouble was to be feared, and in a week you'll have a regiment at your backs. Who has the best horse ? Simpson ? Well, let Simpson carry the word down the valley. If my plans are working well, the news should be at James Town by dawn tomorrow."

The man called Simpson got up, saddled his beast, and waited my bidding. " This is the word to send," said I. " Say that the Cherokees are attacking by the line of the Rappahannock.

Say that I am going into the hills to find if my
fears are justified. Never mind what that means.
Just pass on the words. They will understand
them at James Town. So much for the Governor.
Now I want word sent to Frew's homestead on
the South Fork. Who is to carry it ? "

One old fellow, who chewed tobacco without
intermission, spat out the leaf, and asked me
what news I wanted to send.

" Just that we are attacked," I said.

" That's a simple job," he said cheerfully.
" All down the Border posts we have a signal.
Only yesterday we got word of it from the place
you speak of. A mile from here is a hillock within
hearing of the stockade at Robertson's Ford.
One shot fired there will tell them what you want
them to know. Robertson's will fire twice for
Appleby's to hear, and Appleby's will send on
the message to Dopple's. There are six posts
between here and the South Fork, so when the
folk at Frew's hear seven shots they will know
that the war is on the Rappahannock."

I recognized old Lawrence's hand in this. It
was just the kind of device that he would con-
trive. I hoped it would not miscarry, for I would
have preferred a messenger ; but after all the
Border line was his concern.

Then I spoke aside to Shalah. In his view the
Cherokees would not attack at dawn. They were
more likely to wait till their supports overtook
them, and then to make a dash for the Rappahannock farms. Plunder was more in the line

of those gentry than honest fighting. I spoke
to the leader of the post, and he was for falling
upon them in the narrows of the Rapidan. Their
victory over the Meebaws had fired the blood of
the Borderers, and made them contemptuous of
the enemy. Still, in such a predicament, when we
had to hold a frontier with a handful, the boldest
course was likely to be the safest. I could only
pray that Nicholson's levies would turn up in
time to protect the valley.

"Time passes, brother," said Shalah. "We
came by swiftness, but we return by guile. In
three hours it will be dawn. Sleep till then, for
there is much toil before thee."

I saw the wisdom of his words, and went promptly
to bed in a corner of the stockade. As I was
lying down a man spoke to me, one Rycroft, at
whose cabin I had once sojourned for a day.

"What brings the parson hereaways in these
times ? " he asked.

"What parson ? " I asked.

"The man they call Doctor Blair."

"Great God ! " I cried, " what about him ? "

"He was in Stafford county when I left, hunting
for schoolmasters. Ay, and he had a girl with him."

I sat upright with a start. "Where is he
now ? " I asked.

"I saw him last at Middleton's Ford. I think
he was going down the river. I warned him this
was no place for parsons and women, but he
just laughed at me. It's time he was back in
the Tidewater."

So long as they were homeward-bound I did not care ; but it gave me a queer fluttering of the heart to think that Elspeth but yesterday should have been near this perilous Border. I soon fell asleep, for I was mighty tired, but I dreamed evilly. I seemed to see Doctor Blair hunted by Cherokees, with his coat-tails flying and his wig blown away, and what vexed me was that I could not find Elspeth anywhere in the landscape.

CHAPTER XVIII

OUR ADVENTURE RECEIVES A RECRUIT

AT earliest light, with the dew heavy on the willows and the river line a coil of mist, Shalah woke me for the road. We breakfasted off fried bacon, some of which I saved for the journey, for the Indian was content with one meal a day. As we left the stockade I noted the row of Meebaw scalps hanging, grim and bloody, from the poles. The Borderers were up and stirring, for they looked to take the Indians in the river narrows before the morning was old.

No two Indian war parties ever take the same path, so it was Shalah's plan to work back to the route we had just travelled, by which the Cherokees had come yesterday. This sounds simple enough, but the danger lay in the second party. By striking to right or left we might walk into it, and then good-bye to our hopes of the hills. But the whole thing was easier to me than the cruel toil of yesterday. There was need of stealth and woodcraft, but not of you killing speed.

For the first hour we went up a northern fork
of the Rappahannock, then crossed the water
at a ford, and struck into a thick pine forest.
I was feeling miraculously rested, and found no
discomfort in Shalah's long strides. My mind
was very busy on the defence of the Borders,
and I kept wondering how long the Governor's
militia would take to reach the Rappahannock,
and whether Lawrence could reinforce the northern
posts in time to prevent mischief in Stafford
county. I cast back to my memory of the tales
of Indian war, and could not believe but that
the white man, if warned and armed, would roll
back the Cherokees. 'Twas not them I feared,
but that other force now screened behind the
mountains, who had for their leader some white
madman with a fire in his head and Bible words
on his lips. Were we of Virginia destined to fight
with such fanatics as had distracted Scotland—
fanatics naming the name of God, but leading
in our case the armies of hell ?

It was about eleven in the forenoon, I think,
that Shalah dropped his easy swing and grew
circumspect. The sun was very hot, and the
noon silence lay dead on the woodlands. Scarcely
a leaf stirred, and the only sounds were the twit-
tering grasshoppers and the drone of flies. But
Shalah found food for thought. Again and again
he became rigid, and then laid an ear to the ground.
His nostrils dilated like a horse's, and his eyes
were restless. We were now in a shallow vale,
through which a little stream flowed among broad

reed-beds.　At one point he kneeled on the ground and searched diligently.

"See," he said, "a horse's prints not two hours old—a horse going west."

Presently I myself found a clue.　I picked up from a clump of wild onions a thread of coloured wool.　This was my own trade, where I knew more than Shalah.　I tested the thing in my mouth and between my fingers.

"This is London stuff," I said.　"The man who had this on his person bought his clothes from the Bristol merchants, and paid sweetly for them.　He was no Rappahannock farmer."

Shalah trailed like a bloodhound, following the hoof-marks out of the valley meadow to a ridge of sparse cedars where they showed clear on the bare earth, and then to a thicker covert where they were hidden among strong grasses. Suddenly he caught my shoulder, and pulled me to the ground.　We crawled through a briery place to where a gap opened to the vale on our left.

A party of Indians were passing.　They were young men with the fantastic markings of young braves.　All were mounted on the little Indian horses.　They moved at leisure, scanning the distance with hands shading eyes.

We wormed our way back to the darkness of the covert.　"The advance guard of the second party," Shalah whispered.　"With good fortune, we shall soon see the rest pass, and then have a clear road for the hills."

"I saw no fresh scalps," I said, "so they seem to have missed our man on the horse." I was proud of my simple logic.

All that Shalah replied was, "The rider was a woman."

"How, in Heaven's name, can you tell?" I asked.

He held out a long hair. "I found it among the vines at the level of a rider's head."

This was bad news indeed. What folly had induced a woman to ride so far across the Borders? It could be no settler's wife, but some dame from the coast country who had not the sense to be timid. 'Twas a grievous affliction for two men on an arduous quest to have to protect a foolish female with the Cherokees all about them.

There was no help for it, and as swiftly as possible and with all circumspection Shalah trailed the horse's prints. They kept the high ground, in very broken country, which was the reason why the rider had escaped the Indians' notice. Clearly they were moving slowly, and from the frequent halts and turnings I gathered that the rider had not much purpose about the road.

Then we came on a glade where the rider had dismounted and let the beast go. The horse had wandered down the ridge to the right in search of grazing, and the prints of a woman's foot led to the summit of a knoll which raised itself above the trees.

There, knee-deep in a patch of fern, I saw what I had never dreamed of, what sent the blood from my heart in a cold shudder of fear : a girl, pale and dishevelled, was trying to part some vines. A twig crackled and she looked round, showing a face drawn with weariness and eyes large with terror.

It was Elspeth !

At the sight of Shalah she made to scream, but checked herself. It was well, for a scream would have brought all of us to instant death.

For Shalah at that moment dropped to earth and wriggled into a covert overlooking the vale. I had the sense to catch the girl and pull her after him. He stopped dead, and we two lay also like mice. My heart was going pretty fast and I could feel the heaving of her bosom.

The shallow glen was full of folk, most of them going on foot. I recognized the Cherokee head-dress and the long hickory bows which those carried who had no muskets. 'Twas by far the biggest party we had seen, and, though in that moment I had no wits to count them, Shalah told me afterwards they must have numbered little short of a thousand. Some very old fellows were there, with lean, hollow cheeks, and scanty locks, but the most were warriors in their prime. I could see it was a big war they were out for, since some of the horses carried heavy loads of corn, and it is never the Indian fashion to take much provender for a common raid. In all Virginia's history there had been no such invasion, for the wars of Opechancanough and Berkeley and the fight of Bacon against the Susquehannocks were

mere bickers compared with this deliberate downpour from the hills.

As we lay there, scarce daring to breathe, I
saw that we were in deadly peril. The host was
so great that some marched on the very edge of
our thicket. I could see through the leaves the
brown skins not six yards away. The slightest
noise would bring the sharp Indian eyes peering
into the gloom, and we must be betrayed.

In that moment, which was one of the gravest
of my life, I had happily no leisure to think of
myself. My whole soul sickened with anxiety
for the girl. I knew enough of Indian ways to
guess her fate. For Shalah and myself there
might be torture, and at the best an arrow in our
hearts, but for her there would be things unspeak-
able. I remembered the little meadow on the
Rapidan, and the tale told by the grey ashes.
There was only one shot in my pistol, but I determined that it should be saved for her. In
such a crisis the memory works wildly, and I
remember feeling glad that I had stood up before
Grey's fire. The thought gave me a comforting
assurance of manhood.

Those were nightmare minutes. The girl was
very quiet, in a stupor of fatigue and fear. Shalah
was a graven image, and I was too tensely strung
to have any of the itches and fervours which used
to vex me in hunting the deer when stillness was
needful. Through the fretted greenery I saw
the dim shadows of men passing swiftly. The
thought of the horse worried me. If the con-

founded beast grazed peaceably down the other side of the hill, all might be well. So long as he was out of sight any movement he made would be set down by the Indians to some forest beast, for animals' noises are all alike in a wood. But if he returned to us, there would be the devil to pay, for at a glimpse of him our thicket would be alive with the enemy.

In the end I found it best to shut my eyes and commend our case to our Maker. Then I counted very slowly to myself up to four hundred, and looked again. The vale was empty.

We lay still, hardly believing in our deliverance, for the matter of a quarter of an hour, and then Shalah, making a sign to me to remain, turned and glided up hill. I put my hand behind me, found Elspeth's cheek, and patted it. She stretched out a hand and clutched mine feverishly, and thus we remained till, after what seemed an age, Shalah returned.

He was on his feet and walking freely. He had found the horse, too, and had it by the bridle. "The danger is past," he said gravely. "Let us go back to the glade and rest."

I helped Elspeth to her feet, and on my arm she stumbled to the grassy place in the woods. I searched my pockets, and gave her the remnants of the bread and bacon I had brought from the Rappahannock post. Better still, I remembered that I had in my breast a little flask of eau-de-vie, and a mouthful of it revived her greatly. She put her hands to her head, and began to tidy her dishevelled hair, which is a sure sign in a woman that she is recovering her composure.

" What brought you here ? " I asked gently.

She had forgotten that I was in her black books, and that in her letter she forbade my journey. Indeed, she looked at me as a child in a pickle may look at an upbraiding parent.

" I was lost," she cried. " I did not mean to go far, but the night came down and I could not find the way back. Oh, it has been a hideous nightmare ! I have been almost mad in the dark woods."

" But how did you get here ? " I asked, still hopelessly puzzled.

" I was with Uncle James on the Rappahannock. He heard something that made him anxious, and he was going back to the Tidewater yesterday. But a message came for him suddenly, and he left me at Morrison's farm, and said he would be back by the evening. I did not want to go home before I had seen the mountains where my estate is—you know, the land that Governor Francis said he would give me for my birthday. They told me one could see the hills from near at hand, and a boy that I asked said I would get a rare view if I went to the rise beyond the river. So I had Paladin saddled, and crossed the ford, meaning to be back long ere sunset. But the trees were so thick that I could see nothing from the first rise, and I tried to reach a green hill that looked near. Then it began to grow dark, and I lost my head, and oh ! I don't know where I wandered. I thought every rustle in the bushes was a bear or a panther. I feared the Indians, too, for they told me they were unsafe in this country. All night long I tried to find a valley running east, but the moonlight deceived me, and I must have come farther away every hour. When day came I tied Paladin to a tree and slept a little, and then I rode on to find a hill which would show me the lie of the land. But it was very hot, and I was very weary. And then you came, and those dreadful wild men. And—and——" She broke down and wept piteously.

I comforted her as best I could, telling her that her troubles were over now, and that I should look after her. "You might have met with us in the woods last night," I said, "so you see you were not far from friends." But the truth was that her troubles were only beginning, and I was wretchedly anxious. My impulse was to try to get her back to the Rappahannock; but, on putting this to Shalah, he shook his head.

"It is too late," he said. "If you seek certain death, go towards the Rappahannock. She must come with us to the mountains. The only safety is in the hill-tops."

This seemed a mad saying. To be safe from Indians we were to go into the heart of Indian country. But Shalah expounded it. The tribes, he said, dwelt only in the lower glens of the range, and never ventured to the summits, believing them to be holy land where a great *manitou* dwelt. The Cherokees especially shunned the peaks. If

we could find a way clear to the top we might stay
there in some security, till we learned the issue
of the war, and could get word to our friends.
" Moreover," he said, " we have yet to penetrate
the secret of the hills. That was the object of
our quest, brother."

Shalah was right, and I had forgotten all about
it. I could not suffer my care for Elspeth to
prevent a work whose issue might mean the salvation of Virginia. We had still to learn the
truth about the massing of Indians in the mountains, of which the Cherokee raids were but scouting ventures. The verse of Grey's song came into
my head :—

> " I could not love thee, dear, so much,
>   Loved I not Honour more."

Besides—and this was the best reason—there
was no other way. We had gone too far to turn
back, and, as our proverb says, " It is idle to
swallow the cow and choke on the tail."

I put it all to Elspeth.

She looked very scared. " But my uncle will
go mad if he does not find me."

" It will be worse for him if he is never to find
you again. Shalah says it would be as easy to
get you back over the Rappahannock as for a
child to cross a winter torrent. I don't say it's
pleasant either way, but there's a good hope of
safety in the hills, and there's none anywhere
else."

She sat for a little with her eyes downcast.

"I am in your hands," she said at last. "Oh, the foolish girl I have been! I will be a drag and a danger to you all."

Then I took her hand. "Elspeth," I said, "it's me will be the proud man if I can save you. I would rather be the salvation of you than the King of the Tidewater. And so says Shalah, and so will say all of us."

But I do not think she heard me. She had checked her tears, but her wits were far away, grieving for her uncle's pain, and envisaging the dark future. At the first water we reached she bathed her face and eyes, and using the pool as a mirror, adjusted her hair. Then she smiled bravely. "I will try to be a true comrade, like a man," she said. "I think I will be stronger when I have slept a little."

All that afternoon we stole from covert to covert. It was hot and oppressive in the dense woods, where the breeze could not penetrate. Shalah's eagle eyes searched every open space before we crossed, but we saw nothing to alarm us. In time we came to the place where we had left our party, and it was easy enough to pick up their road. They had travelled slowly, keeping to the thickest trees, and they had taken no pains to cover their tracks, for they had argued that if trouble came it would come from the front, and that it was little likely that any Indian would be returning thus soon and could take up their back trail.

Presently we came to a place where the bold

spurs of the hills overhung us, and the gap we had seen opened up into a deep valley. Shalah went in advance, and suddenly we heard a word pass. We entered a cedar glade, to find our four companions unsaddling the horses and making camp.

The sight of the girl held them staring. Grey grew pale and then flushed scarlet. He came forward and asked me abruptly what it meant. When I told him he bit his lips.

"There is only one thing to be done," he said. "We must take Miss Blair back to the Tidewater. I insist, sir. I will go myself. We cannot involve her in our dangers."

He was once again the man I had wrangled with. His eyes blazed, and he spoke in a high tone of command. But I could not be wroth with him; indeed, I liked him for his peremptoriness. It comforted me to think that Elspeth had so warm a defender.

I nodded to Shalah. "Tell him," I said, and Shalah spoke with him. He took long to convince, but at the end he said no more, and went to speak to Elspeth. I could see that she lightened his troubled mind a little, for, having accepted her fate, she was resolute to make the best of it. I even heard her laugh.

That night we made her a bower of green branches, and as we ate our supper round our modest fire she sat like a queen among us. It was odd to see the way in which her presence affected each of us. With her Grey was the courtly cavalier, ready with a neat phrase and a line from the poets. Donaldson and Shalah were unmoved : no woman could make any difference to their wilderness silence. The Frenchman Bertrand grew almost gay. She spoke to him in his own tongue, and he told her all about the little family he had left and his days in far-away France. But in Ringan was the oddest change. Her presence kept him tongue-tied, and when she spoke to him he was embarrassed into stuttering. He was eager to serve her in everything, but he could not look her in the face or answer readily when she spoke. This man, so debonair and masterful among his fellows, was put all out of countenance by a wearied girl. I do not suppose he had spoken to a gentlewoman for ten years.

CHAPTER XIX

CLEARWATER GLEN

NEXT morning we came into Clearwater Glen.

Shalah spoke to me of it before we started. He did not fear the Cherokees, who had come from the far south of the range and had never been settled in these parts. But he thought that there might be others from the back of the hills who would have crossed by this gap, and might be lying in the lower parts of the glen. It behoved us, therefore, to go very warily. Once on the higher ridges, he thought we might be safe for a time. An invading army has no leisure to explore the rugged summits of a mountain.

The first sight of the place gave me a strong emotion of dislike. A little river brawled in a deep gorge, falling in pools and linns like one of my native burns. All its course was thickly shaded with bushes and knotted trees. On either bank lay stretches of rough hill pasture, lined with dark and tangled forests, which ran up the hill-side till the steepness of the slope broke them

into copses of stunted pines among great bluffs
of rock and raw red scaurs. The glen was very
narrow, and the mountains seemed to beetle above
it so as to shut out half the sunlight. The air
was growing cooler, with the queer, acrid smell in it
that high hills bring. I am a great lover of uplands, and the sourest peat-moss has a charm for
me, but to that strange glen I conceived at once
a determined hate. It is the way of some places
with some men. The senses perceive a hostility
for which the mind has no proof, and in my
experience the senses are right.

Part of my discomfort was due to my bodily
health. I had proudly thought myself seasoned
by the hot Virginian summers, in which I had
escaped all common ailments. But I had forgotten what old hunters had told me, that the
hills will bring out a fever which is dormant in
the plains. Anyhow, I now found that my head
was dizzy and aching, and my limbs had a strange
trembling. The fatigue of the past day had
dragged me to the limits of my strength and made
me an easy victim. My heart, too, was full of
cares. The sight of Elspeth reminded me how
heavy was my charge. 'Twas difficult enough
to scout well in this tangled place, but, forbye my
duty to the dominion, I had the business of taking
one who was the light of my life into this dark
land of bloody secrets.

The youth and gaiety were going out of my
quest. I could only plod along dismally, atten-
tive to every movement of Shalah, praying inces-

santly that we might get well out of it all. To
make matters worse, the travelling became desperate hard. In the Tidewater there were bridle
paths, and in the vales of the foothills the going
had been good, with hard, dry soil in the woods,
and no hindrances save a thicket of vines or a
rare windfall. But in this glen, where the hill
rains beat, there was no end to obstacles. The
open spaces were marshy, where our horses sank
to the hocks. The woods were one medley of
fallen trees, rotting into touchwood, hidden boulders, and matted briers. Often we could not
move till Donaldson and Bertrand with their
hatchets had hewn some sort of road. All this
meant slow progress, and by midday we had not
gone half-way up the glen to the ridge which
meant the neck of the pass.

This was an occasion when Ringan showed
at his best. He had lost his awe of Elspeth,
and devoted himself to making the road easy
for her. Grey, who would fain have done the
same, was no match for the seafarer, and had
much ado to keep going himself. Ringan's cheery
face was better than medicine. His eyes never
lost their dancing light, and he was ready ever
with some quip or whimsy to tide over the worst
troubles. We kept very still, but now and again
Elspeth's laugh rang out at his fooling, and it did
my heart good to hear it.

After midday the glen seemed to grow darker,
and I saw that the blue sky, which I had thought
changeless, was becoming overcast. As I looked

upwards I saw the high ridge blotted out and a white mist creeping down. I had noticed for some time that Shalah was growing uneasy. He would halt us often, while he went a little way on, and now he turned with so grim a look that we stopped without bidding.

He slipped into the undergrowth, while we waited in that dark, lonesome place. Even Ringan was sober now.

Elspeth asked in a low voice what was wrong, and I told her that the Indian was uncertain of the best road.

" Best road ! " she laughed. " Then pray show me what you call the worst."

Ringan grinned at me ruefully. " Where do you wish yourself at this moment, Andrew ? "

" On the top of this damned mountain," I grunted.

" Not for me," he said. " Give me the Dry Tortugas, on a moonlight night when the breaming fires burn along the shore, and the lads are singing ' Spanish Ladies.' Or, better still, the little isle of St. John the Baptist, with the fine yellow sands for careening, and Mother Daria brewing bobadillo and the trades blowing fresh in the tops of the palms. This land is a gloomy sort of business. Give me the bright, changeful sea."

" And I," said Elspeth, " would be threading rowan berries for a necklace in the heather of Medwyn glen. It must be about four o'clock of a midsummer afternoon and a cloudless sky,

except for white streamers over Tinto. Ah,
my own kind countryside ! "

Ringan's face changed.

" You are right, my lady. No Tortugas or
Spanish isles for Ninian Campbell. Give him
the steeps of Glenorchy on an October morn when
the deer have begun to bell. My sorrow, but we
are far enough from our desires—all but Andrew,
who is a prosaic soul. And here comes Shalah
with ugly news ! "

The Indian spoke rapidly to me. " The woods
are full of men. I do not think we are discovered,
but we cannot stay here. Our one hope is to gain
the cover of the mist. There is an open space
beyond this thicket, and we must ride our swiftest.
Quick, brother."

" The men ? " I gasped. " Cherokees ? "

" Nay," he said, " not Cherokees. I think
they are those you seek .from beyond the mountains."

The next half-hour is a mad recollection, wild
and confused and distraught with anxiety. The
thought of Elspeth among savages maddened
me, the more so as she had just spoken of Medwyn
glen, and had sent my memory back to fragrant
hours of youth. We scrambled out of the thicket
and put our weary beasts to a gallop. Happily
it was harder ground, albeit much studded with
clumps of fern, and though we all slipped and
stumbled often, the horses kept their feet. I was
growing so dizzy in the head that I feared every
moment I would fall off. The mist had now

come low down the hill, and lay before us, a line of grey vapour drawn from edge to edge of the vale. It seemed an infinite long way off.

Shalah on foot kept in the rear, and I gathered from him that the danger he feared was behind. Suddenly as I stared ahead something fell ten yards in advance of us in a long curve, and stuck quivering in the soil.

It was an Indian arrow.

We would have reined up if Shalah had not cried on us to keep on. I do not think the arrow was meant to strike us. 'Twas a warning, a grim jest of the savages in the wood.

Then another fell, at the same distance before our first rider.

Still Shalah cried us on. I fell back to the rear, for if we were to escape I thought there might be need of fighting there. I felt in my belt for my loaded pistols.

We were now in a coppice again, where the trees were short and sparse. Beyond that lay another meadow, and, then, not a quarter-mile distant, the welcome line of the mist, every second drawing down on us.

A third time an arrow fell. Its flight was shorter and dropped almost under the nose of Elspeth's horse, which swerved violently, and would have unseated a less skilled horsewoman.

" On, on," I cried, for we were past the need for silence, and when I looked again, the kindly fog had swallowed up the van of the party.

I turned and gazed back, and there I saw a

strange sight. A dozen men or more had come to the edge of the trees on the hill-side. They were quite near, not two hundred yards distant, and I saw them clearly. They carried bows or muskets, but none offered to use them. They were tall fellows, but lighter in the colour than any Indians I had seen. Indeed, they were as fair as many an Englishman, and their slim, golden-brown bodies were not painted in the maniac fashion of the Cherokees. They stood stock still, watching us with a dreadful impassivity which was more frightening to me than violence. Then I, too, was overtaken by the grey screen.

" Will they follow ? " I asked Shalah.

" I do not think so. They are not hill-men, and fear the high places where the gods smoke. Furthermore, there is no need."

" We have escaped, then ? " I asked, with a great relief in my voice.

" Say rather we have been shepherded by them into a fold. They will find us when they desire us."

It was a perturbing thought, but at any rate we were safe for the moment, and I resolved to say nothing to alarm the others. We overtook them presently, and Shalah became our guide. Not that more guiding was needed than Ringan or I could have given, for the lift of the ground gave us our direction, and there was the sound of a falling stream. To an upland-bred man mist is little of a hindrance, unless on a featureless moor.

Ever as we jogged upward the air grew colder. Rain was blowing in our teeth, and the ferny grass

and juniper clumps dripped with wet. Almost it
might have been the Pentlands or the high mosses
between Douglas Water and Clyde. To us coming
fresh from the torrid plains it was bitter weather,
and I feared for Elspeth, who was thinly clad for
the hill-tops. Ringan seemed to feel the cold the
worst of us, for he had spent his days on the hot
seas of the south. He put his horse-blanket over
his shoulders, and cut a comical figure with his
red face peeping from its folds.

"Lord," he would cry, "I wish I was in the
Dry Tortugas or snug in the beach-house at the
Isle o' Pines. This minds me painfully of my
young days, when I ran in a ragged kilt in the
cold heather of Cruachan. I must be getting an
old man, Andrew, for I never thought the hills
could freeze my blood."

Suddenly the fog lightened a little, the slope
ceased, and we had that gust of freer air which
means the top of the pass. My head was less
dizzy now, and I had a momentary gladness that
at any rate we had done part of what we set out
to do.

"Clearwater Gap!" I cried. "Except for old
Studd, we are the first Christians to stand on this
watershed."

Below us lay a swimming hollow of white mist,
hiding I knew not what strange country.

From the vales below I had marked the lie of
the land on each side of the gap. The highest
ground was to the right, so we turned up the
ridge, which was easier than the glen and better

travelling.   Presently we were among pines again, and got a shelter from the driving rain.   My plan was to find some hollow far up the mountain side, and there to make our encampment.   After an hour's riding, we came to the very place I had sought.   A pocket of flat land lay between two rocky knolls, with a ring of good-sized trees around it.   The spot was dry and hidden, and what especially took my fancy was a spring of water which welled up in the centre, and from which a tiny stream ran down the hill.   'Twas a fine site for a stockade, and so thought Shalah and the two Borderers.

There was much to do to get the place ready, and Donaldson and Bertrand fell to with their axes to fell trees for the fort.   Now that we had reached the first stage in our venture, my mind was unreasonably comforted.   With the buoyancy of youth, I argued that since we had got so far we must get farther.   Also the fever seemed to be leaving my bones and my head clearing.   Elspeth was almost merry.   Like a child playing at making house, she ordered the men about on divers errands.   She was a fine sight, with the wind ruffling her hair and her cheeks reddened from the rain.

Ringan came up to me.   " There are three hours of daylight in front of us.   What say you to make for the top of the hills and find Studd's cairn ?   I need some effort to keep my blood running."

I would gladly have stayed behind, for the fever had tired me, but I could not be dared by Ringan and not respond.   So we set off at a great pace up the ridge, which soon grew very steep, and forced us to a crawl. There were places where we had to scramble up loose cliffs amid a tangle of vines, and then we would dip into a little glade, and then once again breast a precipice. By and by the trees dropped away, and there was nothing but low bushes and boulders and rank mountain grasses. In clear air we must have had a wonderful prospect, but the mist hung close around us, the drizzle blurred our eyes, and the most we saw was a yard or two of grey vapour. It was easy enough to find the road, for the ridge ran upwards as narrow as a hog's back.

Presently it ceased, and with labouring breath we walked a step or two on flat ground. Ringan, who was in front, stumbled over a little heap of stones about a foot high.

" Studd had a poor notion of a cairn," he said, as he kicked them down. There was nothing beneath but bare soil.

But the hunter had spoken the truth. A little digging in the earth revealed the green metal of an old powder-flask with a wooden stopper. I forced it open, and shook from its inside a twist of very dirty paper. There were some rude scratchings on it with charcoal, which I read with difficulty.

Salut to Advent^{rs}.
Robbin Studd on ye Sumit of Mountaine ye 3rd dy of June yr 1672 hathe sene ye Promiss^d Lande.

Somehow in that bleak place this scrap of a human message wonderfully uplifted our hearts. Before we had thought only of our danger and cares, but now we had a vision of the reward. Down in the mists lay a new world. Studd had seen it, and we should see it; and some day the Virginian people would drive a road through Clearwater Gap and enter into possession. It is a subtle joy that which fills the heart of the pioneer, and mighty unselfish too. He does not think of payment, for the finding is payment enough. He does not even seek praise, for it is the unborn generations that will call him blessed. He is content, like Moses, to leave his bones in the wilderness if his people may pass over Jordan.

Ringan turned the flask in his hands. " A good man, this old Studd," he said. " I like his words, *Salute to Adventurers*. He was thinking of the folk that should come after him, which is the mark of a big mind, Andrew. Your common fellow would have writ some glorification of his own doings, but Studd was thinking of the thing he had done and not of himself. You say he's dead these ten years. Maybe he's looking down at us and nodding his old head well pleased. I would like fine to drink his health."

We ran down the hill, and came to the encampment at the darkening. Ringan, who had retained the flask, presented it to Elspeth with a bow.

" There, mistress," he says, " there's the key of your new estate."

CHAPTER XX

THE STOCKADE AMONG THE PINES

IT took us a heavy day's work to get the stockade finished. There were only the two axes in the party, besides Shalah's tomahawk, and no one can know the labour of felling and trimming trees till he has tried it. We found the horses useful for dragging trunks, and but for them should have made a poor job of it. Grey's white hands were all cut and blistered, and, though I boasted of my hardiness, mine were little better. Ringan was the surprise, for you would not think that sailing a ship was a good apprenticeship to forestry. But he was as skilful as Bertrand and as strong as Donaldson, and he had a better idea of fortification than us all put together.

The palisade which ran round the camp was six feet high, made of logs lashed to upright stakes. There was a gate which could be barred heavily, and loopholes were made every yard or so for musket fire. On one side—that facing the uplift of the ridge—the walls rose to nine feet. Inside we made a division. In one half the horses were

picketed at night, and the other was our dwelling.
For Elspeth we made a bower in one corner, which
we thatched with pine branches ; but the rest of
us slept in the open round the fire. It was a
rough place, but a strong one, for our water could
not be cut off, and, as we had plenty of ball and
powder, a few men could hold it against a host.
To each was allotted his proper station, in case of
attack, and we kept watch in succession like soldiers in war. Ringan, who had fought in many
places up and down the world, was our general in
these matters, and a rigid martinet we found him.
Shalah was our scout, and we leaned on him
for all woodland work ; but inside the palisade
Ringan's word was law.

Our plan was to make this stockade the centre
for exploring the hills and ascertaining the strength
and purposes of the Indian army. We hoped, and
so did Shalah, that our enemies would have no
leisure to follow us to the high ridges ; that what
risk there was would be run by the men on their
spying journeys ; but that the stockade would be
reasonably safe. It was my intention, as soon as
I had sufficient news, to send word to Lawrence,
and we thought that presently the Rappahannock
forces would have driven the Cherokees southward,
and the way would be open to get Elspeth back
to the Tidewater.

The worst trouble, as I soon saw, was to be the
matter of food. The supplies we had carried were
all but finished by what we ate after the stockade
was completed. After that there remained only a

single bag of flour, another bag of Indian meal, and a pound or two of boucanned beef, besides three flasks of eau-de-vie, which Ringan had brought in a leather casket. The forest berries were not yet ripe, and the only food to be procured was the flesh of the wild game. Happily in Donaldson and Bertrand we had two practised trappers; but they were doubtful about success, for they had no knowledge of what beasts lived in the hills. I have said that we had plenty of powder and ball, but I did not relish the idea of shooting in the woods, for the noise would be a signal to our foes. Still, food we must have, and I thought I might find a secluded place where the echoes of a shot would be muffled.

The next morning I parcelled up the company according to their duties, for while Ringan was captain of the stockade, I was the leader of the venture. I sent out Bertrand and Donaldson to trap in the woods; Ringan, with Grey and Shalah, stayed at home to strengthen still further the stockade and protect Elspeth; while I took my musket and some pack-thongs and went up the hill-side to look for game. We were trysted to be back an hour before sundown, and if some one of us did not find food we should go supperless.

That day is a memory which will never pass from me. The weather was grey and lowering, and though the rain had ceased, the air was still heavy with it, and every bush and branch dripped with moisture. It was a poor day for hunting,

for the eye could not see forty yards; but it
suited my purpose, since the dull air would deaden
the noise of my musket. I was hunting alone in a
strange land among imminent perils, and my aim
was not to glorify my skill, but to find the means
of life. The thought strung me up to a mood
where delight was more notable than care. I was
adventuring with only my hand to guard me in
those ancient, haunted woods, where no white man
had ever before travelled. To experience such
moments is to live with the high fervour which
God gave to mortals before towns and laws laid
their dreary spell upon them.

Early in the day I met a bear—the second I had
seen in my life. I did not want him, and he dis-
regarded me and shuffled grumpily down the hill-
side. I had to be very careful, I remember, to
mark my path, so that I could retrace it, and I
followed the Border device of making a chip here
and there in the bark of trees, and often looking
backward to remember the look of the place when
seen from the contrary side. Trails were easy to
find on the soft ground, but besides the bear I
saw none but those of squirrel and rabbit, and a
rare opossum. But at last, in a marshy glen, I
found the fresh slot of a great stag. For two
hours and more I followed him far north along
the ridge, till I came up with him in a patch of
scrub oak. I had to wait long for a shot, but when
at last he rose I planted a bullet fairly behind his
shoulder, and he dropped within ten paces. His
size amazed me, for he was as big as a cart-horse

in body, and carried a spread of branching antlers
like a forest tree.   To me, accustomed to the little
deer of the Tidewater, this great creature seemed
a portent, and I guessed that he was that elk
which I had heard of from the Border hunters.
Anyhow he gave me wealth of food.   I hid some
in a cool place, and took the rest with me, packed
in bark, in a great bundle on my shoulders.

The road back was easier than I had feared, for
I had the slope of the hill to guide me ; but I was
mortally weary of my load before I plumped it
down inside the stockade.   Presently Bertrand and
Donaldson returned.   They brought only a few
rabbits, but they had set many traps, and in a
hill burn they had caught some fine golden-bellied
trout.   Soon venison steaks and fish were grilling
in the embers, and Elspeth set to baking cakes
on a griddle.   Those left behind had worked
well, and the palisade was as perfect as could
be contrived.   A runlet of water had been led
through a hollow trunk into a trough—also hewn
from a log—close by Elspeth's bower, where she
could make her toilet unperplexed by other eyes.
Also they had led a stream into the horses'
enclosure, so that they could be watered with
ease.

The weather cleared in the evening, as it often
does in a hill country.   From the stockade we had
no prospect save the reddening western sky, but
I liked to think that in a little walk I could see
old Studd's Promised Land.   That was a joy I
reserved for myself on the morrow.   I look back

on that late afternoon with delight as a curious
interlude of peace. We had forgotten that we
were fugitives in a treacherous land, I for one had
forgotten the grim purpose of our quest, and we
cooked supper as if we were a band of careless
folk taking our pleasure in the wilds. Wood-
smoke is always for me an intoxication like strong
drink. It seems the incense of nature's altar,
calling up the shades of the old forest gods, smack-
ing of rest and comfort in the heart of solitude.
And what odour can vie for hungry folk with that
of roasting meat in the clear hush of twilight ?
The sight of that little camp is still in my
memory. Elspeth flitted about busied with her
cookery, the glow of the sunset lighting up her
dark hair. Bertrand did the roasting, crouched
like a gnome by the edge of the fire. Grey
fetched and carried for the cooks, a docile and
cheerful servant, with nothing in his look to
recall the proud gentleman of the Tidewater.
Donaldson sat on a log, contentedly smoking
his pipe, while Ringan, whistling a strathspey,
attended to the horses. Only Shalah stood aloof,
his eyes fixed vacantly on the western sky, and
his ear intent on the multitudinous voices of the
twilit woods.

Presently food was ready, and our rude meal
in that darkling place was a merry one. Elspeth
sat enthroned on a couch of pine branches—I can
see her yet shielding her face from the blaze with
one little hand, and dividing her cakes with the
other. Then we lit our pipes, and fell to the long

tales of the camp-fire. Ringan had a story of a black-haired princess of Spain, and how for love of her two gentlemen did marvels on the seas. The chief one never returned to claim her, but died in a fight off Cartagena, and wrote a fine ballad about his mistress which Ringan said was still sung in the taverns of the Main. He gave a verse of it, a wild, sad thing, with tears in it and the joy of battle. After that we all sang, all but me, who have no voice. Bertrand had a lay of Normandy, about a lady who walked in the apple-orchards and fell in love with a wandering minstrel ; and Donaldson sang a rough ballad of Virginia, in which a man weighs the worth of his wife against a tankard of apple-jack. Grey sang an English song about the north-country maid who came to London, and a bit of the chanty of the Devon men who sacked Santa Fé and stole the Almirante's daughter. As for Elspeth, she sang to a soft Scots tune the tale of the Lady of Cassilis who followed the gipsy's piping. In it the gipsy tells of what he can offer the lady, and lo! it was our own case !—

> " And ye shall wear no silken gown,
>   No maid shall bind your hair ;
> The yellow broom shall be your gem,
>   Your braid the heather rare.
> Athwart the moor, adown the hill,
>   Across the world away !
> The path is long for happy hearts
>   That sing to greet the day,
>   My love,
>   That sing to greet the day."

I remember, too, the last verse of it :—

> " And at the last no solemn stole
> Shall on thy breast be laid ;
> No mumbling priest shall speed thy soul,
> No charnel-vault thee shade.
> But by the shadowed hazel copse,
> Aneath the greenwood tree,
> Where airs are soft and waters sing,
> Thou'lt ever sleep by me,
> My love,
> Thou'lt ever sleep by me."

Then we fell to talking about the things in the West that no man had yet discovered, and Shalah, to whom our songs were nothing, now lent an ear.

" The first Virginians," said Grey, " thought that over the hills lay the western ocean and the road to Cathay. I do not know, but I am confident that but a little way west we should come to water. A great river or else the ocean."

Ringan differed. He held that the land of America was very wide in those parts, as wide as south of the isthmus where no man had yet crossed it. Then he told us of a sea-captain who had travelled inland in Mexico for five weeks and come to a land where gold was as common as chuckie-stones, and a great people dwelt who worshipped a god who lived in a mountain. And he spoke of the holy city of Manoa, which Sir Walter Raleigh sought, and which many had seen from far hill-tops. Likewise of the wonderful kings who once dwelt in Peru, and the little isle in the Pacific where all the birds were nightingales and the Tree of Life flourished ; and the mountain north of the Main which was all one emerald. " I think," he said, " that, though no man has ever had the fruition of these marvels, they are likely to be more true than false. I hold that God has kept this land of America to the last to be the loadstone of adventurers, and that there are greater wonders to be seen than any that man has imagined. The pity is that I have spent my best years scratching like a hen at its doorstep instead of entering. I have a notion some day to travel straight west to the sunset. I think I should find death, but I might see some queer things first."

Then Shalah spoke :—

" There was once a man of my own people who, when he came to man's strength, journeyed westward with a wife. He travelled all his days, and when his eyes were dim with age he saw a great water. His spirit left him on its shore, but on his road he had begotten a son, and that son journeyed back towards the rising sun, and came after many years to his people again. I have spoken with him of what he had seen."

" And what was that ? " asked Ringan, with eager eyes.

" He told of plains so great that it is a lifetime to travel over them, and of deserts where the eagle flying from the dawn dies of drought by midday, and of mountains so high that birds cannot cross them but are changed by cold into stone, and of rivers to which our little waters are as reeds to a forest cedar. But especially he spoke of the fierce warriors that ride like the wind on horses. It seems, brother, that he who would reach that land must reach also the Hereafter."

"That's the place for me," Ringan cried. "What say you, Andrew ? When this affair is over, shall we make a bid for these marvels ? I can cull some pretty adventurers from the Free Companions."

"Nay, I am for moving a step at a time," said I. "I am a trader, and want one venture well done before I begin on another. I shall be content if we safely cross these mountains on which we are now perched."

Ringan shook his head. "That was never the way of the Highlands. 'Better a bone on the far-away hills than a fat sheep in the meadows,' says the Gael. What say you, mistress ? " and he turned to Elspeth.

"I think you are the born poet," said she, smiling, "and that Mr. Garvald is the sober man of affairs. You will leap for the top of the wall and get a prospect while Mr. Garvald will patiently pull it down."

"Oh, I grant that Andrew has the wisdom," said Ringan. "That's why him and me's so well agreed. It's because we differ much, and so fit together like opposite halves of an apple. . . . Is your traveller still in the land of the living ? " he asked Shalah.

But the Indian had slipped away from the fire-side circle, and I saw him without in the moonlight standing rigid on a knoll and gazing at the skies.

Next day dawned cloudless, and Shalah and I spent it in a long journey along the range. We kept to the highest parts, and at every vantage-ground we scanned the glens for human traces. By this time I had found my hill legs, and could keep pace even with the Indian's swift stride. The ridge of mountains, you must know, was not a single backbone, but broken up here and there by valleys into two and even three ranges. This made our scouting more laborious, and prevented us from getting the full value out of our high station. Mostly we kept in cover, and never showed on a sky-line. But we saw nothing to prove the need of this stealth. Only the hawks wheeled, and the wild pigeons crooned ; the squirrels frisked among the branches ; and now and then a great deer would leap from its couch and hasten into the coverts.

But, though we got no news, that journey brought to me a revelation, for I had my glimpse of Studd's Promised Land. It came to me early in the day, as we halted in a little glade, gay with willowherb and goldenrod, which hung on a shelf of the hills looking westwards. The first streamers of morn had gone, the mists had dried up from the valleys, and I found myself looking into a deep cleft and across at a steep pine-clad mountain. Clearly the valley was split by this mountain into two forks, and I could see only the cool depth of it and catch a gleam of broken water a mile or two below. But looking more to the north, I saw where the vale opened, and then I had a vision

worthy of the name by which Studd had baptized
it.   An immense green pasture land ran out to the
dim horizon.   There were forests scattered athwart
it, and single great trees, and little ridges, too, but
at the height where we stood it seemed to the eye
to be one verdant meadow as trim and shapely as
the lawn of a garden.   A noble river, the child of
many hill streams, twined through it in shining
links.   I could see dots, which I took to be herds
of wild cattle grazing, but no sign of any human
dweller.

" What is it ? " I asked unthinkingly.

" The Shenandoah," Shalah said, and I never
stopped to ask how he knew the name.   He was
gazing at the sight with hungry eyes, he whose
gaze was, for usual, so passionless.

That prospect gave me a happy feeling of comfort ; why, I cannot tell, except that the place
looked so bright and habitable.   Here was no sour
wilderness, but a land made by God for cheerful human dwellings.   Some day there would be
orchards and gardens among those meadows, and
miles of golden corn, and the smoke of hearth
fires.   Some day I would enter into that land of
Canaan which now I saw from Pisgah.   Some day
—and I scarcely dared the thought—my children
would call it home.

CHAPTER XXI

A HAWK SCREAMS IN THE EVENING

THOSE two days in the stockade were like a rift of sun in a stormy day, and the next morn the clouds descended. The face of nature seemed to be a mirror of our fortunes, for when I woke the freshness had gone out of the air, and in the overcast sky there was a forewarning of storm. But the little party in the camp remained cheerful enough. Donaldson and Bertrand went off to their trapping; Elspeth was braiding her hair, the handsomest nymph that ever trod these woodlands, and trying in vain to discover from the discreet Ringan where he came from, and what was his calling. The two Borderers knew well who he was; Grey, I think, had a suspicion; but it never entered the girl's head that this debonair gentleman bore the best known name in all the Americas. She fancied he was some exiled Jacobite, and was ready to hear a pitiful romance. This at another time she would have readily got; but Ringan for the nonce was in a sober mood, and though he would talk of Breadalbane, was chary

of touching on more recent episodes. All she
learned was that he was a great traveller, and had
tried most callings that merit a gentleman's interest.

The day before, Shalah and I had explored the
range to the south, keeping on the west side where
we thought the enemy were likely to gather. This
day we looked to the side facing the Tidewater, a
difficult job, for it was eaten into by the upper
glens of many rivers. The weather grew hot and
oppressive, and over the lowlands of Virginia there
brooded a sullen thundercloud. It oppressed my
spirits, and I found myself less able to keep up
with Shalah. The constant sight of the lowlands
filled me with anxiety for what might be happening in those sullen blue flats. Gone was the glad
forgetfulness of yesterday. The Promised Land
might smile as it pleased, but we were still on the
flanks of Pisgah with the Midianites all about us.

My recollection of that day is one of heavy
fatigue and a pressing hopelessness. Shalah behaved oddly, for he was as restive as a frightened
stag. No covert was unsuspected by him, and if
I ventured to raise my head on any exposed ground
a long brown arm pulled me down. He would
make no answer to my questions except a grunt.
All this gave me the notion that the hills were
full of the enemy, and I grew as restive as the
Indian. The crackle of a branch startled me, and
the movement of a scared beast brought my heart
to my throat.

Then from a high place he saw something which

sent us both crawling into the thicket. We made a circuit of several miles round the head of a long ravine, and came to a steep bank of red screes. Up this we wormed our way, as flat as snakes, with our noses in the dusty earth. I was dripping with sweat, and cursing to myself this new madness of Shalah's. Then I found a cooler air blowing on the top of my prostrate skull, and I judged that we were approaching the scarp of a ridge. Shalah's hand held me motionless. He wriggled on a little farther, and with immense slowness raised his head. His hand now beckoned me forward, and in a few seconds I was beside him and was lifting my eyes over the edge of the scarp.

Below us lay a little plain, wedged in between two mountains, and breaking off on one side into a steep glen. It was just such a shelf as I had seen in the Carolinas, only a hundred times greater, and it lay some five hundred feet below us. Every part of the hollow was filled with men. Thousands there must have been, around their fires and tee-pees, and coming or going from the valley. They were silent, like all savages, but the low hum rose from the place which told of human life.

I tried to keep my eyes steady, though my heart was beating like a fanner. The men were of the same light colour and slimness as those I had seen on the edge of the mist in Clearwater Glen. Indeed, they were not unlike Shalah, except that he was bigger than the most of them. I was not learned in Indian ways, but a glance told me that these folk never came out of the Tidewater, and were

no Cherokees of the hills or Tuscaroras from the
Carolinas. They were a new race from the west
or the north, the new race which had so long been
perplexing us. Somewhere among them was the
brain which had planned for the Tidewater a
sudden destruction.

Shalah slipped noiselessly backward, and I followed him down the scree slope, across the ravine,
and then with infinite caution through the sparse
woods till we had put a wide shoulder of hill between us and the enemy. After that we started
running, such a pace as made the rush back to the
Rappahannock seem an easy saunter. Shalah
would avoid short-cuts for no reason that I could
see, and make long circuits in places where I had
to go on hands and feet. I was weary before we
set out, and soon I began to totter like a drunken
man. The Indian's arm pulled me up countless
times, and his face, usually so calm, was now sharp
with care. "You cannot fail here, brother," he
would say. "On our speed hang the lives of all."
That put me on my mettle, for it was Elspeth's
safety I now strove for, and the thought gave life
to my leaden limbs. Every minute the air grew
heavier, and the sky darker, so that when about
five in the afternoon we passed the Gap and
struggled up the last hill to the stockade, it seemed
as if night had already fallen.

Elspeth and Ringan were there, and the two
trappers had just returned. I could do nothing
but pant on the ground, but Shalah cried out for
news of Grey. He heard that he had gone into

the woods with his musket two hours past. At this he flung up his hands with a motion of despair. "We cannot wait," he said to Ringan. "Close the gate and put every man to his post, for the danger is at hand."

Ringan gave his orders. The big log gate was barred, the fire trampled out, and we waited in that thunderous darkness. A long draught of cold water had revived me, and I could think clearly of Elspeth. Her bower was in the safest part of the stockade, but she would not stay there. I could see terror in her eyes, but she gave no sign of it. She made ready our supper of cold meat as if she had no other thought in the world.

Waiting on an attack is a hard trial for mortal nerves. I am not ashamed to confess that in those minutes my courage was little to boast of. I envied Ringan his ease, and Bertrand his light cheerfulness, and Donaldson his unshaken gravity, and especially I envied Shalah his god-like calm. But most of all I envied Elspeth the courage which could know desperate fear and never show it. Most likely I did myself some wrong. Most likely my own face was firm enough, but, if it were, 'twas a poor clue to the brain behind it. I fell to wondering about Grey still travelling in the woods. Was there any hope for him ? Was there hope, indeed, for any one of us penned in a wooden palisade fifty miles from aid, a handful against an army ?

Presently in the lowering silence came the scream of a hawk.

An uncommon sound, half croak, half cry, which only hill dwellers know, but 'tis an eerie noise in the wilderness. It came again, less near, and a third time from a great distance. I thought it queer, for a hawk does not scream twice in the same hour. I looked at Shalah, who stood by the gate, every sinew in his body taut with expectation. He caught my eye.

" That hawk never flew on wings," he said.

Then an owl hooted, and from near at hand came the cough of a deer. The thicket was alive with life, which mimicked the wild things of the woods.

Then came a sound which drowned all others. From the inky sky descended a jagged line of light, and in the same second the crash of the thunder broke. Never have I seen such a storm. Down in the Tidewater we had thunderstorms in plenty during the summer-time, but they growled and passed and scarce ruffled the even blue of the sky. But here it looked as if we had found the home of the lightnings, where all the thunderbolts were forged. It blazed around us like a steady fire. By a miracle the palisade was not struck, but I heard a rending and splintering in the forest where tall trees had met their doom. The noise deafened me, and confused my senses. Out of the loophole I could see the glade that sloped down to the Gap, and it was as bright as if it had been high noonday. The clumps of fern and grass stood out yellow and staring against the inky background of the trees. I remember

I noted a rabbit run confusedly into the open, and then at a fresh flare of lightning scamper back.

Something was crouching and shivering at my side. I found it was Elspeth, whose courage was no match for the terrors of the heavens. She snuggled against me for companionship, and hid her face in the sleeve of my coat.

Suddenly came a cry from Shalah on my left. He pointed his hand to the glade, and in it I saw a man running. A new burst of light sprang up, for some dry tindery creepers had caught fire, and were blazing to heaven. It lit a stumbling figure, which I saw was Grey, and behind him was a lithe Indian running on his trail.

" Open the gate," I cried, and I got my musket in the loophole.

The fugitive was all but spent. He ran, bowed almost to the ground, with a wild back glance ever and again over his shoulder. His pursuer gained on him with great strides, and in his hand he carried a bare knife. I dared not shoot, for Grey was between me and his enemy.

'Twas as well I could not, for otherwise Grey would never have reached us alive. We cried to him to swerve, and the sound of our voices brought up that last flicker of hope which waits till the end in every man. He seemed actually to gain a yard, and now he was near enough for us to see his white face and staring eyes. Then he stumbled, and the man with the knife was almost on him. But he found his feet again, and swerved like a hunted hare in one desperate bound. This gave me my chance, my musket cracked, and the Indian pitched quietly to the ground. The knife flew out of his hand and almost touched Grey's heel.

With the sound Shalah had leaped from the gate, picked up Grey like a child, and in a second had him inside the palisade and the bars down. He was none too soon, for as his pursuer fell a flight of arrows broke from the thicket, and had I shot earlier Grey had died of them. As it was they were too late. The bowmen rushed into the glade, and five muskets from our side took toll of them. My last vision was of leaping yellow devils capering from among blazing trees.

Then without warning it was dark again, and from the skies fell a deluge of rain. In a minute the burning creepers were quenched, and the whole world was one pit of ink, with the roar as of a thousand torrents about our ears. As the vividness of the lightning, so was the weight of the rain. Ringan cried to us to stand to our places, for now was the likely occasion for attack ; but no human being could have fought in such weather. Indeed, we could not hear him, and he had to stagger round and shout his command into each several ear. The might of the deluge almost pressed me to the earth. I carried Elspeth into her bower, but the roof of branches was speedily beaten down, and it was no better than a peat bog.

That overwhelming storm lasted for maybe a quarter of an hour, and then it stopped as suddenly as it came. Inside the palisade the ground swam like a loch, and from the hill-side came the rumour of a thousand swollen streams. That, with the heavy drip of laden branches, made sound enough, but after the thunder and the downpour it seemed silence itself. Presently, when I looked up I saw that the black wrack was clearing from the sky, and through a gap there shone a watery star.

Ringan took stock of our defences, and doled out to each a portion of sodden meat. Grey had found his breath by this time, and had got a spare musket, for his own had been left in the woods. Elspeth had had her wits sorely jangled by the storm, and in the revulsion was on the brink of tears. She was very tender towards Grey's condition, and the sight gave me no jealousy, for in that tense hour all things were forgotten but life and death. Donaldson, at Ringan's bidding, saw to the feeding of the horses as if he were in his own stable on the Rappahannock. It takes all sorts of men to make a world, but I thought at the time that for this business the steel nerves of the Borderer were worth many quicker brains and more alert spirits.

The hours marched sombrely towards midnight, while we stayed every man by his post. I asked Shalah if the enemy had gone, and he shook his head. He had the sense of a wild animal to detect danger in the forest when the eye and ear gave no proof. He stood like a stag, sniffing the night air, and peering with his deep eyes into the gloom. Fortunately, though the moon was all but full, the sky was so overcast that only the faintest yellow glow broke into the darkness of the hill-tops.

It must have been an hour after midnight when we got our next warning of the enemy. Suddenly a firebrand leaped from farther up the hill, and flew in a wide curve into the middle of the stockade. It fell on the partition between the horses and ourselves and hung crackling there. A shower of arrows followed it, which missed us, for we were close to the edges of the palisade. But the sputtering torch was a danger, for presently it would show our position ; so Bertrand very gallantly pulled it down, stamped it out, and got back to his post unscathed.

Yet the firebrand had done its work, for it had showed the savages where the horses stood picketed. Another followed, lighting in their very midst, and setting them plunging at their ropes.

I heard Ringan curse deeply, for we had not thought of this stratagem. And the next second I became aware that there was some one among the horses. At first I thought that the palisade had been stormed, and then I heard a soft voice which was no Indian's. Heedless of orders, I flung myself at the rough gate, and in a trice was beside the voice.

Elspeth was busy among the startled beasts. She had a passion for horses, and had, as we say, the " cool " hand with them, for she would soothe a frightened stallion by rubbing his nose and whispering in his ear. By the time I got to her she had stamped out the torch, and was stroking Grey's mare, which was the worst scared. Her own fear had gone, and in that place of plunging hooves and tossing manes she was as calm as in a summer garden. "Let me be, Andrew," she said. "I am better at this business than you."

She had the courage of a lion, but 'twas a wild courage, without foresight. Another firebrand came circling through the darkness, and broke on the head of Donaldson's pony. I caught the girl and swung her off her feet into safety. And then on the heels of the torch came a flight of arrows, fired from near at hand.

By the mercy of God she was unharmed. I had one through the sleeve of my coat, but none reached her. One took a horse in the neck, and the poor creature screamed pitifully. Presently there was a wild confusion of maddened beasts, with the torch burning on the ground and lighting the whole place for the enemy. I had Elspeth in my arms, and was carrying her to the gate, when over the palisade I saw yellow limbs and fierce faces.

They saw it too—Ringan and the rest—and it did not need his cry to keep our posts to tell us the right course. The inner palisade which shut off the horses must now be our line of defence, and the poor beasts must be left to their fate. But Elspeth and I had still to get inside it.

Her ankle had caught in a picket rope, which in another second would have wrenched it cruelly, had I not slashed it free with my knife. This sent the horse belonging to it in wild career across

the corral, and I think 'twas that interruption
which saved our lives. It held back the savages
for an instant of time, and prevented them blocking
our escape. It all took place in the flutter of an
eyelid, though it takes long in the telling. I pushed
Elspeth through the door, and with all my strength
tore at the bars.

But they would not move. Perhaps the rain
had swollen the logs, and they had jammed too
tightly to let the bar slide in the groove. So I
found myself in that gate, the mad horses and the
savages before me, and my friends at my back,
with only my arm to hold the post.

I had my musket and my two pistols—three
shots, for there would be no time to reload. A
yellow shadow slipped below a horse's belly, and
there came the cry of an animal's agony. Then
another and another, and yet more. But no one
came near me in the gateway. I could not see
anything to shoot at—only lithe shades and
mottled shadows, for the torch lay on the wet
ground, and was sputtering to its end. The
moaning of the horses maddened me, and I sent
a bullet through the head of my own poor beast,
which was writhing horribly. Elspeth's horse got
the contents of my second pistol.

And then it seemed that the raiders had gone.
There was one bit of the far palisade which was
outlined for me dimly against a gap in the trees.
I saw a figure on it, and whipped my musket to
my shoulder. Something flung up its arms and
toppled back among the dying beasts.

Then a hand—Donaldson's, I think—clutched me and pulled me back. With a great effort the bars were brought down, and I found myself beside Elspeth. All her fortitude had gone now, and she was sobbing like a child.

Gradually the moaning of the horses ceased, and the whole world seemed cold and silent as a stone. We stood our watch till a wan sunrise struggled up the hill-side.

CHAPTER XXII

HOW A FOOL MUST GO HIS OWN ROAD

IT was a sorry party that looked at each other in the first light of dawn.

Our eyes were hollow with suspense, and all but Shalah had the hunted look of men caught in a trap. Not till the sun had got above the tree-tops did we venture to leave our posts and think of food. It was now that Elspeth's spirit showed supreme. The courage of that pale girl put us all to the blush. She alone carried her head high and forced an air of cheerfulness. She lit the fire with Donaldson's help, and broiled some deer's flesh for our breakfast, and whistled gently as she wrought, bringing into our wild business a breath of the orderly comfort of home. I had seen her in silk and lace, a queen among the gallants, but she never looked so fair as on that misty morning, her hair straying over her brow, her plain kirtle soiled and sodden, but her eyes bright with her young courage.

During the last hours of that dark vigil my mind had been torn with cares. If we escaped

the perils of the night, I asked myself, what then ?
Here were the seven of us, pinned in a hill-fort,
with no help within fifty miles, and one of · the
seven a woman ! I judged that the Indian force
was large, and there was always the mighty army
waiting farther south in that shelf of the hills.
If they sought to take us, it must be a matter of
a day or two at the most till they succeeded. If
they only played with us—which is the cruel
Indian way—we might resist a little, but starvation would beat us down. Where were we to
get food, with the forests full of our subtle enemies ?
To sit still would mean to wait upon death, and
the waiting would not be long.

There was the chance, to be sure, that the
Indians would be drawn off in the advance towards
the east. But here came in a worse anxiety.
I had come to get news to warn the Tidewater.
That news I had got. The mighty gathering
which Shalah's eyes and mine had beheld in that
upland glen was the peril we had foreseen. What
good were easy victories over raiding Cherokees
when this deadly host waited on the leash ? I
had no doubt that the Cherokees were now broken.
Stafford county would be full of Nicholson's
militia, and Lawrence's strong hand lay on the
line of the Borders. But what availed it ? While
Virginia was flattering herself that she had re-
pelled the savages, and the Rappahannock men
were notching their muskets with the tale of the
dead, a wave was gathering to sweep down the
Pamunkey or the James, and break on the walls

of James Town. I did not think that Nicholson,
even forewarned and prepared, could stem the
torrent ; and if it caught him unawares the proud
Tidewater would break like a rotten reed.

I had been sent to scout. Was I to be false
to the word I had given, and let any risk to myself
or others deter me from taking back the news ?
The Indian army tarried ; why, I did not know—
perhaps some mad whim of their soothsayers,
perhaps the device of a wise general ; but at any
rate they tarried. If a war party could spend a
night in baiting us and slaying our horses, there
could be no very instant orders for the road. If
this were so, a bold man might yet reach the Border line. At that moment it seemed to me a madman's errand. Even if I slipped past the watchers
in the woods and the glens, the land between would
be strewn with fragments of the Cherokee host,
and I had not the Indian craft. But it was very
seriously borne in upon me that 'twas my duty
to try. God might prosper a bold stroke, and in
any case I should be true to my trust.

But what of Elspeth ? The thought of leaving her was pure torment. In our hideous peril
'twas scarcely to be endured that one should go.
I told myself that if I reached the Border I could
get help, but my heart warned me that I lied.
My news would leave no time there for riding
hillward to rescue a rash adventure. We were
beyond the pale, and must face the consequences.
That we all had known and reckoned with, but
we had not counted that our risk would be shared

by a woman. Ah! that luckless ride of Elspeth's! But for that foolish whim she would
be safe now in the cool house at Middle Plantation, with a ship to take her to safety if the worst
befell. And now of all the King's subjects in
that hour we were the most ill-fated, islanded on
a sand heap with the tide of savage war hourly
eating into our crazy shelter.

Before the daylight came, as I stood with my
cheek to my musket, I had come to a resolution.
In a tangle of duties a man must seize the solitary
clear one, and there could be no doubt of what
mine was. I must try for the Tidewater, and I
must try alone. Shalah had the best chance to
get through, but without Shalah the stockade was
no sort of refuge. Ringan was wiser and stronger
than me, but I thought I had more hill-craft,
and, besides, the duty was mine, not his. Grey
had no knowledge of the wilds, and Donaldson
and Bertrand could not handle the news as it
should be handled, in the unlikely event of their
getting through alive. No, there were no two
ways of it. I must make the effort, though in
that leaden hour of weariness and cold it seemed
as if my death-knell were ringing.

Morn showed a grey world, strewn with the
havoc of the storm. The eagles were already
busy among the dead horses, and our first job
was to bury the poor beasts. Just outside the
stockade we dug as best we could a shallow trench,
while the muskets of the others kept watch over
us. There we laid also the body of the man I had

shot in the night. He was a young savage, naked to the waist, and curiously tattooed on the forehead with the device of what seemed to be a rising or setting sun. I observed that Shalah looked closely at this, and that his face wore an unusual excitement. He said something in his own tongue, and, when the trench was dug, laid the dead man in it so that his head pointed westwards.

We wrought in a dogged silence, and Elspeth's cheery whistling was the only sound in that sullen morning. It fairly broke my heart. She was whistling the old tune of "Leezie Lindsay," a merry lilt with the hill wind and the heather in it. The bravery of the poor child was the hardest thing of all to bear when I knew that in a few hours' time the end might come. The others were only weary and dishevelled and ill at ease, but on me seemed to have fallen the burden of the cares of the whole earth.

Shalah had disappeared for a little, and came back with the word that the near forests were empty. So I summoned a council, and talked as we breakfasted.

I had looked into the matter of the food, and found that we had sufficient for three days. We had boucanned a quantity of deer's flesh two days before, and this, with the fruit of yesterday's trapping, made a fair stock in our larder.

Then I announced my plan. "I am going to try to reach Lawrence," I said.

No one spoke. Shalah lifted his head, and looked at me gravely.

" Does any man object ? " I asked sharply,
for my temper was all of an edge.

" Your throat will be cut in the first mile,"
said Donaldson gruffly.

" Maybe it will, but maybe not. At any rate,
I can try. You have not heard what Shalah and I
found in the hills yesterday. Twelve miles south
there is a glen with a plateau at its head, and
that plateau is as full of Indians as a beehive.
Ay, Ringan, you and Lawrence were right. The
Cherokees are the least of the trouble. There's a
great army come out of the West, men that you
and I never saw the like of before, and they are
waiting till the Cherokees have drawn the fire of
the Borderers, and then they will bring hell to
the Tidewater. You and I know that there's
some sort of madman in command, a man that
quotes the Bible and speaks English ; but madman or not, he's a great general, and woe betide
Virginia if he gets among the manors. I was
sent to the hills to get news, and I've got it. Would
it not be the part of a coward to bide here and
make no effort to warn our friends ? "

" What good would a warning do ? " said
Ringan. " Even if you got through to Lawrence—which is not very likely—d'you think a
wheen Borderers in a fort will stay such an army ?
It would only mean that you lost your life on the
South Fork instead of in the hills, and there's
little comfort in that."

" It's not like you to give such counsel," I said
sadly. " A man cannot think whether his duty

will succeed as long as it's there for him to do it. Maybe my news would make all the differ. Maybe there would be time to get Nicholson's militia to the point of danger. God has queer ways of working, if we trust Him with honest hearts. Besides, a word on the Border would save the Tidewater folk, for there are ships on the James and the York to flee to if they hear in time. Let Virginia go down and be delivered over to painted savages, and some day soon we will win it back ; but we cannot bring life to the dead. I want to save the lowland manors from what befell the D'Aubignys on the Rapidan, and if I can only do that much I will be content. Will you counsel me, Ringan, to neglect my plain duty ? "

" I gave no counsel," said Ringan hurriedly. " I was only putting the common sense of it. It's for you to choose."

Here Grey broke in. " I protest against this craziness. Your first duty is to your comrades and to this lady. If you desert us we lose our best musket, and you have as little chance of reaching the Tidewater as the moon. Are you so madly enamoured of death, Mr. Garvald ? " He spoke in the old stiff tones of the man I had quarrelled with.

I turned to Shalah. " Is there any hope of getting to the South Fork ? "

He looked me very full in the face. " As much hope as a dove has who falls broken winged into an eyrie of falcons ! As much hope as the deer when the hunter's knife is at its throat ! Yet the dove may escape, and the deer may yet tread the forest. While a man draws breath there is hope, brother."

"Which I take to mean that the odds are a thousand against one," said Grey.

"Then it's my business to stake all on the one," I cried. "Man, don't you see my quandary? I hold a solemn trust which I have the means of fulfilling, and I'm bound to try. It's torture to me to leave you, but you will lose nothing. Three men could hold this place as well as six, if the Indians are not in earnest, and, if they are, a hundred would be too few. Your danger will be starvation, and I will be a mouth less to feed. If I get to the Border I will find help, for we cannot stay here for ever, and how d'you think we are to get Miss Blair by ourselves to the Rappahannock with every mile littered with fighting clans? I must go, or I will never have another moment's peace in life."

Grey was not convinced. "Send the Indian," he said.

"And leave the stockade defenceless," I cried. "It's because he stays behind that I dare to go. Without him we are all bairns in the dark."

"That's true, anyway," said Ringan, and fell to whittling a stick.

"For three days," I continued, "you have food enough, and if by the end of it you are not attacked you may safely go hunting for more. If nothing happens in a week's time you will know that I have failed, and you can send another messenger. Ringan would be the best."

" That can hardly be," he said, " because I'm coming with you now."

I could only stare blankly.

" Two's better than one for this kind of business, and I am no use here—only *fruges consumere natus*, as I learned from the Inveraray dominie. It's my concern as much as yours, for I brought you here, and I'm trysted with Lawrence to take back word. I'm loath to leave my friends, but my place is at your side, Andrew. So say no more about it."

I knew it was idle to protest. Ringan was as obstinate as a Spanish mule when he chose, and, besides, there was reason in what he said. Two were better than one both for speed in travel and for fighting if the need came, and though I had more woodcraft than him, he had ten times my wisdom. There was something about his matter-of-fact tone which took the enterprise out of the land of impossibilities into a more sober realm. I even began to dream of success.

But when I looked at Elspeth her eyes were so full of grief and care that my spirits sank again.

" Tell me," I cried, " that you think I am doing right. God knows it is hard to leave you, and I carry the sorest heart in Virginia. But you would not have me stay idle when my plain duty commands. Say that you bid me go, Elspeth."

" I bid you go," she said bravely, " and I will pray God to keep you safe." But her eyes belied her voice, for they were swimming with tears. At that moment I got the conviction that I was more to her than a mere companion, that by some miracle I had won a place in that proud and loyal heart. It seemed a cruel stroke of fate that I should get this hope at the very moment when I was to leave her and go into the shadow of death.

But that was no hour to think of love. I took every man apart and swore him, though there was little need, to stand by the girl at all costs.

To Grey I opened my inmost thoughts.

" You and I serve one mistress," I said, " and now I confide her to your care. All that I would have done I am assured you will do. My heart is easier when I know that you are by her side. Once we were foes, and since then we have been friends, and now you are the dearest friend on earth, for I leave you with all I cherish."

He flushed deeply and gave me his hand.

" Go in peace, sir," he said. " If God wills that we perish, my last act will be to assure an easy passage to heaven for her we worship. If we meet again, we meet as honourable rivals, and may that day come soon."

So with pistols in belt, and a supply of cartouches and some little food in our pockets, Ringan and I were enfolded in the silence of the woods.

CHAPTER XXIII

THE HORN OF DIARMAID SOUNDS

WE reached the Gap, and made slantwise across the farther hill. I did not dare to go down Clearwater Glen, and, besides, I was aiming for a point farther south than the Rappahannock. In my wanderings with Shalah I had got a pretty good notion of the lie of the mountains on their eastern side, and I had remarked a long ridge which flung itself like a cape far into the lowlands. If we could leave the hills by this, I thought we might strike the stream called the North Fork, which would bring us in time to the neighbourhood of Frew's dwelling. The ridges were our only safe path, for they were thickly overgrown with woods, and the Indian bands were less likely to choose them for a route. The danger was in the glens, where the trees were sparser and the broad stretches of meadow made better going for horses.

The movement of my legs made me pluck up heart. I was embarked at any rate in a venture, and had got rid of my desperate indecision. The two of us held close together, and chose the duskiest thickets, crawling belly-wise over the little clear patches and avoiding the crown of the ridge like the plague. The weather helped us, for the skies hung grey and low, with wisps of vapour curling among the trees. The glens were pits of mist, and my only guide was my recollection of what I had seen, and the easterly course of the streams.

By midday we had mounted to the crest of a long scarp which fell away in a narrow and broken promontory towards the plains. So far we had seen nothing to give us pause, and the only risk lay in some Indian finding and following our trail. We lay close in a scrubby wood, and rested for a little, while we ate some food. Everything around us dripped with moisture, and I could have wrung pints from my coat and breeches.

" Oh for the Dry Tortugas ! " Ringan sighed. " What I would give for a hot sun and the kindly winds o' the sea ! I thought I pined for the hills, Andrew, but I would not give a clean beach and a warm sou'-wester for all the mountains on earth."

Then again : " Yon's a fine lass," he would say.

I did not reply, for I had no heart to speak of what I had left behind.

" Cheer up, young one," he cried. " There was more lost at Flodden. A gentleman-adventurer must live by the hour, and it's surprising how Fortune favours them that trust her. There was a man I mind, in Breadalbane . . ." And here he would tell some tale of how light came out of black darkness for the trusting heart.

"Man, Ringan," I said, "I see your kindly purpose. But tell me, did ever you hear of such a tangle as ours being straightened out?"

"Why, yes," he said. "I've been in worse myself, and here I am. I have been in a cell at Cartagena, chained to a man that had died of the plague, with the gallows preparing for me at cock-crow. But in the night some friends o' mine came into the bay, and I had the solemn joy of stepping out of yon cell over the corp of the Almirante. I've been mad with fever, and jumped into the Palmas River among the alligators, and not one of them touched me, though I was swimming about crying that the water was burning oil. And then a lad in a boat gave me a clout on the head that knocked the daftness out of me, and in a week I was marching on my own deck, with my bonnet cocked like a king's captain. I've been set by my unfriends on a rock in the Florida Keys, with a keg of dirty water and a bunch of figs, and the sun like to melt my brains, and two bullet holes in my thigh. But I came out of the pickle, and lived to make the men that put me there sorry they had been born. Ay, and I've seen my grave dug, and my dead clothes ready, and in a week I was making napkins out of them. There's a wonderful kindness in Providence to mettled folk."

"Ay, Ringan, but that was only the risk of your own neck. I think I could endure that. But

was there ever another you liked far better than
yourself that you had to see in deadly peril ? "

" No. I'll be honest with you, there never was.
I grant you that's the hardest thing to thole. But
you'll keep a stiff lip even to that, seeing you are
the braver of the two of us."

At that I cried out in expostulation, but Ringan
was firm.

" Ay, the braver by far, and I'll say it again.
I'm a man of the dancing blood, with a rare appe-
tite for frays and forays. You are the sedate soul
that would be happier at home in the chimney
corner. And yet you are the most determined of
the lot of us, though you have no pleasure in it.
Why ? Just because you are the bravest. You
can force yourself to a job when flesh and spirit
cry out against it. I let no man alive cry down
my courage, but I say freely that it's not to be
evened with yours."

I was not feeling very courageous. As we sped
along the ridge in the afternoon I seemed to myself
like a midge lost in a monstrous net. The dank,
dripping trees and the misty hills seemed to muffle
and deaden the world. I could not believe that
they ever would end ; that anywhere there was a
clear sky and open country. And I had always
the feeling that in those banks of vapour lurked
deadly enemies who any moment might steal out
and encompass us.

But about four o'clock the weather lightened,
and from the cock's-comb on which we moved we
looked down into the lower glens. I saw that we

had left the main flanks of the range behind us,
and were now fairly on a cape which jutted out
beyond the other ridges. It behoved us now to
go warily, and where the thickets grew thin we
moved like hunters, in every hollow and crack
that could shelter a man. Ringan led, and led
well, for he had not stalked the red deer on the
braes of Breadalbane for nothing. But no sign of
life appeared in the green hollows on either hand,
neither in the meadow spaces nor by the creeks of
the growing streams. The world was dead silent ;
not even a bird showed in the whole firmament.

Lower and lower we went, till the end of the
ridge was before us, a slope which melted into the
river plains. A single shaft of bright sunshine
broke from the clouds behind us, and showed the
tumbled country of low downs and shallow vales
which stretched to the Tidewater border. I had a
momentary gleam of hope, as sudden and transient
as that ray of light. We were almost out of the
hills, and, that accomplished, we were most likely
free of the Indian forces that gathered there. I
had come to share the Rappahannock men's opinion about the Cherokees. If we could escape the
strange tribes from the west, I looked for no trouble
at the hands of those common raiders.

The thicket ended with the ridge, and there was
a quarter-mile of broken meadow before the forest
began. It was a queer place, that patch of green
grass set like an arena for an audience on the
mountain side. A fine stream ran through it, coming down the glen on our right, and falling after-

wards into a dark, woody ravine. I mistrusted the look of it, for there was no cover, and 'twas in full view of the whole flanks of the hills.

Ringan, too, was disturbed. " 'Twould be wiser like to wait for darkness before trying that bit," he said. " We'll be terrible kenspeckle to the gentry we ken of."

But I would not hear of delay. Now that we were all but out of the hills I was mad to get forward. I thought foolishly that every minute we delayed there we increased our peril, and I longed for the covering of the lowland forest. Besides, I thought that by using some of the crinkles in the meadow we could be sheltered from any eyes on the slopes.

Ringan poked his head out of the covert and took a long gaze. "The place seems empty enough, but I cannot like it. Have you your pistols handy, Andrew? I see what looks like an Indian track, and if we were to meet a brave or two, it would be a pity to let them betray us."

I looked at my pistols to see if the damp woods had spoiled the priming.

" Well, here's for fortune," said Ringan, and we scrambled off the ridge and plunged into the lush grasses of the meadow.

Had we kept our heads and crossed as prudently as we had made the morning's journey, all might have been well. But a madcap haste seemed to possess us. We tore through the herbage as if we had been running a race in the yard of a peaceful manor. The stream stayed us a little, for it could not be forded without a wetting, and I went in up to the waist. As we scrambled up the far bank some impulse made me turn my head.

There, coming down the water, was a band of Indians.

They were still some distance off, but they saw us, and put their horses to the gallop. I cried to Ringan to run for the shelter of the woods, for in the open we were at their mercy. He cast one glance over his shoulder, and set a pace which came near to foundering me.

We got what we wanted earlier than we had hoped. The woods in front rose in a high bluff, and down a little ravine a burn trickled. The sides were too steep and matted for horses to travel, and he who stood in the ravine had his back and flanks defended.

" Now for a fight, Andrew lad," cried Ringan, his eyes dancing. " Stick you to the pistols, and I'll show them something in the way of sword-play."

The Indians wheeled up to the edge of the ravine, and I saw to my joy that they did not carry bows. One had a musket, but it looked as if he had no powder left, for it swung idly on his back. They had tomahawks at their belts and long shining knives with deerhorn handles. I only got a glimpse of them, but 'twas enough to show me they were of that Western nation that I dreaded.

They were gone in an instant.

" That looks bad for us, Andrew," Ringan said. " If they had come down on us yelling for our scalps, we would have had a merry meeting. But they've either gone to bring their friends or they're trying to take us in the back. I'll guard the front, and you keep your eyes on the hinder parts, though a jackdaw could scarcely win over these craigs."

A sudden burst of sun came out, while Ringan and I waited uneasily. The great blue roll of mountain we had left was lit below the mist with a glory of emerald and gold. Ringan was whistling softly through his teeth, while I scanned the half moon of rock and matted vines which made our shelter. There was no sound in the air but the tap of a woodpecker and the trickling of the little runlets from the wet sides.

The mind in a close watch falls under a spell, so that while the senses are alert, the thoughts are apt to wander. As I have said before, I have the sharpest sight, and as I watched a point of rock it seemed to move ever so slightly. I rubbed my eyes and thought it fancy, and a sudden noise above made me turn my head. It was only a bird, and as I looked again at the rock it seemed as if a spray of vine had blown athwart it which was not there before. I gazed intently, and, following the spray into the shadow, I saw something liquid and mottled like a toad's skin. As I stared it flickered and shimmered. 'Twas only the light on a wet leaf, I told myself; but surely it had not been there before. A sudden suspicion seized me, and I lifted my pistol and fired.

There was a shudder in the thicket, and an Indian shot through the head, rolled into the burn.

At the sound I heard Ringan cry out, and there came a great war-whoop from the mouth of the ravine. I gave one look, and then turned to my own business, for as the dead man fell another leaped from the matted cliffs.

My second pistol missed fire. In crossing the stream I must have damped the priming.

What happened next is all confusion in my mind. I dodged the fall of the knife, and struck hard with my pistol butt at the uplifted arm. I felt no fear, only intense anger at my folly in not having looked better to my priming. But the shock of the man's charge upset me, and the next I knew of it we were wrestling on the ground.

I had his right arm by the wrist, but I was no match for him in suppleness, and in the position in which we lay I could not use the weight of my shoulders. The most I could do was to keep him from striking, and to effect that my strength was stretched to its uttermost. My eyes filmed with weariness, and my breath came in gasps, for, remember, I had been up all night, and that day had already travelled many miles. I remember yet the sickly smell of his greasy skin and the red hate of his eyes. As we struggled I could see Ringan holding the mouth of the ravine with his sword. One of his foes he had shot, and the best blade in the Five Seas was now engaged with three Indian knives. I heard his happy whistling, and a grunt now and then from a wounded foe. He had enough to do, and could give me no aid. And as I realized this I felt the grip of my arms growing slacker, and knew that in a second or two I should feel that long Indian steel.

I made a desperate effort, and swung round so that I got my left shoulder on his knife arm. That brought my right shoulder close to his mouth, and he bit me to the bone. The wound did me good, for it maddened me, and I got a knee loose, and forced it into his loins. For a moment I dreamed of victory, but I had not counted on the wiles of a savage. He lay quite limp for a second, and, as I relaxed my effort a little, seized the occasion to slip from beneath me and let me roll into the burn. The next instant he was above me, and I saw the knife against the sky.

I thought that all was over. He pushed back his hair from his eyes, and the steel quivered. And then something thrust between me and the point, there was a leap and a shudder, and I was gazing at emptiness.

I lay gazing, for I seemed bereft of wits. Then a voice cried, " Are you hurt, Andrew ? " and I got to my feet.

My enemy lay in the pool of the burn, with a hole through his throat from Ringan's sword. A little farther off lay the savage I had shot. At the mouth of the ravine lay three dead Indians. The last of the six must have fled.

Ringan had sheathed his blade, and was looking at me with a queer smile on his face.

" Yon was a merry bout, Andrew," he said, and his voice sounded very far away. Then he swayed into my arms, and I saw that his vest was dark with blood.

"What is it?" I cried in wild fear. "Are you hurt, Ringan?" I laid him on a bed of moss, and opened his shirt. In his breast was a gaping wound from which the bright blood was welling.

He lay with his eyes closed while I strove to stanch the flow. Then he choked, and as I raised his head there came a gush of blood from his lips.

"That man of yours . . ." he whispered. "I got his knife before he got my sword. . . . I doubt it went deep. . . ."

"O Ringan," I cried, "it's me that's to blame. You got it trying to save me. You're not going to leave me, Ringan?"

He was easier now, and the first torrent of blood had subsided. But his breath laboured, and there was pain in his eyes.

"I've got my call," he said faintly. "Who would have thought that Ninian Campbell would meet his death from an Indian shabble? They'll no believe it at Tortuga. Still and on. . . ."

I brought him water in my hat, and for a moment he breathed freely. He motioned me to put my ear close.

"You'll send word to the folk in Breadalbane. . . . Just say that I came by an honest end. . . . Cheer up, lad. You'll live to see happy days yet. . . . But keep mind of me, Andrew. . . . Man, I liked you well, and would have been blithe to keep you company a bit longer. . . ."

I was crying like a child. There was a little

gold charm on a cord round his neck, now dyed with his blood. He motioned me to look at it.

"Give it to the lass," he whispered. "I had once a lass like yon, and I aye wore it for her sake. I've had a roving life, with many ill deeds in it, but doubtless the Almighty will make allowances. Can you say a bit prayer, Andrew ? "

As well as I could, I repeated that Psalm I had said over the graves by the Rapidan. He looked at me with eyes as clear and honest as a child's.

" ' In death's dark vale I will fear no ill,' " he repeated after me. " That minds me of lang syne. I never feared muckle on earth, and I'll not begin now."

I saw that the end was very near. The pain had gone, and there was a queer innocence in his lean face. His eyes shut and opened again, and each time the light was dimmer.

Suddenly he lifted himself. "The Horn of Diarmaid has sounded," he cried, and dropped back in my arms.

That was the last word he spoke.

I watched by him till the dark fell, and long after. Then as the moon rose I bestirred myself, and looked for a place of burial. I would not have him lie in that narrow ravine, so I carried him into the meadow, and found a hole which some wild beast had deserted. Painfully and slowly with my knife I made it into a shallow grave, where I laid him, with some boulders above. Then I think I flung myself on the earth and wept my fill. I had lost my best of friends, and the ache of regret and loneliness was too bitter to bear. I asked for nothing better than to join him soon on the other side.

After a while I forced myself to rise. He had praised my courage that very day, and if I was to be true to him I must be true to my trust. I told myself that Ringan would never have countenanced this idle grief. I girt on his sword, and hung the gold charm round my neck. Then I took my bearings as well as I could, re-loaded my pistols, and marched into the woods, keeping to the course of the little river.

As I went I remember that always a little ahead I seemed to hear the merry lilt of Ringan's whistling.

CHAPTER XXIV

I SUFFER THE HEATHEN'S RAGE

AS I stumbled through the moonlit forest I heard Ringan's tunes ever crooning among the trees. First it was the old mad march of "Bundle and go," which the pipers play when the clans are rising. Then it changed to the lilt of "Colin's Cattle," which is an air that the fairies made, and sung in the ear of a shepherd who fell asleep in one of their holy places. And then it lost all mortal form, and became a thing as faint as the wind in the tree-tops or the humming of bees in clover. My weary legs stepped out to this wizard music, and the spell of it lulled my fevered thoughts into the dull patience of the desperate.

At an open space where I could see the sky I tried to take further bearings. I must move southeast by east, and in time I must come to Lawrence. I do not think I had any hope of getting there, for I knew that long ere this the man who escaped must have returned with others, and that now they would be hot on my trail. What could one lad do in a wide woodland against the cunningest trackers on earth ? But Ringan had praised my courage, and I could not fail him. I should go on till I died, and I did not think that would be very long. My pistols, re-loaded, pressed against my side, and Ringan's sword swung by my thigh. I was determined to make a good ending, since that was all now left to me. In that hour I had forgotten about everything—about the peril of Virginia, even about Elspeth and the others in the fort on the hill-top. There comes a time to every one when the world narrows for him to a strait alley, with Death at the end of it, and all his thoughts are fixed on that waiting enemy of mankind.

My senses were blunted, and I took no note of the noises of the forest. As I passed down a ravine a stone dropped behind me, but I did not pause to wonder why. A twig crackled on my left, but it did not disquiet me, and there was a rustling in the thicket which was not the breeze. I marked nothing, as I plodded on with vacant mind and eye. So when I tripped on a vine and fell, I was scarcely surprised when I found I could not rise. Men had sprung up silently around me, and I was pinned by many hands.

They trussed me with ropes, binding my hands cruelly behind my back, and swathing my legs till not a muscle could move. My pistols hung idle, and the ropes drove the hafts into my flesh. This is the end, thought I, and I did not even grieve at my impotence. My courage now was of the passive kind, not to act but to endure. Always I kept telling myself that I must be brave, for Ringan had praised my courage, and I had a conviction that nothing that man could do would shake me. Thanks be to God, my quick fancy was dulled, and I did not try to look into the future. I lived for the moment, and I was resolved that the moment should find me unmoved.

They carried me to where their horses were tied up in a glade, and presently we were galloping towards the hills, myself an inert bundle strapped across an Indian saddle. The pain of the motion was great, but I had a kind of grim comfort in bearing it. After a time I think my senses left me, and I slipped into a stupor, from which I woke with a fiery ache at every joint and eyes distended with a blinding heat. Some one tossed me on the ground, where I lay with my cheek in a cool, wet patch of earth. Then I felt my bonds being unloosed, and a strong arm pulled me to my feet. When it let go I dropped again, and not till many hands had raised me and set me on a log could I look round at my whereabouts.

I was in a crook of a hill glen, lit with a great radiance of moonlight. Fires dotted the flat, and Indian tents, and there seemed to me hundreds of savages crowding in on me. I do not suppose that I showed any fear, for my bodily weakness had made me as impassive as any Indian.

Presently a voice spoke to me, but I could not understand the words. I shook my head feebly, and another spoke. This time I knew that the tongue was Cherokee, a speech I could recognize but could not follow. Again I shook my head, and a third took up the parable. This one spoke the Powhatan language, which I knew, and I replied in the same tongue.

There was a tall man wearing in his hair a single great feather, whom I took to be the chief. He spoke to me through the interpreter, and asked me whence I came.

I told him I was a hunter who had strayed in the hills. He asked where the other was.

"He is dead," I said, "dead of your knives. But five of your braves atoned for him."

"You speak truth," he said gravely. "But the Children of the West Wind do not suffer the death of their sons to go unrewarded. For each one of the five, three Palefaces shall eat the dust in the day of our triumph."

"Be it so," said I stoutly, though I felt a dreadful nausea coming over me. I was determined to keep my head high, if only my frail body would not fail me.

"The Sons of the West Wind," he spoke again, "have need of warriors. You can atone for the slaughter you have caused, and the blood feud will be forgotten. In the space of five suns we shall sweep the Palefaces into the sea, and rule all the land to the Eastern waters. My brother is a man of his hands, and valour is dear to the heart of Onotawah. If he casts in his lot with the Children of the West Wind a wigwam shall be his, and a daughter of our race to wife, and six of our young men shall follow his commands. Will my

brother march with us against those whom God
has delivered to us for our prey ? "

" Does the eagle make terms with the kite ? " I
asked, " and fly with them to raid his own eyrie ?
Yes, I will join with you, and march with you till
I have delivered you to, perhaps, a score of the
warriors of my own people. Then I will aid them
in making carrion of you."

Heaven knows what wrought on me to speak
like this, I, a poor, broken fellow, face to face
with a hundred men-at-arms. I think my mind
had forsaken me altogether, and I spoke like a
drunken man with a tongue not my own. I had
only the one idea in my foolish head—to be true
to Ringan, and to meet the death of which I was
assured with an unflinching face. Yet perhaps my
very madness was the course of discretion. You
cannot move an Indian by pity, and he will show
mercy only to one who, like a gamecock, asks
nothing less.

The chief heard me gravely, and spoke to the
others. One cried out something in a savage
voice, and for a moment a fierce argument was
raised, which the chief settled with uplifted hand.

" My brother speaks bold words," he said.
" The spirits of his fathers cry out for the companionship of such a hero. When the wrongs
of our race have been avenged, I wish him good
hunting in the Kingdom of the Sunset."

They took me and stripped me mother naked.
Has any man who reads this tale ever faced an
enemy in his bare feet ? If so, he will know that

the heart of man is more in his boots than philoso-
phers wot of. Without them he feels lost and
unprepared, and the edge gone from his spirit.
But without his clothes he is in a far worse case.
The winds of heaven play round his nakedness ;
every thorn and twig is his assailant, and the whole
of him seems a mark for the arrows of his foes.
That stripping was the thing that brought me to
my senses. I recognized that I was to be the
subject of those hellish tortures which the Indians
use, the tales of which are on every Borderer's
lips.

And yet I did not recognize it fully, or my
courage must have left me then and there. My
imagination was still limping, and I foresaw only
a death of pain, not the horrid incidents of its
preparation. Death I could face, and I summoned
up every shred of my courage. Ringan's voice
was still in my ear, his airy songs still sang themselves in my brain. I would not shame him, but
oh ! how I envied him lying, all troubles past, in
his quiet grave !

The night was mild, and the yellow radiance
of the moon seemed almost warmth-giving. I
sat on that log in a sort of stupor, watching my
enemies preparing my entertainment. One thing
I noted, that there were no women in the camp.
I remembered that I had heard that the most
devilish tortures were those which the squaws
devised, and that the Indian men were apt to be
quicker and more merciful in their murderings.

Then I was lifted up and carried to a flat space

beside the stream, where the trunk of a young pine had been set upright in the ground. A man, waving a knife, and singing a wild song, danced towards me. He seized me by the hair, and I actually rejoiced, for I knew that the pain of scalping would make me oblivious of all else. But he only drew the sharp point of the knife in a circle round my head, scarce breaking the skin.

I had grace given me to keep a stout face, mainly because I was relieved that this was to be my fate. He put the knife back in his girdle, and others laid hold on me.

They smeared my lower limbs with some kind of grease which smelt of resin. One savage who had picked up a brand from one of the little fires dropped some of the stuff on it, and it crackled merrily. He grinned at me—a slow, diabolical grin.

They lashed me to the stake with ropes of green vine. Then they piled dry hay a foot deep around me, and laid above it wood and green branches. To make the fuel still greener, they poured water on it. At the moment I did not see the object of these preparations, but now I can understand it. The dry hay would serve to burn my legs, which had already been anointed with the inflammable grease. So I should suffer a gradual torture, for it would be long ere the flames reached a vital part. I think they erred, for they assumed that I had the body of an Indian, which does not perish till a blow is struck at its heart; whereas I am confident that any white man would be dead of the anguish long ere the fire had passed beyond his knees.

I think that was the most awful moment of my life. Indeed I could not have endured it had not my mind been drugged and my body stupid with fatigue. Men have often asked me what were my thoughts in that hour, while the faggots were laid about my feet. I cannot tell, for I have no very clear memory. The Power which does not break the bruised reed tempered the storm to my frailty. I could not envisage the future, and so was mercifully enabled to look only to the moment. I knew that pain was coming ; but I was already in pain, and the sick man does not trouble himself about degrees of suffering. Death, too, was coming ; but for that I had been long ready. The hardest thing that man can do is to endure, but this was to me no passive endurance ; it was an active struggle to show a fortitude worthy of the gallant dead.

So I must suppose that I hung there in my bonds with a motionless face and a mouth which gave out no cry. They brought the faggots, and poured on water, and I did not look their way. Some score of braves began a war dance, circling round me, waving their tomahawks, and singing their wild chants. For me they did not break the moonlit silence. I was hearing other sounds and seeing far other sights. An old sad song of Ringan's was in my ears, something about an exile who cried out in France for the red heather and the salt winds of the Isles.

"*Nevermore the deep fern,*" it ran, "*or the bell of the dun deer, for my castle is wind-blown sands, and my homelands are a stranger's.*" And the air brought back in a flash my own little house on the grey hill-sides of Douglasdale, the cluck of hens about the doors on a hot summer morn, the crying of plovers in the windy Aprils, the smell of peat-smoke when the snow drifted over Cairntable. Home-sickness has never been my failing, but all at once I had a vision of my own land, the cradle of my race, well-beloved and unforgotten over the leagues of sea. Somehow the thought strengthened me. I had now something besides the thought of Ringan to keep my heart firm. If all hell laid hold on me, I must stand fast for the honour of my own folk.

The edge of the pile was lit, and the flames crackled through the hay below the faggots. The smoke rose in clouds, and made me sneeze. Suddenly there came a desperate tickling in my scalp where the knife had pricked. Little things began to tease me, notably the ache of my swollen wrists, and the intolerable cramp in my legs.

Then came a sharp burst of pain as a tongue of flame licked on my anointed ankles. Anguish like hell-fire ran through my frame. I think I would have cried out if my tongue had had the power. Suddenly I envisaged the dreadful death which was coming. All was wiped from my mind, all thought of Ringan, and home, and honour ; everything but this awful fear. Happily the smoke hid my face, which must have been distraught with panic. The seconds seemed endless. I prayed that unconsciousness would come. I prayed for death, I prayed for respite. I was mad with the furious madness of a tortured animal, and the immortal soul had fled from me and left only a husk of pitiful and shrinking flesh.

Suddenly there came a lull. A dozen buckets of water were flung on the pile, and the flames fell to smouldering ashes. The smoke thinned, and I saw the circle of my tormentors.

The chief spoke, and asked me if my purpose still held.

With the cool shock of the water one moment of bodily comfort returned to me, and with it a faint revival of my spirit. But it was of no set intention that I answered as I did. My bones were molten with fright, and I had not one ounce of bravery in me. Something not myself took hold on me, and spoke for me. Ringan's tunes, a brisk one this time, lilted in my ear.

I could not believe my own voice. But I rejoice to say that my reply was to consign every Indian in America to the devil.

I shook with fear when I had spoken. I looked to see them bring dry fuel and light the pile again. But I had played a wiser part than I knew. The chief gave an order, the faggots were cleared, my bonds were cut, and I was led away from the stake.

The pain of my cramped and scorched limbs was horrible, but I had just enough sense left to shut my teeth and make no sound.

The chief looked at me long and calmly as I drooped before him, for there was no power in my legs. He was an eagle-faced savage, with the most grave and searching eyes.

" Sleep, brother," he said. " At dawn we will take further counsel."

I forced some kind of lightness into my voice. " Sleep will be grateful," I said, " for I have come many miles this day, and the welcome I have got this evening has been too warm for a weary man."

The Indian nodded. The jest was after his own taste.

I was carried to a teepee and shown a couch of dry fern. A young man rubbed some oil on my scorched legs, which relieved the pain of them. But no pain on earth could have kept me awake. I did not glide but pitched headforemost into sleep.

CHAPTER XXV

EVENTS ON THE HILL-SIDE

M Y body was too sore to suffer me to sleep
dreamlessly, but my dreams were pleasant.
I thought I was in a sunny place with Elspeth,
and that she had braided a coronet of wild flowers
for her hair. They were simple flowers, such as
I had known in childhood and had not found
in Virginia—yarrow, and queen of the meadow,
and bluebells, and the little eyebright. A great
peace filled me, and Ringan came presently to us
and spoke in his old happy speech. 'Twas to the
accompaniment of Elspeth's merry laughter that
I wakened, to find myself in a dark, strange-
smelling place, with a buffalo robe laid over me,
and no stitch of clothing on my frame.

That wakening was bitter indeed. I opened
my eyes to another day of pain and peril, with
no hope of deliverance. For usual I am one of
those who rise with a glad heart and a great zest
for whatever the light may bring. Now, as I moved
my limbs, I found aches everywhere, and but
little strength in my bones. Slowly the events

of the last day came back to me—the journey
in the dripping woods, the fight in the ravine, the
death of my comrade, the long horror of the hours
of torture. No man can be a hero at such an
awakening. I had not the courage of a chicken
in my soul, and could have wept with weakness
and terror.

I felt my body over, and made out that I had
taken no very desperate hurt. My joints were
swollen with the bonds, and every sinew seemed as
stiff as wire. The skin had been scorched on my
shins and feet, and was peeling off in patches,
but the ointment which had been rubbed on it
had taken the worst ache out of the wounds. I
tottered to my feet, and found that I could stand,
and even move slowly like an old man. My clothes
had been brought back and laid beside me, and
with much difficulty I got into them ; but I gave
up the effort to get my stockings and boots over
my scorched legs. My pistols, too, had been
restored, and Ringan's sword, and the gold amulet
he had entrusted to me. Somehow, in the handling
of me, my store of cartouches had disappeared
from my pockets. My pistols were loaded and
ready for use, but that was the extent of my defences, for I was no more good with Ringan's sword
than with an Indian bow.

A young lad brought me some maize porridge
and a skin of water. I could eat little of the food,
but I drank the water to the last drop, for my
throat was as dry as the nether pit. After that I
lay down on my couch again, for it seemed to me

that I would need to treasure every atom of my strength. The meal had put a little heart in me—heart enough to wait dismally on the next happening.

Presently the chief whom they called Onotawah stood at the tent door, and with him a man who spoke the Powhatan tongue.

" Greeting, brother," he said.

" Greeting," I answered, in the stoutest tone I could muster.

"I come from the council of the young men, where the blood of our kin cries for the avenger. The Sons of the West Wind have seen the courage of the stranger, and would give him the right of combat as a free man and a brave. Is my brother ready to meet our young men in battle ? "

I was about as fit to fight as an old horse to leap a fence, but I had the wit to see that my only hope lay in a bold front. At any rate, a clean death in battle was better than burning, and my despair was too deep to let me quibble about the manner of leaving this world.

" You see my condition," I said. " I am somewhat broken with travel and wounds, but, such as I am, I am willing to meet your warriors. Send them one at a time or in battalions, and I am ready for them."

It was childish brag, but I think I must have delivered it with some spirit, for I saw approbation in his eye.

" When we fight, we fight not as butchers but as men-at-arms," he said. " The brother of one of the dead will take on himself the cause of our tribe. If he slay you, our honour is avenged. If he be slain, we save you alive, and carry you with us as we march to the rising sun."

"I am content," I said, though I was very little content. What earthly chance stood I against a lithe young brave, accustomed from his childhood to war? I thought of a duel hand-to-hand with knives or tomahawks, for I could not believe that I would be allowed to keep my pistols. It was a very faint-hearted combatant who rose and staggered after Onotawah into the clear morning. The cloudy weather had gone, and the glen where we lay was filled with sun and bright colours Even in my misery I saw the fairness of the spec-tacle, and the cool plunge of the stream was grate-ful to my throbbing eyes.

The whole clan was waiting, a hundred warriors as tall and clean-limbed as any captain could desire. I bore no ill-will to my captors; indeed, I viewed them with a respect I had never felt for Indians before. They were so free in their walk, so slim and upstanding, so hawklike in eye and feature, and withal so grave, that I could not but admire them. If the Tidewater was to perish, 'twould be at the hands of no unworthy foes.

A man stood out from the others, a tall savage with a hard face, who looked at me with eyes of hate. I recognized my opponent, whom the chief called by some name like Mayoga.

Before us on the hill-side across the stream was a wood, with its limits cut as clear on the meadow as a coppice in a nobleman's park. 'Twas maybe half a mile long as it stretched up the slope, and about the same at its greatest width. The shape was like a stout bean with a hollow on one side, and down the middle ran the gorge of a mountain stream.

Onotawah pointed to the wood. "Hearken, brother, to the customs of our race in such combats. In that thicket the twain of you fight. Mayoga will enter at one end and you at the other, and once among the trees it is his business to slay you as he pleases and as he can."

"What are the weapons?" I asked.

"What you please. You have a sword and your little guns."

Mayoga laughed loud. "My bow is sufficient," he cried. "See, I leave knife and tomahawk behind," and he cast them on the grass.

Not to be outdone, I took off my sword, though that was more an encumbrance than a weapon.

"I have but the two shots," I said.

"Then I will take but the two arrows," cried my opponent, shaking the rest out of his quiver; and at this there was a murmur of applause. There were some notions of decency among these Western Indians.

I bade him take a quiverful. "You will need them," said I, looking as truculent as my chicken heart would permit me.

They took me to the eastern side of the wood, and there we waited for the signal, which was a musket shot, telling me that Mayoga was ready to enter at the opposite end. My companions were friendly enough, and seemed to look on the duel as a kind of sport. I could not understand their tongue, but I fancy that they wagered among themselves on the issue, if, indeed, that was in doubt, or, at any rate, on the time before I should fall. They had forgotten that they had tortured me the night before, and one clapped me on the shoulder and seemed to encourage me. Another pointed to my raw shins, and wound some kind of soft healing fibre round my feet and ankles. I did my best to keep a stout face, and when the shot came, I waved my hand to them and plunged boldly into the leafy darkness.

But out of the presence of men my courage departed, and I became the prey of dismal fear. How was I, with my babyish woodcraft, to contend for a moment against an Indian who was as subtle and velvet-footed as a wild beast ? The wood was mostly of great oaks and chestnuts, with a dense scrub of vines and undergrowth, and in the steepest parts of the hill-side many mossgrown rocks. I found every movement painful in that rough and matted place. For one thing, I made an unholy noise. My tender limbs shrank from every stone and twig, and again and again I rolled over with the pain of it. Sweat blinded my eyes, and the fatigues of yesterday made my breath labour like a foundered horse.

My first plan—if the instinct of blind terror can be called a plan—was to lie hid in some thick place and trust to getting the first shot at my

enemy when he found me. But I realized that
I could not do this. My broken nerves would
not suffer me to lie hidden. Better the torture
of movement than such terrible patience. So I
groped my way on, starting at every movement
in the thicket. Once I roused a deer, which broke
off in front of me towards my adversary. That
would tell him my whereabouts, I thought, and
for some time I lay still with a palpitating heart.
But soon the silence resumed its sway, a death-
like silence, with far off the faint tinkle of water.

By and by I reached the stream, the course
of which made an open space a few yards wide
in the trees. The sight of its cool foaming cur-
rent made me reckless. I dipped my face in it,
drank deep of it, and let it flow over my burning
legs. Then I scrambled up the other bank, and
entered my enemy's half of the wood. He had
missed a fine chance, I thought, in not killing
me by the water's edge; and this escape, and the
momentary refreshment of the stream, heartened
me enough to carry me some way into his territory.

The wood was thinner here, and the ground
less cumbered. I moved from tree to tree, crawling in the open bits, and scanning each circle of
green dusk before I moved. A red-bird fluttered
on my right, and I lay long watching its flight.
Something moved ahead of me, but 'twas only a
squirrel.

Then came a mocking laugh behind me. I
turned sharply, but saw nothing. Far up in
the branches there sounded the slow flap of an

owl's flight. Many noises succeeded, and suddenly came one which froze my blood—the harsh
scream of a hawk. My enemy was playing with
me, and calling the wild things to mock me.

I went on a little, and then turned up the hill
to where a clump of pines made a darker patch
in the woodland. All was quiet again, and my
eyes searched the dusk for the sign of human life.
Then suddenly I saw something which stiffened
me against a trunk.

Forty paces off in the dusk a face was looking
from behind a tree. It was to the west of me,
and was looking downhill towards a patch of
undergrowth. I noted the long feather, the black
forelock, the red skin of the forehead.

At the sight, for the first time the zest of the
pursuit filled me, and I forgot my pain. Had
I outwitted my wily foe, and by some miracle
stolen a march on him? I dared not believe
it; but yet, as I rubbed my eyes, I could not
doubt it. I had got my chance, and had taken
him unawares. The face still peered intently
downhill. I lifted a pistol, took careful aim,
and fired at the patch of red skin.

A thousand echoes rang through the wood.
The bullet had grazed the tree trunk, and the
face was gone. But whither? Did a dead man
lie behind the trunk, or had a wounded man
crawled into cover?

I waited breathlessly for a minute or two, and
then went forward, with my second pistol at the
cock.

There was nothing behind the tree. Only a piece of red bark with a bullet hole through it, some greasy horsehair, and a feather. And then from many quarters seemed to come a wicked laughter. I leaned against the trunk, with a deadly nausea clutching at my heart. Poor fool, I had rejoiced for a second, only to be dashed into utter despair !

I do not think I had ever had much hope, but now I was convinced that all was over. The water had made my burns worse, and disappointment had sapped the little remnants of my strength. My one desire was to get out of this ghoulish thicket and die by the stream-side. The cool sound of it would be a fitting dirge for a foolish fellow who had wandered far from his home.

I could hear the plunge of it, and struggled towards it. I was long past taking any care. I stumbled and slipped along the hill-side, my breath labouring, and a moaning at my lips from sheer agony and weakness. If an arrow sped between my ribs I would still reach the water, for I was determined to die with my legs in its flow.

Suddenly it was before me. I came out on a mossy rock above a deep, clear pool, into which a cascade tumbled. I knelt feebly on the stone, gazing at the blue depths, and then I lifted my eyes.

There on a rock on the other side stood my enemy.

He had an arrow fitted to his bow, and as I looked he shot. It struck me on the right arm, pinning it just above the elbow. The pistol, which

I had been carrying aimlessly, slipped from my nerveless hand to the moss on which I kneeled.

That sudden shock cleared my wits. I was at his mercy, and he knew it. I could see every detail of him twenty yards off across the water. He stood there as calm and light as if he had just arisen from rest, his polished limbs shining in the glow of the sun, the muscles on his right arm rippling as he moved his bow. Madman that I was, ever to hope to contend with such a dauntless youth, such tireless vigour! There was a cruel, thin-lipped smile on his face. He had me in his clutches like a cat with a mouse, and he was going to get the full zest of it. I kneeled before him, with my strength gone, my right arm crippled. He could choose his target at his leisure, for I could not resist. I saw the gloating joy in his eyes. He knew his power, and meant to miss nothing of its savour.

Yet in that fell predicament God gave me back my courage. But I took a queer way of showing it.

I began to whimper as if in abject fear. Every limb was relaxed in terror, and I grovelled on my knees before him. I bent back my right wrist and made feeble plucks at the arrow in my right arm, while my shoulder drooped almost to the sod. But all the time my other hand was behind my back, edging its way to the pistol. My fingers clutched at the butt, and slowly I began to withdraw it till I had it safe in the shadow of my pocket.

My enemy did not know that I was left-handed.

He fitted a second arrow to his bow, while his lips curved maliciously. All the demoniac, panther-like cruelty of his race looked at me out of his deep eyes. He was taking his time about it, unwilling to lose the slightest flavour of his vengeance. I played up to him nobly, squirming as if in an agony of terror. But by this time I had got a comfortable posture on the rock, and my left shoulder was towards him.

At last he made his choice, and so did I. I never thought that I could miss, for if I had had any doubt I should have failed. I was as confident in my sureness as any saint in the mercy of God.

He raised his bow, but it never reached his shoulder. My left arm shot out, and in the same second my last bullet went through his brain.

He toppled forward and plunged into the pool. The grease from his body floated up, and made a scum on the surface.

Then I broke off the arrow and pulled it out of my arm, putting the pieces in my pocket. The water cleared, and I could see him lying in the cool blue depths, his eyes staring, his mouth open, and a little dark eddy about his forehead.

CHAPTER XXVI

SHALAH

I CAME out of the wood a new being. My wounded arm and my torn and inflamed limbs were forgotten. I held my head high, and walked like a free man. It was not that I had slain my enemy and been delivered from deadly peril, nor had I any clearer light on my next step. But I had suddenly got the conviction that God was on my side, and that I need not fear what man could do unto me. You may call it the madness of a lad whose body and spirit had been tried to breaking-point. But, madness or no, it gave me infinite courage, and in that hour I would have dared every savage on earth.

I found some Indians at the edge of the wood, and told one who spoke Powhatan the issue of the fight. I flung the broken arrow on the ground. "That is my token," I said. "You will find the other in the pool below the cascade."

Then I strode towards the tents, looking every man I passed squarely in the eyes. No one spoke, no one hindered me ; every face was like a graven image.

I reached the teepee in which I had spent the night, and flung myself down on the rude couch. In a minute I was sunk in a heavy sleep.

I woke to see two men standing in the tent door. One was the chief Onotawah, and the other a tall Indian who wore no war paint.

They came towards me, and the light fell on the face of the second. To my amazement I recognized Shalah. He put a finger on his lip, and, though my heart clamoured for news, I held my peace.

They squatted on a heap of skins and spoke in their own tongue. Then Shalah addressed me in English.

"The maiden is safe, brother. There will be no more fighting at the stockade. Those who assaulted us were of my own tribe, and yesterday I reasoned with them."

Then he spoke to the chief, and translated for me.

"He says that you have endured the ordeal of the stake, and have slain your enemy in fight, and that now you will go before the great Sachem for his judgment. That is the custom of our people."

He turned to Onotawah again, and his tone was high and scornful. He spoke as if he were the chief and the other were the minion, and, what was strangest of all, Onotawah replied meekly. Shalah rose to his feet and strode to the door, pointing down the glen with his hand. He seemed to menace the other, his nostrils quivered with contempt, and his voice was barbed with passion. Onotawah bowed his head and said nothing.

Then he seemed to dismiss him, and the proud chief walked out of the teepee like a disconsolate schoolboy.

Instantly Shalah turned to me and inquired about my wounds. He looked at the hole in my arm and at my scorched legs, and from his belt took a phial of ointment, which he rubbed on the former. He passed his cool hands over my brow, and felt the beating of my heart.

" You are weary, brother, and somewhat scarred, but there is no grave hurt. What of the Master ? "

I told him of Ringan's end. He bent his head, and then sprang up and held his hands high, speaking in a strange tongue. I looked at his eyes and they were ablaze with fire.

" My people slew him," he cried. " By the shades of my fathers, a score shall keep him company as slaves in the Great Hunting-ground."

" Talk no more of blood," I said. " He was amply avenged. 'Twas I who slew him, for he died to save me. He made a Christian end, and I will not have his memory stained by more murders. But oh, Shalah, what a man died yonder ! "

He made me tell every incident of the story, and he cried out, impassive though he was, at the sword-play in the neck of the gorge.

" I have seen it," he cried. " I have seen his bright steel flash and men go down like ripe fruit. Tell me, brother, did he sing all the while, as was his custom ? Would I had been by his side ! "

Then he told me of what had befallen at the stockade.

" The dead man told me a tale, for by the mark on his forehead I knew that he was of my own house. When you and the Master had gone I went into the woods and picked up the trail of our foes. I found them in a crook of the hills, and went among them in peace. They knew me, and my word was law unto them. No living thing will come near the stockade save the wild beasts of the forest. Be at ease in thy mind, brother."

The news was a mighty consolation, but I was still deeply mystified.

" You speak of your tribe. But these men were no Senecas."

He smiled gravely. " Listen, brother," he said. " The white men of the Tidewater called me Seneca, and I suffered the name. But I am of a greater and princelier house than the Sons of the Cat. Some little while ago I spoke to you of the man who travelled to the Western Seas, and of his son who returned to his own people. I am the son of him who returned. I spoke of the doings of my own kin."

" But what is your nation, then ? " I cried.

" One so great that these little clanlets of Chero-kee and Monacan, and even the multitudes of the Long House, are but slaves and horseboys by their side. We dwelt far beyond these moun-tains towards the setting sun, in a plain where the rivers are like seas, and the cornlands wider than all the Virginian manors. But there came trouble in our royal house, and my father returned to find a generation which had forgotten the deeds of their forefathers. So he took his own tribe, who still remembered the House of the Sun, and, because his heart was unquiet with longing for that which is forbidden to man, he journeyed eastward, and found a new home in a valley of these hills. Thine eyes have seen it. They call it the Shenandoah."

I remembered that smiling Eden I had seen from that hill-top, and how Shalah had spoken that very name.

"We dwelt there," he continued, "while I grew to manhood, living happily in peace, hunting the buffalo and deer, and tilling our cornlands. Then the time came when the Great Spirit called for my father, and I was left with the kingship of the tribe. Strange things meantime had befallen our nation in the West. Broken clans had come down from the north, and there had been many battles, and there had been blight, and storms, and sickness, so that they were grown poor and harassed. Likewise men had arisen who preached to them discontent, and other races of a lesser breed had joined themselves to them. My own tribe had become fewer, for the young men did not stay in our valley, but drifted back to the West, to that nation we had come from, or went north to the wars with the white man, or became lonely hunters in the hills. Then from the south along the mountain crests came another people, a squat and murderous people, who watched us from the ridges and bided their chance."

" The Cherokees ? " I asked.

" Even so. I speak of three hundred moons back, when I was yet a stripling, with little experience in war. I saw the peril, but I could not think that such a race could vie with the Children of the Sun. But one black night, in the Moon of Wildfowl, the raiders descended in a torrent and took us unprepared. What had been a happy people dwelling with full barns and populous wigwams became in a night a desolation. Our wives and children were slain or carried captive, and on every Cherokee belt hung the scalps of my warriors. Some fled westwards to our nation, but they were few that lived, and the tribe of Shalah went out like a torch in a roaring river.

" I slew many men that night, for the gods of my fathers guided my arm. Death I sought, but could not find it ; and by and by I was alone in the woods, with twenty scars and a heart as empty as a gourd. Then I turned my steps to the rising sun and the land of the white man, for there was no more any place for me in the councils of my own people.

" All this was many moons ago, and since then I have been a wanderer among strangers. While I reigned in my valley I heard of the white man's magic and of the power of his gods, and I longed to prove them. Now I have learned many things which were hid from the eyes of our oldest men. I have learned that a man may be a great brave, and yet gentle and merciful, as was the Master. I have learned that a man may be a lover of peace and quiet ways and have no lust of battle in his heart, and yet when the need comes be more valiant than the best, even as you, brother. I have learned that the God of the white men was Himself a man who endured the ordeal of the stake for the welfare of His enemies. I have seen cruelty and cowardice and folly among His worshippers; but I have also seen that His faith can put spirit into a coward's heart, and make heroes of mean men. I do not grudge my years of wandering. They have taught me such knowledge as the Sachems of my nation never dreamed of, and they have given me two comrades after my own heart. One was he who died yesterday, and the other is now by my side."

These words of Shalah did not make me proud, for things were too serious for vanity. But they served to confirm in me my strange exaltation. I felt as one dedicated to a mighty task.

" Tell me, what is the invasion which threatens the Tidewater ? "

" The whole truth is not known to me; but from the speech of my tribesmen, it seems that the Children of the West Wind, twelve moons ago, struck their tents and resolved to seek a new country. There is a restlessness comes upon all Indian peoples once in every five generations. It fell upon my grandfather, and he travelled towards the sunset, and now it has fallen upon the whole race of the Sun. As they were on the eve

of journeying there came to them a prophet, who
told them that God would lead them not towards
the West, as was the tradition of the elders, but
eastwards to the sea and the dwellings of the Palefaces."

"Is that the crazy white man we have heard
of ? "

"He is of your race, brother. What his spell
is I know not, but it works mightily among my
people. They tell me that he hath bodily converse
with devils, and that God whispers His secrets
to him in the night-watches. His God hath told
him—so runs the tale—that He hath chosen the
Children of the Sun for His peculiar people, and
laid on them the charge of sweeping the white
men off the earth and reigning in their stead from
the hills to the Great Waters."

"Do you believe in this madman, Shalah ? "
I asked.

"I know not," he said, with a troubled face.
"I fear one possessed of God. But of this I am
sure, that the road of the Children of the West
Wind lies not eastward but westward, and that no
good can come of war with the white man. This
Sachem hath laid his magic on others than our
people, for the Cherokee nation and all the broken
clans of the hills acknowledge him and do his
bidding. He is a soldier as well as a prophet,
for he has drilled and disposed his army like a
master of war."

"Will your tribe ally themselves with Cherokee murderers ? "

" I asked that question of this man Onotawah, and he liked it little. He says that his people distrust this alliance with a race they scorn, and I do not think they pine for the white man's war. But they are under the magic of this prophet, and presently, when blood begins to flow, they will warm to their work. In time they will be broken, but that time will not be soon, and meanwhile there will be nothing left alive between the hills and the bay of Chesapeake."

" Do you know their plans ? " I asked.

" The Cherokees have served their purpose," he said. " Your forecast was right, brother. They have drawn the fire of the Border, and been driven in a rabble far south to the Roanoke and the Carolina mountains. That is as the prophet planned. And now, while the white men hang up their muskets and rejoice heedlessly in their triumph, my nation prepares to strike. To-night the moon is full, and the prophet makes intercession with his God. To-morrow at dawn they march, and by twilight they will have swarmed across the Border."

" Have you no power over your own people ? "

" But little," he answered. " I have been too long absent from them, and my name is half-forgotten. Yet, were they free of this prophet, I think I might sway them, for I know their ways, and I am the son of their ancient kings. But for the present his magic holds them in thrall. They listen in fear to one who hath the ear of God."

I arose stretched my arms, and yawned.

" They carry me to this Sachem," I said. " Well
and good. I will outface this blasphemous liar,
whoever he may be. If he makes big magic, I
will make bigger. The only course is the bold
course. If I can humble this prophet man, will
you dissuade your nation from war and send them
back to the sunset ? "

" Assuredly," he said wonderingly. " But what
is your plan, brother ? "

" None," I answered. " God will show me
the way. Honesty may trust in Him as well
as madness."

" By my father's shade, you are a man, brother,"
and he gave me the Indian salute.

" A very weary, feckless cripple of a man," I
said, smiling. " But the armies of Heaven are on
my side, Shalah. Take my pistols and Ringan's
sword. I am going into this business with no
human weapons."

And as they set me on an Indian horse and the
whole tribe turned their eyes to the higher glens,
I actually rejoiced. Light-hearted or light-headed,
I know not which I was, but I know that I had
no fear.

CHAPTER XXVII

HOW I STROVE ALL NIGHT WITH THE DEVIL

IT was late in the evening ere we reached the shelf in the high glens which was the head-quarters of the Indian host. I rode on a horse, between Onotawah and Shalah, as if I were a chief and no prisoner. On the road we met many bands of Indians hastening to the trysting-place, for the leader had flung his outposts along the whole base of the range, and the chief warriors returned to the plateau for the last ritual. No man spoke a word, and when we met other companies the only greeting was by uplifted hands.

The shelf was lit with fires, and there was a flare of torches in the centre. I saw an immense multitude of lean, dark faces—how many I cannot tell, but ten thousand at the least. It took all my faith to withstand the awe of the sight. For these men were not the common Indian breed, but a race nurtured and armed for great wars, discip-lined to follow one man, and sharpened to a needle-point in spirit. Perhaps if I had been myself a campaigner I should have been less awed by the spectacle ; but having nothing with which to compare it, I judged this a host before which the scattered Border stockades and Nicholson's scanty militia would go down like stubble before fire.

At the head of the plateau, just under the brow of the hill, and facing the half-circle of level land, stood a big tent of skins. Before it was a square pile of boulders about the height of a man's waist, heaped on the top with brushwood so that it looked like a rude altar. Around this the host had gathered, sitting mostly on the ground with knees drawn to the chin, but some few standing like sentries under arms. I was taken to the middle of the half-circle, and Shalah motioned me to dismount, while a stripling led off the horses. My legs gave under me, for they were still very feeble, and I sat hunkered up on the sward like the others. I looked for Shalah and Onotawah, but they had disappeared, and I was left alone among those lines of dark, unknown faces.

I waited with an awe on my spirits against which I struggled in vain. The silence of so vast a multitude, the sputtering torches lighting the wild amphitheatre of the hills, the strange clearing with its altar, the mystery of the immense dusky sky, and the memory of what I had already endured—all weighed on me with the sense of impending doom. I summoned all my fortitude to my aid. I told myself that Ringan had believed in me, and that I had the assurance that God would not see me cast down. But such courage as I had was now a resolve rather than any exhilaration of spirits. A brooding darkness lay on me like a cloud.

Presently the hush grew deeper, and from the tent a man came. I could not see him clearly, but the flickering light told me that he was very tall, and that, like the Indians, he was naked to the middle. He stood behind the altar, and began some incantation.

It was in the Indian tongue which I could not understand. The voice was harsh and discordant, but powerful enough to fill that whole circle of hill. It seemed to rouse the passion of the hearers, for grave faces around me began to work, and long-drawn sighs came from their lips.

Then at a word from the figure four men advanced, bearing something between them, which they laid on the altar. To my amazement I saw that it was a great yellow panther, so trussed up that it was impotent to hurt. How such a beast had ever been caught alive I know not. I could see its green cat's-eyes glowing in the dark, and the striving of its muscles, and hear the breath hissing from its muzzled jaws.

The figure raised a knife and plunged it into the throat of the great cat. The slow lapping of blood broke in on the stillness. Then the voice shrilled high and wild. I could see that the man had marked his forehead with blood, and that his hands were red and dripping. He seemed to be declaiming some savage chant, to which my neighbours began to keep time with their bodies. Wilder and wilder it grew, till it

ended in a scream like a seamew's. Whoever
the madman was, he knew the mystery of Indian
souls, for in a little he would have had that host
lusting blindly for death. I felt the spell myself,
piercing through my awe and hatred of the spell-
weaver, and I won't say but that my weary
head kept time with the others to that weird
singing.

A man brought a torch and lit the brushwood
on the altar. Instantly a flame rose to heaven,
through which the figure of the magician showed
fitfully like a mountain in mist. That act broke
the wizardry for me. To sacrifice a cat was monstrous and horrible, but it was also uncouthly
silly. I saw the magic for what it was, a maniac's
trickery. In the revulsion I grew angry, and my
anger heartened me wonderfully. Was this stupen-
dous quackery to bring ruin to the Tidewater ?
Though I had to choke the life with my own hands
out of that warlock's throat, I should prevent it.

Then from behind the fire the voice began again.
But this time I understood it. The words were
English. I was amazed, for I had forgotten that
I knew the wizard to be a white man.

" *Thus saith the Lord God*," it cried, " *Woe to
the bloody city ! I will make the pile great for fire.
Heap on wood, kindle the fire, consume the flesh, and
spice it well, and let the bones be burned.*"

He poked the beast on the altar, and a bit of
burning yellow fur fell off and frizzled on the
ground.

It was horrid beyond words, lewd and savage

and impious, and desperately cruel. And the strange thing was that the voice was familiar.

"*O thou that dwellest upon many waters,*" it went on again, "*abundant in treasures, thine end is come, and the measure of thy covetousness. The Lord of Hosts hath sworn by Himself, saying, Surely I will fill thee with men as with caterpillars. . . .*"

With that last word there came over me a flood of recollection. It was spoken not in the common English way, but in the broad manner of my own folk. . . . I saw in my mind's eye a wet moorland, and heard a voice inveighing against the wickedness of those in high places. . . . I smelled the foul air of the Canongate Tolbooth, and heard this same man testify against the vanity of the world. . . . "*Cawterpillars !*" It was the voice that had once bidden me sing "Jenny Nettles."

Harsh and strident and horrible, it was yet the voice I had known, now blaspheming Scripture words behind that gruesome sacrifice. I think I laughed aloud. I remembered the man I had pursued my first night in Virginia, the man who had raided Frew's cabin. I remembered Ringan's tale of the Scots redemptioner that had escaped from Norfolk county, and the various strange writings which had descended from the hills. Was it not the queerest fate that one whom I had met in my boyish scrapes should return after six years and many thousand miles to play once more a major part in my life ! The nameless general in the hills was Muckle John Gib, once a mariner of Borrowstoneness, and some time leader of the

Sweet-Singers. I felt the smell of wet heather, and the fishy odours of the Forth; I heard the tang of our country speech, and the swirl of the gusty winds of home.

But in a second all thought of mirth was gone, and a deep solemnity fell upon me. God had assuredly directed my path, for He had brought the two of us together over the widest spaces of earth. I had no fear of the issue. I should master Muckle John as I had mastered him before. My awe was all for God's mysterious dealing, not for that poor fool posturing behind his obscene sacrifice. His voice rose and fell in eldritch screams and hollow moans. He was mouthing the words of some Bible Prophet.

"*A Sword is upon her horses, and upon her chariots, and upon all the mingled people that are in the midst of her, and they shall become as women. A Sword is upon her treasures, and they shall be robbed; a drought is upon her waters, and they shall be dried up; for it is the land of graven images, and they are mad upon their idols.*"

Every syllable brought back some memory. He had the whine and sough in his voice that our sectaries prized, and I could shut my eyes and imagine I was back in the little kirk of Lesmahagow on a hot summer morn. And then would come the scream of madness, the high wail of the Sweet-Singer.

"*Thus saith the Lord God: Behold, I will bring a King of kings from the north, with horses and with chariots, and with horsemen and companies and much*

*people. He shall slay with the sword thy daughters
in the field . . ."*

" Fine words," I thought, " but Elspeth laid
her whip over your shoulders, my man."

. . ." *With the hoofs of his horses shall he tread
down all thy streets. He shall slay thy people by
the sword, and thy strong garrisons shall go down
to the ground. . . . And I will cause the music of
thy songs to cease, and the sound of thy harps shall
no more be heard."*

I had a vision of Elspeth's birthday party when
we sat round the Governor's table, and I had
wondered dismally how long it would be before
our pleasant songs would be turned to mourning.

The fires died down, the smoke thinned, and the
full moon rising over the crest of the hills poured
her light on us. The torches flickered insolently in
that calm radiance. The voice, too, grew lower and
the incantation ceased. Then it began again in the
Indian tongue, and the whole host rose to their
feet. Muckle John, like some old priest of Diana,
flung up his arms to the heavens, and seemed to be
invoking his strange gods. Or he may have been
blessing his flock—I know not which. Then he
turned and strode back to his tent, just as he had
done on that night in the Cauldstaneslap. . . .

A hand was laid on my arm and Onotawah stood
by me. He motioned me to follow him, and led
me past the smoking altar to a row of painted
white stones around the great wigwam. This he
did not cross, but pointed to the tent door. I
pushed aside the flap and entered.

An Indian lamp—a wick floating in oil—stood on a rough table. But its thin light was unneeded, for the great flood of moonshine, coming through the slits of the skins, made a clear yellow twilight. By it I marked the figure of Muckle John on his knees.

" Good evening to you, Mr. Gib," I said.

The figure sprang to its feet and strode over to me.

" Who are ye," it cried, " who speak a name that is no more spoken on earth ? "

" Just a countryman of yours, who has for-gathered with you before. Have you no mind of the Cauldstaneslap and the Canongate Tol-booth ? "

He snatched up the lamp and peered into my face, but he was long past recollection.

" I know ye not. But if ye be indeed one from that idolatrous country of Scotland, the Lord hath sent you to witness the triumph of His servant. Know that I am no longer the man John Gib, but the chosen of the Lord, to whom He hath given a new name, even Jerubbaal, saying let Baal plead against him, because he hath thrown down his altar."

" That's too long a word for me to remember, Mr. Gib, so by your leave I'll call you as you were christened."

I had forced myself to a slow coolness, and my voice seemed to madden him.

" Ye would outface me," he cried. " I see ye are an idolater from the tents of Shem, on whom

judgment will be speedy and surprising. Know ye
not what the Lord hath prepared for ye ?   Down
in your proud cities ye are feasting and dicing
and smiling on your paramours, but the writing
is on the wall, and in a little ye will be crying like
weaned bairns for a refuge against the storm of
God.   Your strong men shall be slain, and your
virgins shall be led captive, and your little children shall be dashed against a stone.   And in the
midst of your ruins I, even I, will raise a temple
to the God of Israel, and nations that know me
not will run unto me because of the Lord my
God."

I had determined on my part, and played it
calmly.

" And what will you do with your Indian
braves ? " I asked.

" Sharon shall be a fold of flocks, and the valley
of Achor a place to lie down in, for my people
that have sought me," he answered.

" A bonny spectacle," I said.   " Man, if you
dare to cross the Border you will be whipped at
a cart-tail and clapped into Bedlam as a crazy
vagabond."

" Blasphemer," he shrieked, and ran at me with
the knife he had used on the panther.

It took all my courage to play my game.   I
stood motionless, looking at him, and his hand
fell.   Had I moved he would have struck, but to
his mad eyes my calmness was terrifying.

" It sticks in my mind," I said, " that there
is a commandment, Do no murder.   You call

yourself a follower of the Lord. Let me tell you that you are no more than a bloody-minded savage, a thousandfold more guilty than those poor creatures you are leading astray. You serve Baal, not God, John Gib, and the devil in hell is banking his fires and counting on your company."

He gibbered at me like a bedlamite, but I knew what I was doing. I raised my voice, and spoke loud and clear, while my eyes held his in that yellow dusk.

"Priest of Baal," I cried, "lying prophet! Go down on your knees and pray for mercy. By the living God, the flames of hell are waiting for you. The lightnings tremble in the clouds to scorch you up and send your black soul to its own place."

His hands pawed for my throat, but the horror was descending on him. He shrieked like a wild beast, and cast fearful eyes behind him. Then he rushed into the dark corners, stabbing with his knife, crying that the devils were loosed. I remember how horribly he frothed at the mouth.

"Avaunt," he howled. "Avaunt, Mel and Abaddon! Avaunt, Evil-Merodach and Baal-Jezer! Ha! There I had ye, ye muckle goat. The stink of hell is on ye, but ye shall not take the elect of the Lord."

He crawled on his belly, stabbing his knife into the ground. I easily avoided him, for his eyes saw nothing but his terrible phantoms. Verily Shalah had spoken truth when he said that this man had bodily converse with the devils.

Then I threw him—quite easily, for his limbs were going limp in the extremity of his horror. He lay gasping and foaming, his eyes turning back in his head, while I bound his arms to his sides with my belt. I found some cords in the tent, and tied his legs together. He moaned miserably for a little, and then was silent.

I think I must have sat by him for three hours. The world was very still, and the moon set, and the only light was the flickering lamp. Once or twice I heard a rustle by the tent door. Some Indian guard was on the watch, but I knew that no Indian dared cross the forbidden circle.

I had no thoughts, being oppressed with a great stupor of weariness. I may have dozed a little, but the pain of my legs kept me from slumbering. Once or twice I looked at him, and I noticed that the madness had gone out of his face, and that he was sleeping peacefully. I wiped the froth from his lips, and his forehead was cool to my touch.

By and by, as I held the lamp close, I observed that his eyes were open. It was now time for the gamble I had resolved on. I remembered that morning in the Tolbooth, and how the madness had passed, leaving him a simple soul. I unstrapped the belt, and cut the cords about his legs.

" Do you feel better now, Mr. Gib ? " I asked, as if it were the most ordinary question in the world.

He sat up and rubbed his eyes. "Was it a dwam ? " he inquired. " I get them whiles."

" It was a dwam, but I think it has passed."

He still rubbed his eyes, and peered about him, like a big collie dog that has lost its master.

" Who is it that speirs ? " he said. " I ken the voice, but I havena heard it this long time."

" One who is well acquaint with Borrowstoneness and the links of Forth," said I.

I spoke in the accent of his own countryside, and it must have woke some dim chord in his memory. I made haste to strike while the iron was hot.

" There was a woman at Cramond . . ." I began.

He got to his feet and looked me in the face. " Ay, there was," he said, with an odd note in his voice. " What about her ? " I could see that his hand was shaking.

" I think her name was Alison Steel."

" What ken ye of Alison Steel ? " he asked fiercely. " Quick, man, what word have ye frae Alison ? "

" You sent me with a letter to her. D'you not mind your last days in Edinburgh, before they shipped you to the Plantations ? "

" It comes back to me," he cried. " Ay, it comes back. To think I should live to hear of Alison ! What did she say ? "

" Just this. That John Gib was a decent man if he would resist the devil of pride. She charged me to tell you that you would never be out of her prayers, and that she would live to be proud of you. 'John will never shame his kin,' quoth she."

"Said she so-? " he said musingly. "She was aye a kind body. We were to be married at Martinmas, I mind, if the Lord hadna called me."

"You've need of her prayers," I said, "and of the prayers of every Christian soul on earth. I came here yestereen to find you mouthing blasphemies, and howling like a mad tyke amid a parcel of heathen. And they tell me you're to lead your savages on Virginia, and give that smiling land to fire and sword. Think you Alison Steel would not be black ashamed if she heard the horrid tale ? "

" 'Twas the Lord's commands," he said gloomily, but there was no conviction in his words.

I changed my tone. "Do you dare to speak such blasphemy ? " I cried. "The Lord's commands ! The devil's commands ! The devil of your own sinful pride ! You are like the false prophets that made Israel to sin. What brings you, a white man, at the head of murderous savages ? "

"Israel would not hearken, so I turned to the Gentiles," said he.

"And what are you going to make of your Gentiles ? Do you think you've put much Christianity into the heart of the gentry that were watching your antics last night ? "

"They have glimmerings of grace," he said.

"Glimmerings of moonshine ! They are bent

on murder, and so are you, and you call that the Lord's commands. You would sacrifice your own folk to the heathen hordes. God forgive you, John Gib, for you are no Christian, and no Scot, and no man."

" Virginia is an idolatrous land," said he ; but he could not look up at me.

" And are your Indians not idolaters ? Are you no idolater, with your burnt offerings and heathen gibberish ? You worship a Baal and a Moloch worse than any Midianite, for you adore the devils of your own rotten heart."

The big man, with all the madness out of him, put his towsy head in his hands, and a sob shook his great shoulders.

" Listen to me, John Gib. I am come from your own country-side to save you from a hellish wickedness. I know the length and breadth of Virginia, and the land is full of Scots, men of the Covenant you have forsworn, who are living an honest life on their bits of farms, and worshipping the God you have forsaken. There are women there like Alison Steel, and there are men there like yourself before you hearkened to the devil. Will you bring death to your own folk, with whom you once shared the hope of salvation ? By the land we both have left, and the kindly souls we both have known, and the prayers you said at your mother's knee, and the love of Christ who died for us, I adjure you to flee this great sin. For it is the sin against the Holy Ghost, and that knows no forgiveness."

The man was fairly broken down. "What must I do ? " he cried. "I'm all in a creel. I'm but a pipe for the Lord to sound through."

"Take not that Name in vain, for the sounding is from your own corrupt heart. Mind what Alison Steel said about the devil of pride, for it was that sin by which the angels fell."

"But I've His plain commands," he wailed. "He hath bidden me cast down idolatry, and bring the Gentiles to His kingdom."

"Did He say anything about Virginia ? There's plenty idolatry elsewhere in America to keep you busy for a lifetime, and you can lead your Gentiles elsewhere than against your own kin. Turn your face westward, John Gib. I, too, can dream dreams and see visions, and it is borne in on me that your road is plain before you. Lead this great people away from the little shielings of Virginia, over. the hills and over the great mountains and the plains beyond, and on and on till you come to an abiding city. You will find idolaters enough to dispute your road, and you can guide your flock as the Lord directs you. Then you will be clear of the murderer's guilt who would stain his hands in kindly blood."

He lifted his great head, and the marks of the sacrifice were still on his brow.

"D'ye think that would be the Lord's will ? " he asked innocently,

"I declare it unto you," said I. "I have been sent by God to save your soul. I give you your marching orders, for though you are half a madman

you are whiles a man.   There's the soul of a leader
in you, and I would keep you from the shame of
leading men to hell.   To-morrow morn you will
tell these folk that the Lord has revealed to you
a better way, and by noon you will be across the
Shenandoah.   D'you hear my word ? "

" Ay," he said.   " We will march in the morning."

" Can you lead them where you will ? "

His back stiffened, and the spirit of a general
looked out of his eyes.

" They will follow where I bid.   There's no a
man of them dare cheep at what I tell them."

" My work is done," I said.   " I go to whence
I came.   And some day I shall go to Cramond
and tell Alison that John Gib is no disgrace to
his kin."

" Would you put up a prayer ? " he said timidly.
" I would be the better of one."

Then for the first and last time in my life I
spoke aloud to my Maker in another's presence, and
it was surely the strangest petition ever offered.

" Lord," I prayed, " Thou seest Thy creature,
John Gib, who by the perverseness of his heart
has come to the edge of grievous sin.   Take the
cloud from his spirit, arrange his disordered wits,
and lead him to a wiser life.   Keep him in mind
of his own land, and of her who prays for him.
Guide him over hills and rivers to an enlarged
country, and make his arm strong against his
enemies, so be they are not of his own kin.   And
if ever he should hearken again to the devil, do

23

Thou blast his body with Thy fires, so that his soul may be saved."

" Amen," said he, and I went out of the tent to find the grey dawn beginning to steal up the sky.

Shalah was waiting at the entrance, far inside the white stones. 'Twas the first time I had ever seen him in a state approaching fear.

" What fortune, brother ? " he asked, and his teeth chattered.

" The Tidewater is safe. This day they march westwards to look for their new country."

" Thy magic is as the magic of Heaven," he said reverently. " My heart all night has been like water, for I know no charm which hath prevailed against the mystery of the Panther."

" 'Twas no magic of mine," said I. " God spoke to him through my lips in the night watches."

We took our way unchallenged through the sleeping host till we had climbed the scarp of the hills.

" What brought you to the tent door ? " I asked.

" I abode there through the night. I heard the strife with the devils, and my joints were loosened. Also I heard thy voice, brother, but I knew not thy words."

" But what did you mean to do ? " I asked again.

" It was in my mind to do my little best to see that no harm befell thee. And if harm came, I had the thought of trying my knife on the ribs of yonder magician."

CHAPTER XXVIII

HOW THREE SOULS FOUND THEIR HERITAGE

IN that hour I had none of the exhilaration of success. So strangely are we mortals made that, though I had won safety for myself and my people, I could not get the savour of it. I had passed too far beyond the limits of my strength. Now that the tension of peril was gone, my legs were like touchwood, which a stroke would shatter, and my foolish head swam like a merry-go-round. Shalah's arm was round me, and he lifted me up the steep bits till we came to the crown of the ridge. There we halted, and he fed me with sops of bread dipped in eau-de-vie, for he had brought Ringan's flask with him. The only result was to make me deadly sick. I saw his eyes look gravely at me, and the next I knew I was on his back. I begged him to set me down and leave me, and I think I must have wept like a bairn. All pride of manhood had flown in that sharp revulsion, and I had the mind of a lost child.

As the light grew some strength came back to and presently I was able to hobble a little on my rickety shanks. We kept the very crest of the range, and came by and by to a promontory of clear ground, the same, I fancy, from which I had first seen the vale of the Shenandoah. There we rested in a nook of rock, while the early sun warmed us, and the little vapours showed us in glimpses the green depths and the far-shining meadows.

Shalah nudged my shoulder, and pointed to the south, where a glen debouched from the hills. A stream of mounted figures was pouring out of it, heading for the upper waters of the river where the valley broadened again. For all my sickness my eyes were sharp enough to perceive what manner of procession it was. All were on horseback, riding in clouds and companies without the discipline of a march, but moving as swift as a flight of wildfowl at twilight. Before the others rode a little cluster of pathfinders, and among them I thought I could recognize one taller than the rest.

" Your magic hath prevailed, brother," Shalah said. " In an hour's time they will have crossed the Shenandoah, and at nightfall they will camp on the farther mountains."

That sight gave me my first assurance of success. At any rate, I had fulfilled my trust, and if I died in the hills Virginia would yet bless her deliverer.

And yet my strongest feeling was a wild regret. These folk were making for the untravelled lands of the sunset. You would have said I had got my bellyful of adventure, and should now have sought only a quiet life. But in that moment of bodily weakness and mental confusion I was shaken with a longing to follow them, to find what lay beyond the farthest cloud-topped mountain, to cross the wide rivers, and haply to come to the infinite and mystic Ocean of the West.

" Would to God I were with them ! " I sighed.

" Will you come, brother ? " Shalah whispered, a strange light in his eyes. " If we twain joined the venture, I think we should not be the last in it. Shalah would make you a king. What is your life in the muddy Tidewater but a thing of little rivalries and petty wrangles and moping over paper ? The hearth will soon grow cold, and the bright eyes of the fairest woman will dull with age, and the years will find you heavy and slow, with a coward's shrinking from death. What say you, brother ? While the blood is strong in the veins shall we ride westward on the path of a king ? "

His eyes were staring like a hawk's over the hills, and, light-headed as I was, I caught the infection of his ardour. For, remember, I was so low in spirit that all my hopes and memories were forgotten, and I was in that blank apathy which is mastered by another's passion. For a little the life of Virginia seemed unspeakably barren, and I quickened at the wild vista which Shalah offered. I might be a king over a proud people, carving a fair kingdom out of the wilderness, and ruling it justly in the fear of God. These western Indians were the stuff of a great nation. I, Andrew Garvald, might yet find that empire of which the old adventurers dreamed.

With shame I set down my boyish folly. It

did not last long, for to my dizzy brain there came the air which Elspeth had sung, that song of Montrose's which had been, as it were, the star of all my wanderings.

> " For, if Confusion have a part,
> Which virtuous souls abhor—"

Surely it was confusion that had now overtaken me. Elspeth's clear voice, her dark, kind eyes, her young and joyous grace, filled again my memory. Was not such a lady better than any savage kingdom ? Was not the service of my own folk nobler than any principate among strangers ? Could the rivers of Damascus vie with the waters of Israel ?

" Nay, Shalah," I said. " Mine is a quieter destiny. I go back to the Tidewater, but I shall not stay there. We have found the road to the hills, and in time I will plant the flag of my race on the Shenandoah."

He bowed his head. " So be it. Each man to his own path, but I would ours had run together. Your way is the way of the white man. You conquer slowly, but the line of your conquest goes not back. Slowly it eats its way through the forest, and fields and manors appear in the waste places, and cattle graze in the coverts of the deer. Listen, brother. Shalah has had his visions when his eyes were unsealed in the night watches. He has seen the white man pressing up from the sea, and spreading over the lands of his fathers. He has seen the glens of the hills parcelled out like

the meadows of Henricus, and a great multitude
surging ever on to the West. His race is doomed
by God to perish before the stranger ; but not yet
awhile, for the white man comes slowly. It hath
been told that the Children of the West Wind
must seek their cradle, and while there is time he
would join them in that quest. The white men
follow upon their heels, but in his day and in that
of his son's sons they will lead their life according
to the ancient ways. He hath seen the wisdom of
the stranger, and found among them men after
his own heart ; but the Spirit of his fathers calls,
and now he returns to his own people."

" What will you do there ? " I asked.

" I know not. I am still a prince among them,
and will sway their councils. It may be fated
that I slay yonder magician and reign in his stead."

He got to his feet and looked proudly westward.

" In a little I shall overtake them. But I would
my brother had been of my company."

Slowly we travelled north along the crests, for
though my mind was now saner, I had no strength
in my body. The hill mists came down on us,
and the rain drove up from the glens. I was
happy for all my weakness, for I was lapped in a
great peace. The raw weather, which had once
been a horror of darkness to me, was now something kindly and homelike. The wet smells minded
me of my own land, and the cool buffets of the
squalls were a tonic to my spirit. I wandered
into pleasant dreams, and scarce felt the rough-

ness of the ground on my bare feet and the aches in every limb.

Long ere we got to the Gap I was clean worn out. I remember that I fell constantly, and could scarcely rise. Then I stumbled, and the last power went out of will and sinew. I had a glimpse of Shalah's grave face as I slipped into unconsciousness.

I woke in a glow of firelight. Faces surrounded me, dim wraith-like figures still entangled in the meshes of my dreams. Slowly the scene cleared, and I recognized Grey's features, drawn and constrained, and yet welcoming. Bertrand was weeping after his excitable fashion.

But there was a face nearer to me, and with that face in my memory I went off into pleasant dreams. Somewhere in them mingled the words of the old spaewife, that I should miss love and fortune in the sunshine and find them in the rain.

The strength of youth is like a branch of yew, for if it is bent it soon straightens. By the third day I was on my feet again, with only the stiffness of healing wounds to remind me of those desperate passages. When I could look about me I found that men had arrived from the Rappahannock, and among them Elspeth's uncle, who had girded on a great claymore, and looked, for all his worn face and sober habit, a mighty man of war. With them came news of the rout of the Cherokees, who had been beaten by Nicholson's militia in Stafford county and driven down the long line of the

Border, paying toll to every stockade. Midway Lawrence had fallen upon them and forced the remnants into the hills above the head waters of the James. It would be many a day, I thought, before these gentry would bring war again to the Tidewater. The Rappahannock men were in high feather, convinced that they had borne the brunt of the invasion. 'Twas no business of mine to enlighten them, the more since of the three who knew the full peril, Shalah was gone and Ringan was dead. My tale should be for the ear of Lawrence and the Governor, and for none else. The peace of mind of Virginia should not be broken by me.

Grey came to me on the third morning to say good-bye. He was going back to the Tidewater with some of the Borderers, for to stay longer with us had become a torture to him. There was no ill feeling in his proud soul, and he bore defeat as a gentleman should.

" You have fairly won, Mr. Garvald," he said. " Three nights ago I saw clearly revealed the inclination of the lady, and I am not one to strive with an unwilling maid. I wish you joy of a great prize. You staked high for it, and you deserve your fortune. As for me, you have taught me much for which I owe you gratitude. Presently, when my heart is less sore, I desire that we should meet in friendship, but till then I need a little solitude to mend broken threads."

There was the true gentleman for you, and I sorrowed that I should ever have misjudged him.

He shook my hand in all brotherliness, and went down the glen with Bertrand, who longed to see his children again.

Elspeth remained, and concerning her I fell into my old doubting mood. The return of my strength had revived in me the passion which had dwelt somewhere in my soul from the hour she first sang to me in the rain. She had greeted me as girl greets her lover, but was that any more than the revulsion from fear and the pity of a tender heart ? Doubts oppressed me, the more as she seemed constrained and uneasy, her eyes falling when she met mine, and her voice full no longer of its frank comradeship.

One afternoon we went to a place in the hills where the vale of the Shenandoah could be seen. The rain had gone, and had left behind it a taste of autumn. The hill berries were ripening, and a touch of flame had fallen on the thickets.

Soon the great valley lay below us, running out in a golden haze to the far blue mountains.

" Ah ! " she sighed, like one who comes from a winter night into a firelit room. She was silent, while her eyes drank in its spacious comfort.

" That is your heritage, Elspeth. That is the birthday gift to which old Studd's powder-flask is the key."

" Nay, yours," she said, " for you won it."

The words died on her lips, for her eyes were abstracted. My legs were still feeble, and I had leaned a little on her strong young arm as we came up the hill, but now she left me and climbed on a

rock, where she sat like a pixie. The hardships of
the past month had thinned her face and deepened
her eyes, but her grace was the more manifest.
Fresh and dewy as morning, yet with a soul of
steel and fire—surely no lovelier nymph ever
graced a woodland. I felt how rough and common was my own clay in contrast with her bright
spirit.

"Elspeth," I said hoarsely, "once I told you
what was in my heart."

Her face grew grave. "And have you not seen
what is in mine?" she asked.

"I have seen and rejoiced, and yet I doubt."

"But why?" she asked again. "My life is
yours, for you have preserved it. I would be
graceless indeed if I did not give my best to you
who have given all for me."

"It is not gratitude I want. If you are only
grateful, put me out of your thoughts, and I will
go away and strive to forget you. There were
twenty in the Tidewater who would have done
the like."

She looked down on me from the rock with the
old quizzing humour in her eyes.

"If gratitude irks you, sir, what would you
have?"

"All," I cried; "and yet, Heaven knows, I am
not worth it. I am no man to capture a fair girl's
heart. My face is rude and my speech harsh, and
I am damnably prosaic. I have not Ringan's
fancy, or Grey's gallantry; I am sober and tongue-
tied and uncouth, and my mind runs terribly on

facts and figures. O Elspeth, I know I am no hero of romance, but a plain body whom Fate has forced into a month of wildness. I shall go back to Virginia, and be set once more at my accompts and ladings. Think well, my dear, for I will have nothing less than all. Can you endure to spend your days with a homely fellow like me ? "

" What does a woman desire ? " she asked, speaking as if to herself, and her voice was very soft as she gazed over the valley. " Men think it is a handsome face or a brisk air or a smooth tongue. And some will have it that it is a deep purse or a high station. But I think it is the honest heart that goes all the way with a woman's love. We are not so blind as to believe that the glitter is the gold. We love romance, but we seek it in its true home. Do you think I would marry you for gratitude, Andrew ? "

" No," I said.

" Or for admiration ? "

" No," said I.

" Or for love ? "

" Yes," I said, with a sudden joy.

She slipped from the rock, her eyes soft and misty. Her arms were about my neck, and I heard from her the words I had dreamed of and yet scarce hoped for, the words of the song sung long ago to a boy's ear, and spoken now with the pure fervour of the heart—" My dear and only love."

Years have flown since that day on the hills,

and much has befallen; but the prologue is the kernel of my play, and the curtain which rose after that hour revealed things less worthy of chronicle. Why should I tell of how my trade prospered, and of the great house we built at Middle Plantation; of my quarrels with Nicholson, which were many; of how we carved a fair estate out of Elspeth's inheritance, and led the tide of settlement to the edge of the hills? These things would seem a pedestrian end to a high beginning. Nor would I weary the reader with my doings in the Assembly, how I bearded more Governors than one, and disputed stoutly with His Majesty's Privy Council in London. The historian of Virginia—now by God's grace a notable land—may, perhaps, take note of these things, but it is well for me to keep silent. It is of youth alone that I am concerned to write, for it is a comfort to my soul to know that once in my decorous progress through life I could kick my heels and forget to count the cost; and as youth cries farewell, so I end my story and turn to my accompts.

Elspeth and I have twice voyaged to Scotland. The first time my uncle and mother were still in the land of the living, but they died in the same year, and on our second journey I had the task of settling their estates. My riches being now considerable, I turned my attention to the little house of Auchencairn, which I enlarged and beautified, so that if we have the wish we may take up our dwelling there. We have found in the West a goodly heritage, but there is that in a man's birth-place which keeps tight fingers on his soul, and I think that we desire to draw our last breath and lay our bones in our own grey country-side. So, if God grants us length of days, we may haply return to Douglasdale in the even, and instead of our noble forests and rich meadows, look upon the bleak mosses and the rainy uplands which were our childhood's memory.

That is the fancy at the back of both our heads. But I am very sure that our sons will be Virginians.

THE END